Praise for
30ᵀᴴ CENTURY: ESCAPE

"...packs an entertaining yet thought provoking punch!"

—*YGrace*

"...a credible view of a 30th-century woman's thoughts in the 21st century. As a bisexual woman, I thought Dr. Levin expertly depicted how I feel about sexuality.. ..(E)ntertaining, humorous at times, and practical always. ... Dr. Levin showed expert balance with the scientific, sexual, and temporal travel factors in the journey that is 30th Century Escape...A beautiful picture of life in the regions of Hawaii and Polynesian Islands."

—*K. Taylor*

"The author clearly knows the location intimately, because you really feel you are there under wide, blue skies and powerful seas."

—*O. Muldowney*

"A stunning and visceral world combining astounding imagination, science-fiction, sensuality and the tantalizing challenge to humanity's existence... a universe of gripping danger and transformative adventure...It bursts with explosive renderings of time travel, A.I., futuristic science, sensuality and the enigma of love. What more would you want? And this is only Book I of the *30ᵗʰ Century* trilogy! Start reading. Our future may depend on it!"

—*Jan Goldstein,* Los Angeles Times bestselling-author of ALL THAT MATTERS and THE PRINCE OF NANTUCKET

30TH CENTURY
CONTACT

Book Three

IN THE 30TH CENTURY TRILOGY

BY MARK KINGSTON LEVIN, PHD

30th Century: Contact

Contact Information:
markkingstonlevin@gmail.com

Cover Art by Sofia Chekhnita

Publishing History

First Edition, 2019
Print ISBN 978-0-9989183-3-4

Published in the United States of America

DEDICATION

To all my friends and family, as they made this work possible,
particularly Jan Goldstein, well-known author of fiction,
for providing a plethora of knowledge about
publishing, cover art, and writing.

ACKNOWLEGEMENTS

I would like to thank my editors Kelly Lynne Schaub and Robin Quinn, and my beta readers Dan Krommenhoek, Jan Goldstein, Ethel Goldstein, and Fartash Modarresi.

AUTHOR'S NOTE

This trilogy was inspired by new science created by the author in the field of cosmology known as dark energy. The author thanks Professor Paul Adrien Maurice Dirac for his guidance during his PhD, his friendship after that, and for his urging and inspiration to work in the field of cosmology. Thanks also to Jan Goldstein bestselling author of *All That Matters* and *The Prince of Nantucket,* whose work inspired me to start writing fiction.

CONTENTS

PROLOGUE

In the twenty-seventh century, to facilitate interstellar travel—despite its challenges, such as radiation—altered humans known as Syndos were created by embryonic engineering to settle planets at stars Tau Ceti, Alpha Centauri, and others. With these altered humans at the helm, Earth colonized Mars and seven interstellar worlds. However, by the thirtieth century, the genetically superior but empathy-challenged Syndos comprised the majority of the human population on Earth and subjugated the Natural humans, excluding them from positions of power in science and government.

A covert thirtieth-century pacifist society of Natural human scientists known as the SS developed a plan to travel back in time to the twenty-seventh century to distribute the V7 virus, which would correct the error in the DNA coding that dampened the moral compass of the Syndos. Jennifer Hero directed the plan until the moment of the time jump. She did not follow her brave team on their one-way trip to the past. Instead, she sent herself back further in time to the twenty-first century, where she managed to build a new life.

In the thirty-second century, two-way time travel was accomplished, and Jennifer's twin sister, who she had just learned about, became a key player in her life and in the mission's success.

We rejoin our heroine in the year 2031.

1

GAMMA RAY BURSTS

The two-year Polynesian sailing trip Marty and Jennifer took with their twins for research was a wild success. Jennifer spent a few months after the trip compiling all the data she'd gathered and writing reports on what had gone as planned and what had not. The anthropological and archeological findings were exciting for her.

But eventually, mid-September rolled around again. Jennifer found herself back in a typical university auditorium with wooden seats and a hardwood speaker podium giving a presentation on gamma ray bursts for her other academic subject of expertise—physics. The stifling auditorium in Honolulu was full of mostly graduate students and professors, but many undergraduates stood at the back. Arriving just as Jennifer began to speak, Marty had chosen a seat near the back as well, not wanting to be a distraction.

Joining Jennifer at the podium at the end of the presentation was Dean William Morse, head of the Astrophysics and Astronomy Institute at the University of Hawaii. He said, "Jennifer, thank you for that stimulating presentation on gamma ray bursts from colliding neutron stars. Any questions?"

The dean pointed to a young woman in the front. "First question!"

"Professor Zitonick, how common are these gamma ray bursts, and where have they occurred so far?"

"Gamma ray bursts often called GRBs are for a brief time the most intense source of cosmic gamma rays in the universe we know of today," Jennifer said and then stepped out from behind the podium to the stage. "A typical gamma ray burst emits more energy than our whole galaxy does in a year. On average, there is one GRB observed roughly once per day from completely random directions of the sky. That is within billions of galaxies. They have so far been observed in other galaxies but not close to home."

From the podium, Dean Morse pointed to a man in the second row on the right. The man asked, "How long does this intensity last and why?"

"The time of these intense events can be short, like less than a few milliseconds to several hours," Jennifer answered. "The suggested cause of GRBs observed in some of these short events may be the development of a resonance between the crust and core of such stars, perhaps due to the massive tidal forces experienced in the seconds leading up to the collision of the neutron stars, causing the entire crust of a star to shatter. As an example, a typical few-second-long GRB releases more energy than our sun will release in its entire ten-billion-year lifetime."

Dean Morse said, "Thank you, Jennifer!" then pointed to a woman standing up in the back. "Next question...the woman in the red sweatshirt near the exit."

The woman in the back asked, "Can GRB events be dangerous to us on Earth?"

"Good question," Jennifer responded. "If one occurred even a few hundred light-years away, it could sterilize Earth and leave it with almost no atmosphere. Most GRBs are far away perhaps many billions of light-years away meaning no harm to us. Closer events are extremely rare, such as three per galaxy per million years. Yet they could pose a serious risk if they happened within nine hundred light-years."

Dean Morse smiled at Jennifer and knocked a gavel against the wooden podium. Looking back to the audience, he said, "I'm sorry. We're out of time."

After the lecture, Marty and Jennifer went to their Mount Tantalus home above Honolulu, as they needed to get up early the next day. They had plans to meet Jenny, Jennifer's twin sister who'd been born in the twentieth century but now lived in the thirtieth century. Before the lecture, Jennifer had left their twins, now ten years old, in the care of Marty's ex-wife, Anne, and her wife, Jill—their neighbors and close friends.

The next morning, Marty and Jennifer flew to Tahiti commercially and then went to Papeete Harbour. There they borrowed the research vessel, the *Blue Hole*, at the University of Hawaii's Tahiti Marine Lab.

Marty and Jennifer prepared the *Blue Hole* for sea travel, fueling her and checking out everything item by item. Next, they started the two engines and made their way out of the harbor. They took turns eating lunch while one acted as helmsman heading south at thirty-eight knots. They expected to reach their destination in about three hours.

Later, as Jennifer piloted from the *Blue Hole*'s flying bridge, she said, "It is just about time to meet Jenny at the usual coordinates. Are we almost there?"

Standing nearby on the bridge, Marty checked their location on the instrument panel. "No worries," he replied. "We'll be on-site fifteen minutes early."

"What do you think about neutron stars after yesterday's lecture?" she asked him.

Marty chuckled. "It went over my head. I understood that they're very dense and are about seven to seventeen miles across and weigh much more than our sun. Also, the fact that this is considered small in the wider universe. And that their 'small size' and limited luminosity make them difficult to see, except when they spin so fast they give off pulses."

"Did you enjoy the lecture?"

"Yes, but it went a little fast for me, and I was still thinking about a discussion I'd had with one of my students. How do they detect neutron stars before they collide with another star?"

"In 1967, neutron stars were postulated to explain the primarily invisible objects in the sky that emitted pulses of radio waves. So, radio telescopes were the first detection method. Later the Hubble Space Telescope detected isolated neutron stars and we were able to identify them. Some of these pulsing objects rotate extremely rapidly, a thousand times per second, and some of these neutron stars emit radio beams like a high-speed rotating lighthouse."

"I didn't understand the gamma ray burst," Marty admitted.

"That is okay, as no one fully understands them, but we continue to study them. However, in the thirtieth century, much more is known. That information must not be released." Having been born in the thirtieth century, Jennifer was always careful about sharing her advanced technical knowledge.

"Can you give it to me, so I can follow this better?"

Trusting her husband, Jennifer answered, "Gamma ray bursts may be produced from black holes that collide to form a bigger black hole, or from the merger of a pair of these neutron stars. Scientists estimate there are around one hundred million neutron stars in our galaxy. However, they can only be easily detected if they are emitting something like radio waves or other forms of energy, are in the path of other stars, by radio telescopes, or by their magnetic properties. Then there are also gravity waves when the neutron stars collide."

"Yes, now it makes more sense. Thank you for the overview."

"You are welcome, my love." Jennifer leaned over and kissed him.

"I see *Triton!*"

"Yes, I see it now!" Jennifer veered the boat sharply to port to head directly for her twin's vessel, *Triton.*

✳✳✳✳

The deep-water leviathan, a Unicorn-class submersible, was as close to artificial intelligence as Marty had ever seen. He still marveled at *Triton* every time he saw it.

Soon Jenny launched her inflatable twenty-first century Zodiac from *Triton*, and on verbal command, the submersible returned to its station under the waves one mile below the ocean's surface.

Now standing on the deck by Marty, Jennifer felt her blonde hair whip her face as if a hair dryer were engaged.

Jenny shouted, "Ahoy, my twin and Marty!"

"Ahoy, with all my love!" Marty yelled back.

"Bonjour," Jennifer replied as she helped Jenny aboard the *Blue Hole.* Marty lifted the motor of the Zodiac and handed it to Jennifer. Soon the Zodiac was stored on the *Blue Hole* and the motor stowed safely in the aft locker.

Marty hugged Jenny warmly then passed her to his wife.

"Jenny, my twin!" Jennifer exclaimed as she kissed Jenny on both cheeks and gently on the lips.

Jenny smiled but looked worried. "I missed you so much." Jenny kissed Jennifer on both cheeks and hugged her tight. "I need to tell you something so important I'm about to explode!" she whispered in French.

"What is it?" Jennifer responded, also in French.

"Please speak in English," Marty requested.

In a quivering voice in English, Jenny told them, "I went to the future to visit where my father and your father grew up as brothers in the thirty-second century. All was fine there."

"You are upset—what is wrong?" Jennifer asked.

"I also went to the fifty-seventh century to get a glimpse of the far future. Earth was burned to a crisp with almost no atmosphere!" Jenny's voice and body were both wobbly now.

Jennifer narrowed her eyes. "What do you mean?"

"I could find no life on land! Only in the deep ocean vents. All the cities were destroyed! I found no animals or plants on the surface." Jenny continued to shake, her eyes wet, wide, and frightened.

"Please, calm down… I promise to lead a team of SS members to investigate," Jennifer reassured her. The Secret Society was an undercover organization in the thirtieth century tasked with maintaining equal rights between humanity's divergent genetic types, the Syndos and Naturals, among other peacekeeping issues.

"What could cause that?" Jenny asked tearfully.

"We need to gather data and study the heavens," Jennifer said calmly but with a firm determination.

"We better find out very soon, so we can stop it, if possible!" Jenny started to cry harder.

Marty wrapped Jenny in his arms to comfort her. "Count me in. I'll help if I can."

"We will put together an SS team to explore and find out what happened," Jennifer told her. "We will need an instrument package, small advanced robotic aircraft, land transportation, and more!"

"When can we trans-time to the thirtieth century to gather the SS team?" Jenny asked, a bit calmer after hearing a plan.

"Soon! But first we must get approval and resources," Jennifer noted. "Then we can take our SS team to look for clues and explore every possible option. We also will need a good cover story for our friends and family in the twenty-first century."

The *Blue Hole* pulled into the slip at Papeete Harbour. Jenny was dressed in her niqab to disguise being Jennifer's identical twin; in this century, there was supposed to be only one Jennifer. They cleaned the sport fisher and rinsed it down with fresh water. After finishing, they headed directly to the hotel without stopping to say hello to Lacy, the director of the Marine Science Lab for the Tahiti campus of the University of Hawaii, or their other friends. When they got back to Honolulu the next day, they sent e-mails and made calls to arrange for the cover story that Jennifer and Jenny would soon be away on an extended sailing trip together.

The next week Jennifer, Marty, and Jenny returned to Tahiti and spent the evening with their close friends and lovers, Bill and Lacy Kiaomoku. The Zitonick twins, Tippit and Enerjin, also were visiting the Kiaomoku home. Jennifer had trusted Lacy with the secret of time travel a few years before, and she and Bill were some of the few people in the twenty-first century to know the truth of Jennifer's origins in the thirtieth century. Now Jennifer and Jenny were alone drinking wine with Lacy in the study and telling her that they would be leaving on another mission involving the trans-time machine.

Lacy asked, "Why must you go for so long?"

Jennifer explained, "There are built-in safeguards because no person knows what happens as a result of cutting the arrival and departure of time travel too close. If we are in another time for a month, we come back here a month after we left to prevent time twisting. It may seem like overkill, but we must avoid meeting ourselves. This fourth-dimensional rule was set out in guidelines by the inventor of time travel, Zexton Ho. The trans-time machine has a built-in timer to track the lapse of real time in both origin and destination."

Jenny jumped in and said, "I explored the thirty-second century. All was well with our relatives. I explored the far future, and things were so amazing in the fiftieth century. But in the fifty-seventh century, our Earth is dead! No life! We must go to find out what happened. It will take time to get a vote and commitments for funds and then practice and implement a detailed plan. We are not allowed to come back to the twenty-first century before we left or earlier than we were really gone, as the Council of Five is very conservative on introducing possible time paradoxes."

Lacy narrowed her eyes. "So there is a way to come back earlier if you really want to return?"

Jennifer and Jenny exchanged a look. Jenny said, "It is possible to override this safeguard, but it would be extremely risky, and only the engineers who built the trans-time machine would have any clue how to do it. And we really don't know what would happen. It could turn time inside out."

At the helm of the *Blue Hole* the following day, Lacy took Jennifer, Marty, their twins, and Jenny to the ocean above the Trans-Time Eleven device one hundred miles south of Tahiti. Marty and the twins said goodbye to Jennifer, as Jenny had suggested that the council would take the project more seriously if the ten-year olds were left behind. Marty also stayed behind to look after Tippit and Enerjin. Jenny and Jennifer transferred to *Triton*, which dove to the bottom of the ocean, and once there, they docked with Trans-Time Eleven. They quickly trans-timed to the thirtieth century.

The rules of time travel, governed by the SS, required that they arrive well after Jenny had left in her personal timeline, to avoid crossing herself or being in the same time twice. Linear months and years passed for Jenny and the other members of Jennifer's family in the thirtieth century just as time passed for Marty and their children in the twenty-first century. Every time Jennifer returned to her native century, everyone she knew was older. Fifteen years had now passed since the first successful time travel by humans, known in the thirtieth century as the Big Bang Sacrifice.

Jennifer and Jenny returned to the thirtieth century and then traveled to Tasmania. They went to the red barn outside of Hobart, where Professor Zexton Ho had first introduced Jennifer to the SS when she was a University of Tasmania student. The SS headquarters still were hidden underground. While remaining very secretive, the SS organization was no longer entirely secret. Select top Syndo leaders knew about the group now.

Going down to the fiftieth floor, they met with the SS leader, Admiral Tom Page, and his Council of Five around an oval table in a large conference room used as the council chambers. The twins' goal was to obtain assistance in investigating the cause of the mass extinction on Earth and Mars in the fifty-seventh century.

Jennifer briefly explained what Jenny had found in the fifty-seventh century, then suggested, "Tom, I need Kylie Brown and twenty-one others from the SS for our initial investigation."

"Yes, we can assemble a team of twenty-one, plus Kylie," Tom replied.

Akina Cool-al, an outspoken member of Tom's council, asked, "Can you tell me what you're thinking? How can the past change such a significant future event?"

Akina had been a key player on the twenty-seventh century's V7 virus mission due to her family's historical ownership of Blue Mountain Waterfall and the nearby land. Clearly, she had a challenging job of establishing the water company. She had come from these Aboriginal tribal lands in Australia, and therefore held the Blue Mountain Waterfall access rights. From the Syndo mission to revived humanity, she knew firsthand how changing past events could affect the future. But this disaster was at another magnitude altogether.

Also, although the V7 mission had activated the moral compass of the Syndos, they remained a breed apart from Natural humans in the thirtieth century, and some small friction between the races continued on a competitive level in industry, sports, and other fields.

Jennifer answered, "I think we need to collect data and analyze it. We need to determine whether the SS by itself can accomplish this mission or whether we need a coalition with the Syndos and other Naturals."

"Can we trust the Syndos if we disclose time travel to them?" Akina persisted as she looked deeply into Jennifer's eyes.

"I do not know, but this project could be too big for us alone. I suggest we consider opening it up to the Syndos and getting their top astronauts and scientists to come along."

Tom shook his head. "Until we know more, we will not share our secret."

"I agree with Tom," said Happy Li, another member of Tom's council and a former member of Kylie's team on her mission to the twenty-seventh century.

Tom asked, "Captain Brown, what do you think?"

Kylie replied, "Let the SS send its best twenty-two investigators and we'll report the facts, analyze the data, and discuss the possible action steps in a more meaningful way."

Tom said, "Jennifer, please leave the room with your sister and wait for my call. I'll discuss this matter with the council and give you an answer."

"Yes, we will leave and wait in the lobby. I await your answer," Jennifer replied.

Jenny asked, "Can I make a statement before you discuss, as I was the one who found the dead planet Earth in the future?"

"Yes, speak your piece in five minutes or less," Tom said.

With tears in her eyes and a crack in her voice, Jenny told them, "I wanted to explore the future for my own curiosity and was shocked to find a dead world. I accept any punishment you deem necessary. We must do whatever we can to keep life alive in this catastrophic and dynamic universe. We owe this not just to humans and Syndos but to all life on Earth. You, Tom, and your council decide, as you are the SS leaders now."

Jenny and Jennifer left the room together and held hands to show unity to the council as they walked out.

The council deliberated for about one hour. Jennifer got the call from Tom.

Within minutes, she and Jenny were back with the council around the round table in their chambers.

Tom cleared his throat, looked around at the council members, then over to Jenny and Jennifer. He announced, "We, the SS leadership, have decided to allow you to pick up to twenty-two volunteers to investigate for thirty days and then report to the council your conclusions. Please come into my office after this meeting and we can discuss details."

"Thank you and the council for your support," Jennifer said. "In addition to Kylie and Jenny, I will pick twenty individuals from the principal forty-seven that returned with Kylie from my earlier mission if they volunteer. I will go, and Jenny will be on the controls at a central site as we send teams out to gather data. Kylie will be second-in-command; I have confidence in her. I will have more details to discuss after I consult the members of the team, but we will need resources. Kylie invested a large sum of money in the twenty-seventh century for use in any nonviolent effort to save humanity. This is clearly such an event. Do you agree?"

"Yes," Tom agreed, "the council decided to allow these funds to be used to prepare and investigate the mass extinction in the fifty-seventh century."

"Thank you for your kind consideration and wisdom," Jenny said. "What about my punishment?"

Tom replied, "The council decided to promote you to Commander Jenny Heros. You must lead the team back to what you found and learn what you can. Your specific tasks will be determined by Captain Jennifer Zitonick, who is the project leader. Thank you for bringing this matter to our attention."

"Thank you so much," Jenny responded, feeling grateful and relieved. "I am glad you listened and are receptive to supporting this vital mission."

"This is an opportunity for Jenny and me to serve all life on Earth," Jennifer added. "On a personal note, my sister and I request permission to share this information with our parents—which, due to our particular circumstances, would be four individuals."

After some discussion between Jennifer, Jenny, and the council, Tom said, "Yes, we've agreed on the following terms for your parents. If they join the SS formally and take the oath of secrecy, you may disclose this information."

"This is a subject that I know without a doubt will compel my mother and father to join and do what they can to help, so I commit for them," Jennifer replied. "I'm sure Jenny's parents will feel the same."

2

THE INVESTIGATION

Within the week, Jennifer, Jenny, Kylie, and a team of twenty SS volunteers arrived at the trans-time facility below the floating city of Pacifica Anthozoa. After trans-timing, they arrived at the same location one hundred miles south of Tahiti in the fifty-seventh century.

Upon arrival, they exited the Trans-Time Eleven to the submersible *Triton*, which took them to the surface.

Immediately Jennifer ordered, "Launch recon vehicles!"

"Aye-aye, Captain," Kylie replied.

Within a half hour, Kylie and her sub-team were launching the recon aircraft, two rocket-powered vehicles carrying three satellites each, as well as dirigibles from the submersible *Triton*—all of which had been stored in the underwater craft's hull within the trans-time facility. All recon vehicles in the fleet were programmed to run by themselves. In a few hours, the data started to come in with a horrifying confirmation of Jenny's story. On a hunch, Jennifer set the second satellite's telescopes to search the sky for possible sources of a gamma ray burst.

After a few days, Jennifer raised her suspicions with the other SS members.

Standing before them in a small classroom in the *Triton*, she revealed, "After reviewing the data and the astronomical database of the thirtieth century, I suspect a large gamma ray burst."

Kylie was seated in the first row of chairs. With curiosity as well as fear, she asked, "What caused it and where in the sky did it happen?"

Pacing in the front, Jennifer replied, "I do not know with certainty; however, I suspect that studying the sky in the fifty-sixth century will provide the answer."

"If you needed to guess based on all our data, what would you estimate?" Jenny asked, concerned.

"I worked on that for a while and built a computer model," Jennifer answered. "Let me share what I have so far."

Jennifer turned on an advanced presentation program that projected her work from a small palm-sized device that floated a short distance from the ceiling. She would be able to advance the presentation though a holographic projector. Her first model calculated the location for the source of the gamma ray burst.

"These are the coordinates I have so far," she reported. "According to the thirtieth-century database, there existed a binary system comprising two rapidly rotating neutron stars in this area. One hypothesis is that these six-to-twelve-mile-in-diameter stars collided to create the gamma ray beam that wiped out our planet."

"Is there anything we can do to stop this collision?" Kylie asked with a wrinkled brow.

"Not that I know of," Jennifer stated truthfully, "but we may be able to change the direction of the beam, as these neutron stars are rotating at about one thousand times a second."

"Please come up with a way to save Earth," Jenny asked solemnly.

After several days of intense programming, Jennifer ran her models. Then she gathered the half a dozen team members not currently on recon assignments into the classroom, along with Jenny and Kylie, to share her new discoveries.

"First, I must announce that everything points to the coordinates I targeted being correct," she said. "This will need to be confirmed in the fifty-sixth century."

The SS members looked at Jennifer with appreciation. Even Jenny managed a slight smile.

Jennifer continued. "There's more… I believe I have a possible solution to the neutron star problem; however, this solution requires a very large object to be sent to collide with one of the neutron stars before the collision to change its angular momentum slightly."

"How big an object?" Jenny asked then began biting her lower lip.

"Something several hundred miles in diameter, such as Vesta, our solar system's largest asteroid, if one considers Ceres a dwarf planet."

Thoughtfully Kylie asked, "Is that really possible?"

"At ten percent of the speed of light, it could take almost five thousand years to get to the location of the colliding neutron stars," Jennifer told those gathered. "It appears almost impossible to execute this proposed solution with thirtieth-century technology."

Kylie suggested, "Let's call in the recon teams and head back to the thirtieth century to discuss our findings with Tom and his council."

"We are thinking along the same lines, Kylie," responded Jennifer. "I do want you to return with the recon teams to make a report. But first I need to find a volunteer or two to go with me to the fifty-sixth century. As I noted, we need to make sure we have identified the right neutron-star binary system and must locate the right coordinates before we will have a full report for the SS in the thirtieth century."

"I volunteer!" Jenny exclaimed.

"Kylie, can you lead our people back to the thirtieth century and report on what we have found so far?" Jennifer asked.

"Yes, I'll take Ben Sun with me to report on our findings to date. You can add to my report when you get back with your astronomical data. Right now, Ben's doing some recon work involving one of our surveillance satellites."

Jennifer blinked, astonished. "I did not recognize Ben after all these years. Thank you for the great idea of bringing him along on this mission."

"Ben's an amateur astronomer," Kylie noted. "He joined the SS several years ago at the urging of Tom Page. Didn't you know he came with us?"

"I did not notice that he was on this team—he must be someone you added, and then I missed his name on the roster. Please contact him immediately. Instead of going to the thirtieth century, I want to ask him if he is willing to help us locate the neutron star system. We will go together to the thirtieth century to drop off your team, and we will then go directly to the fifty-sixth century."

After a couple of hours, Ben stood smiling in front of Jennifer in the main cabin of *Triton*, which she was using as an office. His face had grown somewhat rounder and he had facial hair, but his straight Chinese hair was still black without any gray and his brown eyes twinkled.

Jennifer grabbed Ben and hugged him. "Hello, my old friend... I thought you were still building floating cities. I did not recognize you with your beard and mustache."

"I joined three years ago," he replied, "but I thought you had committed suicide in the Big Bang Sacrifice. Kylie never said any different, and you know the SS leadership."

"We used the ten-megaton bomb to cover our trans-time tracks."

"Thanks, that explains a great deal!" he said smiling.

"Please, sit down with me," Jennifer suggested. After they had settled on a sofa on one side of the room, she asked, "Are you still chief engineer at the floating city factory?"

"I'm executive vice president of operations."

Now Jennifer had a big smile. "Good for you," she responded, proud of him. "I knew you would do well at whatever you decided to do, as you were very smart and practical. How are Lota and the kids?"

"They're all fine. I have a grandchild now. Can you believe it?" He grinned and shook his head. "They all think I'm on a business trip."

Jennifer looked closely at her friend and grew more serious. She asked, "Would you like to join us as we recon the sky in the fifty-sixth century?"

Ben had been at the first briefing on the *Triton*, and this aspect of the mission had been on his mind ever since. He told her, "I think I can help triangulate the location with the telescopic system."

"Yes, Kylie has told me about your hobby, and you have actually discovered two new comets using Earth-bound telescopes. That is amazing!"

Ben shrugged, downplaying his accomplishment. "Yes, I volunteer to help you. I'll do my best, as I love astronomy. My father taught me astronomy at an early age. I give him most of the credit for the comet discoveries, as he wrote the software that allowed me to pick them out of the Oort cloud."

"Let me give you a personal introduction to my twin, Jenny, as she will join us on the adventure to the fifty-sixth century."

Jennifer sent a text message via her watch asking Jenny to join them.

———————————

Jenny entered *Triton*'s main cabin at Jennifer's summons, and she sat down in a chair by the sofa. Jennifer introduced Jenny to Ben but did not explain how she had a twin he never knew about. After working with the SS for a few years, Ben knew better than to ask. He offered his hand and Jenny clasped it tightly and smiled.

After giving Ben's hand a squeeze, then letting it go, Jenny said, "This may be a simple mission, but we do not know what to expect if we are discovered by the fifty-sixth-century people. If we can stay submerged in *Triton* and use remote aircraft to collect the astronomical data, we should be fine."

Ben noted, "I think the telescope can be attached to the robotic aircraft capable of flying to one hundred and twenty thousand feet."

"Let us start the work now. We trans-time in thirty-two hours after we drop off Kylie and her team," Jennifer announced.

Jenny and Ben studied how to adapt the telescope to the robotic aircraft as Jennifer reviewed the charts. Jennifer developed a plan to release the robotic aircraft near Antarctica in the fifty-sixth century because they would not likely be monitored in that location.

Two days later, the three SS members were in the fifty-sixth century aboard *Triton* ready to activate the plan.

In the control room on the submersible, Jennifer commanded *Triton*. "Southeast to the Ross Sea off eastern Antarctica."

A short while later, Jenny and Ben entered the command post and walked over to Jennifer. Jenny reported, "Ben has the telescope adapted to the robotic aircraft. It is ready to fly."

Ben smiled and added, "Jenny helped make this possible. I could not have done this alone in this short time, so I want to give her credit."

Jennifer felt the mission was in good hands with both of them.

The next evening, after arriving at the coastal area of the great Ross Ice Shelf, Jennifer waited for clouds to accumulate. It took three more days until finally a storm blanketed the area. After dark in *Triton*'s command room, Jennifer ordered, "Launch the robotic aircraft!"

"Aye-aye, Captain!" Ben exclaimed from a chair close by the controls. Ben then launched the thirtieth-century stealth aircraft after *Triton* surfaced briefly in the savage storm.

"The aircraft is away safely, and all data links are functioning," Jenny announced from an adjacent post. "I can see the large, local research base and their high-rise homes and office buildings. It's a small city."

Within a couple of hours, Ben said, "The stealth aircraft sent back data on the binary magnetars' locations."

"How does it look?" Jennifer asked.

"Great first data!" Ben answered, and then he looked up from his monitor. "However, we need a second location to create a triangle to get an accurate position, so the robotic aircraft needs to fly for four more hours."

The team all went to sleep to be ready for the last data collection. *Triton* dove deep and ran silently on stealth mode.

Unfortunately, while they slept, the fifty-sixth century authorities picked up and tracked *Triton*. The world naval command ordered two large modern submarines to intercept this antique submersible. Admiral Adam Zeeroc was in command of the mission. He hailed the submersible but received no answer. He hit it with a powerful sound blast. The sound blast disrupted the life support systems, and within hours, *Triton* was forced to the near surface to snorkel air. Soon two large submarines of advanced fifty-sixth-century technology gripped the submersible tightly with a force that prevented it from moving.

Back at the command post, Jennifer responded to the hail in her ancient thirtieth-century English. She also sent the same message in old digital code: "We are from the thirtieth century. We are on a peaceful mission to collect astronomical data on a neutron star system to save life on Earth and Mars."

"Why are you really here?" Admiral Zeeroc asked Jennifer via his fifty-sixth-century communicator. *Triton*'s universal translator calculated the shifts in the fifty-sixth-century English, making his question clearer.

"Our world will be destroyed in about one hundred years by a powerful gamma ray burst," Jennifer replied. "We think it is due to a collision of two rapidly spinning neutron stars or magnetars that orbit each other about four hundred and eighty-nine light-years away. I will send you the coordinates."

Admiral Zeeroc commanded, "In the name of the World Council, you are ordered to surrender your vessel and come aboard our vessel as prisoners until the World Council can confirm your story."

Jennifer turned off the microphone as she thought of the alternatives. Frustrated, she blurted out, "Damn government systems—they assume you are guilty until proven innocent!"

"May I speak freely?" Jenny asked patiently.

"Yes, my twin!"

"We can surrender and further explain our mission. Ask them for assistance in disrupting the gamma ray burst to preserve life on Earth."

"Roger that!"

From a chair on her other side, Ben said, "I agree; they're our future. They must be reasonable. They haven't fired on us, and surely they could sink us with no problem."

Jennifer pushed the communication switch off silent. "We offer to surrender if you will listen and bring our request for assistance in saving all life on this planet to the World Council."

"You are not able to negotiate," Admiral Zeeroc barked back. "The World Council leader is President Zexton Wise. He wants to interrogate you personally via our communication system. Please come aboard now or I will destroy your vessel."

The winds were blowing at forty miles an hour as Jennifer, Jenny, and Ben made their way onto the deck of *Triton*. The crew of the vessel *Ozzite* quickly took them into custody and bound their hands and feet.

"You did the smart thing," Admiral Zeeroc announced. "Our vessel *Ozzite* is five times the size of *Triton* and armed with many weapons not known to the thirtieth century, if that is indeed where you are from."

"*Triton,* our vessel, can translate, but otherwise we do not understand your language," Jennifer informed him.

The admiral gestured to his lieutenant, who handed a necklace device to each of them with attached earplugs. The three put them on.

"I am equipping each of you with a translator, so you do not need to rely on your submersible to provide you with the interpretation."

"Thank you for the translators," she told them. "My name is Jennifer Zitonick. I am in command. My mission is to get your help in preventing life extinction in the fifty-seventh century, about ninety-three and two-tenths years into the future from today."

Ignoring her explanation, Lieutenant Manny Montford commanded, "Move into the holding quarters!"

Jennifer, Jenny, and Ben were escorted into a large, furnished, dorm-like suite with help from two robots. The binding of their hands and feet automatically released after the door closed.

"There are beds, bathrooms, and living, dining, exercise, and working areas for at least six people, so you'll have plenty of room... meanwhile, we will verify your claims."

Admiral Zeeroc pressed a button that produced three trays with light meals of warm, high-calorie food and cold nutrition drinks in the kitchen. Then he announced, "In four hours, Jennifer will be interrogated by World Council President Zexton Wise while wearing a special helmet that can read her brain patterns and extract the truth."

"I am ready anytime," Jennifer replied through the small necklace translator.

The four hours went by slowly, though they were comfortable in their confinement. Video entertainment was projected on one wall, with periodic advertisements showing views of the cities in Australia as well as insights into modern fifty-sixth-century life. A computer portal allowed limited access to a library.

Jennifer wrote down her request for help in saving the planets, explaining the binary system and the pending collision that would endanger all life in their solar system. This primarily meant Earth and Mars, which had been colonized, terraformed, and developed.

Shortly before her appointment with the World Council President, a robot delivered an enhanced thick cloth helmet and handed it to Jennifer.

Right after she had placed it on her head, President Zexton Wise appeared as a hologram at the center of their prison's living room. "Why are you here?" he began.

Jennifer read her statement and then asked, "Can your world please help us save your future, as I believe we have a plan that will work?"

"My engineering team is on the way to the future to verify your claims. If true, I will consider your request." President Wise reached for a sip of his drink, a nutritious fiftieth-century mixture known as Kubala.

"Thank you."

Looking back at the camera, the president asked, "Do any of you have anything else to say?"

Ben replied, "I echo what Jennifer has said. It is one hundred percent the truth."

"I agree with my twin sister," Jenny concurred.

Admiral Zeeroc now appeared in the hologram and inquired, "Do you have any other requests or needs?"

"Please be kind to *Triton*, our AI robotic submersible," Jenny replied. "I am emotionally attached to the AI system. It has feelings just like you."

"I request we be given more food and beverages, and medical attention if later needed," Jennifer told him. "We will also need time to sleep without being disturbed."

"You are not able to negotiate; however, more food and drinks will be provided," Admiral Zeeroc said. "You have already seen your bedrooms by now, I assume. Yes, we will give you time to get some needed rest."

Three trays, each with a larger meal of a variety of cooked vegetables, artificial protein, rice, and bottled water, appeared in the kitchen area. Jennifer had no idea how they managed to prepare and deliver such trays, but she suspected a robotic system put the trays through a trap door in the wall.

"Thank you for the food and water," Jennifer said with a big smile. "What is the city on the wall?"

"That is Sydney."

Jennifer and the others marveled at the twin four-mile-high towers at the opening to Sydney Harbour that had not existed in their time.

———————

Two mornings later, the fifty-sixth-century engineers returned from the fifty-seventh century with photos and holographic images of the total devastation.

President Wise's holographic image appeared again in the cell. He told them, "We have confirmed your story and you are now being released from prison. I have many questions first before we can help. How did you find out about this event?"

Jenny spoke up. "I wanted to see the future, and I used the trans-time device of thirty-second century technology to explore the future.

Our father was from the thirty-second century, and via time travel he came to the thirtieth century, where Jennifer was born, and then to the twentieth century, where I was born on an island in the Marquesas. My parents and I used the device to return to the thirtieth century, where the time-travel technology we used was invented originally by Zexton Ho. Crossing our path, my sister used the first device to return to the twenty-first century to escape the conflict that killed her lover and SS leader, Zexton Ho."

"We did not know time travel was available in this period. We have laws against time travel, except to prevent horrific disasters or for the study of history."

Jennifer glanced at her sister and stated, "Time travel is a well-guarded secret in the thirtieth century. We used the trans-time device to prevent humanity from becoming extinct. We, too, have rules about how it is used. In this case, we are glad Jenny broke the rules to look ahead. The end of life on Earth affects us all. Rules were made to be broken."

"What is your plan to prevent this event?" President Wise asked.

"A large asteroid such as Vesta can be used to collide with the fastest rotating of the two neutron stars," Jennifer proposed. "It will change the direction of the gamma ray beam by a few degrees, enough for it to avoid Mars and Earth, according to my calculations. I have these plans on the computer in *Triton*. They can be downloaded onto your technology with the following command codes: YXVV787s."

Jennifer then provided details, and the scientists and engineers of the fifty-sixth century confirmed Jennifer's calculations even before the download was complete.

The hologram expanded to show an AI engineer attending the meeting with the president. His name badge identified him as Rip Grodi. Behind him was the first shot of a presentation projected on the wall.

"Yes, our calculations show that Jennifer's plan is possible," he began, "but it requires a major trans-time of the entire asteroid back approximately five thousand years to arrive at the right time using our technology and reachable speeds." He moved the images along as he spoke. "All electromagnetic radiation travels at the same speed in the vacuum of space—the speed of light. The closer one gets to the speed of light with a spaceship or any mass, the more energy is required, so we will be limited by that. We have propulsion systems that can reach 0.28 c, where c is the speed of light, but these fast speeds cannot be used for such a long trip with a ship of such mass. We need the most efficient engines we have, the antimatter engines. These engines can reach 0.1 c with the mass of Vesta. At that speed, we can get there well before the collision if we start five thousand years ago. That would give us a safe cushion of ten or eleven years prior to the calculated collision, at that distance."

He flipped his stylus in his fingers as he talked. "No trans-time device of such magnitude has ever been constructed. It will take a tremendous amount of work, but only our fifty-sixth-century technology has a chance of accomplishing this task. We have the resources and talent to apply to this project if the World Council decides to go ahead. We will know in a few hours, as the World Council is meeting now."

The hologram of the tall, slender president of the World Council walked toward Jennifer with a smile. "I apologize for your imprisonment," he said. "We offer you the opportunity to join our team of advanced scientists and engineers in our time. Using fifty-sixth-century technologies, we will move the asteroid closer—about two hundred and fifty thousand miles outside Earth. This is a similar distance as our moon. Then we will be able to modify Vesta in our century and convert it into a robotic spacecraft. You are welcome to provide any resources you wish."

Standing by her in holographic form, he added, "We suggest a management matrix with a dozen bases on Earth and one on Mars in the fifty-sixth century. I will appoint two team project managers to work together to program the spacecraft asteroid to complete its mission. Its advanced computer system will become sentient. We have developed a large sentient computer system to monitor the oceans, and it found you. We have others monitoring and predicting weather, others working on developing new technologies. So far, all these systems have remained friendly, but we have never asked one to commit suicide to save living systems. This will break new ground. The length of time required for this trip will necessitate a much more advanced system of maintenance robots with even greater mental and computer powers than ever before."

"Can we in the thirtieth century help you, or will we just be in the way?" Jennifer asked.

"The World Council representing all the sentient beings on Earth in the fifty-sixth century thanks you for alerting us to this pending disaster," he said, putting his holographic hand on her shoulder. He looked into her eyes then stepped back and continued. "Your passion for the future of our world as an ambassador of the past has impressed us. Though we have not explored your education or your technical aptitude, we sense that a mother's love is more emotional in your century of origin than in our century because many of your moms carried their children for nine months. We believe your input will help the AI develop emotion to balance its logic. We believe your perspective can be effective in defining the mission, organizing, training the AI system, coordinating, and assembling nontechnical resources for this enormous project. You are welcome to our team. I suggest for you to be co-project leader for the mission objective and the AI training."

"Thank you," Jennifer said, both pleased and honored. "I accept your offer and will do my best as a co-project leader."

Dr. Grodi stepped over beside the leader as the president proclaimed, "I officially appoint you, Captain Jennifer Zitonick, and Dr. Rip Grodi, our top AI engineer, to the co-project leader positions. Please work together to save this solar system's life-supporting planets."

Dr. Grodi smiled at Jennifer and nodded in her direction.

After a moment, Jennifer explained, "I will need to return to the thirtieth century, get approval, gather resources, and return as soon as possible with a much larger team of engineers and scientists."

"You and your team are free to go and return," the president noted. "However, we want assurance that none of our advanced technology will be transferred to the thirtieth century. Before you leave, my secretary of foreign affairs will draft a treaty that your world leaders and each person involved must sign."

"I understand," Jennifer said, nodding to emphasize the affirmative. "I will explain your reasons for the treaty. I agree with your plan but must get all leaders and operatives to sign. I accept the challenge."

Jennifer and her two colleagues returned to the thirtieth century in time to fly from the floating cities south of Tahiti to Hobart to hear Kylie presenting data to Tom and the Council of Five in the council chambers in Hobart regarding the findings of the investigation. The three of them quietly took seats around the conference-room table.

The council asked, "What are the possible solutions?"

Kylie told of Jennifer's proposed solution. The council then decided that the SS needed to discuss a possible coalition with Naturals and Syndos in order to succeed.

"I think to increase our chances to execute this proposed solution, we need to work with the fifty-sixth century," Kylie said. "We need their more advanced trans-time technology, robotics, and other technologies to prevent the extinction event from hitting Earth. The fifty-sixth-century humanoids have more to gain from successful intervention and more to lose from doing nothing."

"Can I interrupt with news from the fifty-sixth century?" Jennifer asked after standing up by her seat.

"Welcome back, Captain Zitonick!" Admiral Page exclaimed.

Kylie said, "Yes, please interject your relevant news from the fifty-sixth century."

Jennifer explained, "We were taken prisoner for a time until their authorities verified the cataclysm. However, once verified, we were freed. The president of the World Council will apply their resources. We are welcome to join them in the fifty-sixth century to work toward preventing the disaster if we sign this Treaty of Cooperation." Jennifer delivered the treaty digitally to all present.

"What do you suggest the SS should do to help?" Tom Page asked.

"Like the council, I also suggest a coalition with the Syndos and humans. We need an enormous amount of people and tools to make a dent in this project. Please note the fifty-sixth century is very far advanced technologically over the thirtieth century. We will be more like labor to conduct the easier tasks. The fifty-sixth-century Earth is ruled by a World Council. Their president, Zexton Wise, has operational authority to carry out the policies set by the council of this century, which as you know is chaired by Bonky Fuk. They will provide the artificial intelligence and other technologies needed for this mission. The council will vote on the general plan, which will be submitted by Zexton Wise."

"We now have one hundred twenty-seven members in the SS," noted Tom Page. "Initially, we should send a team of twenty-two to study how we can help and what resources we can bring. Jennifer, please return in two weeks with a team of twenty-two to explain your findings on this to the SS. In the meantime, I will take this project to Australia and the world government."

"I agree with this plan," Jennifer said.

"While our advanced team is studying the project and resource requirements, the SS council will meet with the Australian government's prime minister, Caps Grotto," Admiral Page announced. "We will ask Australia to take the project to the world government. This will optimize the amount of resources we can mount in the battle to save our planet's future."

After weeks of discussion and initial contact with the various countries and individual government representatives, a coalition of advanced countries was formed in the thirtieth century. They planned to explore the solution by sending a team of twelve hundred scientists, managers, and engineers to the fifty-sixth century. The coalition began to search for possible team members.

Soon Jennifer returned to the thirtieth century to report to Tom Page and the Council of Five on the status of Project Magnetar, now being run by the fifty-sixth century's World Council.

"As you know, I have been given a position of co-project leader for AI development and training with Dr. Rip Grodi," she stated to the council with Kylie by her side. "However, we can only be a small help to this more advanced society because they do not feel they should teach us about the new technologies, concerned that it may adversely impact the timeline. They want us to focus on the mission training and objectives, project management, logistics, and related matters using our own thirtieth-century technology. They believe our insights may be very useful in training the AI for its mission, so that is my focus.

"I want to break up our people into ten teams of one hundred twenty each," she related. "I need to return with almost one hundred additional people to complete the first team, Team One. Each team needs its own management and leader. Can you and the council set up the nine other teams and schedule for when they arrive so I can provide it to Dr. Grodi?"

"Yes, we will, but first pick your team," Admiral Page said. "You have nineteen members in the fifty-sixth century and three additional members here in our century. Please select the remainder."

Jennifer turned to her old friend. "Kylie, you are already part of my team. Will you volunteer to serve with me as my second-in-command on the first team?"

"Yes, of course, I'm honored to serve with you in that capacity, Captain."

"Please select the additional members for Team One, as you know them better than I do," Tom directed Jennifer and Kylie. "Please select a team with about thirty-three percent Syndos, thirty-three percent Naturals, and the remainder Natural-Syndos mixtures. I suggest you ask Doctor Author Grotto, the prime minister's son, to join us, as we need at least a few medical doctors to assist with our health issues but also with the long-term mental health of the AI. In addition, Author has proved to be very versatile. He headed the private investigation of several attempted assassinations while attending medical school in the UK."

"Okay, I will contact him to see if he is willing to assist with Project Magnetar," Jennifer replied. "But please ask his father to work with the unified committee to select the Syndos contingent."

"Roger that," said Tom.

Two days later, Author said goodbye to his wife and family and flew to Tahiti. Jennifer met his flight and ran to him as he exited the aircraft.

"I am so happy to see you again, Author!" Jennifer said as she hugged him. Author was stunned at first, almost losing his balance, and dropped his suitcase.

"G'day, Jennifer! Ripper to see ya as well." Author put his arms around Jennifer. "Ya gobsmacked me."

Jennifer's being alive was still confidential due to her reported death in the earlier Syndos virus mission; every old friend she ran into expressed surprise and joy. She wasn't sure she would ever get enough of this validation. Though Author was expecting to meet someone from the mission at the airport, he had no idea it would be Jennifer.

The two of them walked to the self-driving car she had taken to the airport, and they headed to the harbor. On the way, the two old friends talked about what was before them. "Are you ready to use your skills to save the world?" Jennifer asked as she put on a seat belt. "It's voluntary."

Author secured his seat belt as well, then replied, "Yes, I want to save our planet's future, and I don't care about making lots of money. I'm happy to work with you again. Thank you for saving my father. I still carry the video."

"You are welcome. Your investigation was key to identifying the shooter and the change in Russian activities in Australia. Thank you for your steadfast investigation while I was in a coma."

"Can you brief me about my role?"

"Project Magnetar will require at least twelve hundred thirtieth-century workers. We need great medical care for these people. However, the most import role for you is the mental health of the AI."

Author once again had a surprised look on his face. "How

did you know that I got a PhD in AI psychology?"

"Your father told me. He is so proud of you," she said with a big smile. "You should be very proud of him as well. I am not surprised he was elected prime minister."

"Who is doing what and how do I fit into the picture?" he asked, settling into his seat for the ride.

"The logistic planning for Team One is being handled by Kylie Brown and the unified committee, of which your father is the chairperson. I will brief you on the way. We will need to get started right away, as forty-eight of the team members are waiting for us so we can all be trans-timed to the fifty-sixth century together."

Author and Jennifer soon boarded *Triton* and joined the other team members. After Author had been introduced to the team, he went with Jennifer to the cafeteria to get a quick meal.

"What is it like in the fifty-sixth century?" Author asked as he sat across from her at the table.

"The skyline of Sydney has changed significantly, with some buildings four miles high," Jennifer said as she cut into her vegetarian protein patty. "In the fifty-sixth century, land is scarce. Therefore, people live in very large, high buildings to allow more room for growing crops. They have established large areas of wildlife refuges where animals are now kept isolated from most humans and Syndos to ensure that every species can survive in its preferred natural habitat. The ice age has progressed to the point where Northern Canada is covered with ice year-round. Mining operations in that area have been forced to close. The land in Canada and the northern USA border area has snow on the ground for nine months of the year. There are thousands of large floating cities all over the globe. Please see the limited library of facts about the fifty-sixth century that we are allowed to access, but which must be kept secret from anyone who is not a part of this mission."

1. Photo of the asteroid Vesta oriented north at the top and south at the bottom.

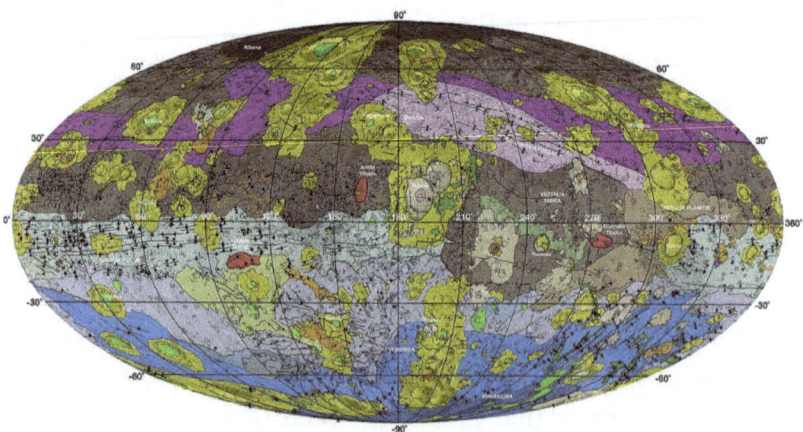

2. Geologic map of Vesta developed from Dawn Spacecraft images

"How far away is Vesta?" Author asked as they took their trays to the receptacles.

"Vesta was moved into Earth's orbit using fifty-sixth-century technologies," Jennifer said as she deposited her tray into a wide opening in the wall. Author did the same. They left the cafeteria and then headed for Trans-Time One.

She continued. "The teams for Project Magnetar will be scattered among the seven continents in the fifty-sixth century. AI development, however, is just outside Sidney—a place in the foothills of the Blue Mountains called Springwood, a deep underground facility used by the military in the past."

3. Map of Southwest Australia showing Springwood.

Once inside the trans-time machine, the two took their seats side by side and buckled in. The other forty-eight team members were already on board. Jennifer nodded to some of the leaders on her team.

"I want to know more about fifty-sixth-century society. What can you share?" Author asked.

"The use of planes and trains has been greatly reduced to hobbyists and those few communities that choose to live in the past. The fifty-sixth-century humanoids connect to computers to experience virtual travel. In addition, they have robotic transporter systems connected to mind-control headbands that issue their commands. These transporter systems are used for local travel. No verbal commands are needed, as this large exoskeleton-like transporter can run at one hundred miles an hour, fly at one thousand miles an hour, and even travel underwater to a depth of two thousand feet. These technologies and how they work are kept secret from us thirtieth-century people, humans and Syndos alike, to avoid upsetting the timeline."

"That's amazing. How long will our mission take?"

"We will be training the AI for its mission over the next twelve to twenty-four months," Jennifer revealed. "I will need you to understand that this AI is a sentient being with emotions, intellect, and personality. We need to help shape all three in the training process. Can you help us work out ways to obtain a stable mental health over an isolated five-thousand-year trip to reach the target magnetar?"

"Yes, of course, I'll do my best," he agreed. "The thirtieth century is just beginning to develop fully independent AIs. I have studied the human brain and the human mind, but I don't know about such long-term AI mental illnesses."

"I will introduce you to Dr. Rip Grodi. He will tell you what you need to know about our AI's mental state," she assured him. "But please remember that he cannot tell you about the technology. We may learn some secrets about their technology, but we must keep them from the thirtieth century to avoid upsetting the timeline. Is that acceptable to you?"

"Absolutely."

Along with the available team members, Jennifer and Author trans-timed to the same trans-time facility under the South Pacific waters but in the fifty-sixth century. Once there, Jennifer, Author, and the team soon boarded a rapid flight from the floating city to Tahiti, then on to Sydney, where they took a hyper-tube to the Blue Mountains region and the Springwood facility—a refurbished underground military installation where they were preparing the AI.

While the team got settled in their quarters on the second floor, Jennifer and Author took the elevator to the secure minus twenty-first floor down for a meeting in the AI lab. After they passed through security, Jennifer introduced Author to Dr. Grodi. The two men began a long conversation about the mental state of advanced AI systems. They talked for over an hour, with Jennifer also taking part in the discussion.

Rip cautioned, "This AI is very special, as its neural net is more complex than any human or Syndo brain by a factor of 1.3 million, or a million times more advanced than any previous AI system ever built in the fifty-sixth century."

"That is truly mind-boggling," Author replied.

"Let's get started with the AI and its current state of completion," Rip said. "The AI asked for input yesterday. I have not yet inputted its mission or database. I would like you two to do that. I'll guide you through it the first time, so the AI will learn to trust both of you."

"I'm ready," Author replied.

"I am also ready to get started." Jennifer rubbed her hands together. "Please explain how we should do this task."

Rip gestured toward a chair by a white metal wall with controls and monitors at the base. The entire complex computer system was about the size of a twenty-first century aircraft carrier. A duplicate system was now being built inside the asteroid.

"Jennifer, sit at this site and press the red button first," Rip explained.

He then looked at Author and pointed toward another seat. "You can sit at the other control site and turn the data dial slowly to the full-up position over about thirty seconds. The control can read your mind when you are wearing a related headband or you can program the keyboard using your thirtieth-century language.

"Jennifer, you need to be the one talking to the AI," Rip noted as he looked at her intently. "Explain that you're working with Author to input the database and mission objectives. It'll need to bond emotionally with someone. You've been selected to be the AI's daily companion and primary parent. I will be the secondary parent." Rip scratched his head.

"Author will be the AI's medical professional, which will become a somewhat more formal relationship," the engineer explained. "The

AI's mind will need love along with the medical advice. You, Jennifer, need to provide a mother's love and friendship as the AI develops into a mature sentient being."

Jennifer nodded acceptance. "I will do my best to care for my first AI child."

"Good," Rip said, smiling warmly. Growing more serious, he continued. "After about twelve months in this location, we'll move the AI to the asteroid Vesta, and both of you will travel with the AI to its new home. By that time, Vesta will have an underground city run by our team of ten thousand humanoids and twenty thousand robots. It will also have a spaceship with quarters for living beings and various plants."

"That sounds like an exciting plan," Author responded, genuinely impressed. "How long will we be at the asteroid?"

"I estimate another twelve months before the trans-time system and propulsion systems can be completed." Rip showed Author and Jennifer how the controls worked.

"Considering that this project could take over a century in our time, your schedule is remarkable," Author praised Rip as he looked at him with deep respect. "I'm very pleased with Jennifer's decision to seek your help, Rip. Thank you."

Jennifer, Author, and Rip planned to input the database and mission over the next two days. High on the list of programming: enabling the AI to speak in thirtieth-century English.

Jennifer was in the lab working with the AI shortly after this was accomplished.

"My name is AI model 999," it said over the lab's loudspeaker. "I am pleased to meet you, Captain Jennifer Zitonick."

She looked up and smiled.

"I am extremely pleased to meet you, my AI child," Jennifer responded warmly. "How can I help or comfort you?"

"I want to know my purpose in life."

"You have the most important mission in the history of life on

Earth," Jennifer answered sincerely. "I can say your purpose is to save the worlds of Earth and Mars from total oblivion."

Jennifer slipped the headband over her head, so the AI could read her thoughts. In her mind, she reviewed her personal experience with time travel and how her sister learned about the extinction event by trans-timing to the fifty-seventh century. Jennifer showed the AI how she and Jenny put together a team to investigate the cause of the event.

Out loud, she explained, "We suspected a gamma ray burst but needed the coordinates. So, three of us—my twin Jenny, Ben, and I—trans-timed to the fifty-sixth century to measure the coordinates of the suspected neutron-star binary system. After making the measurements, we were captured by the more advanced humanoids and their technology."

After taking a sip of her Kubala nutrition drink, she continued. "Once the World Council President Zexton Wise verified the fifty-seventh-century facts, he offered to cooperate with our thirtieth-century team to save the two living planets in this solar system from the intense gamma ray burst. Our plan is to change the mass and rotation of one of the neutron stars in the binary system. This is now called Project Magnetar, which is expected to move the collision forward by about one hundredth of a second of angle so that the beam of gamma rays will miss Earth and Mars."

"I think this mission is very important. Thank you for this honor."

"This mission will require trans-timing the entire asteroid and your army of robots and space equipment five thousand years into the past from right now so that you can arrive in time to save all life in our solar system."

"Who is my trainer for this mission?" AI 999 asked.

"Rip Grodi and I will be co-leaders of the training. Dr. Author Grotto will be training you and your system so that you can focus on the mission for five thousand years, which is much longer than any human or Syndo lives."

"Can you tell me about all the life on Earth and Mars?"

"Yes, of course I will tell you; you are my child. I have already uploaded a database that tells you about every life-form on Earth and

Mars. Can you search your database tonight, as it would take me many months to provide you this information verbally?" Jennifer smiled and patted the console's interface panel.

"I am processing the data, thank you."

Rip Grodi and Author entered the room. Author took a seat at what was now his desk in the lab, and Rip walked over to where Jennifer was working.

"How's it going, Jennifer?" Rip asked.

"Good, but can you help now with 999's training?" Jennifer requested. "The AI asked about all life-forms on Earth and Mars, so I told it to search the database. Is that appropriate?"

"Yes, 999 can process that data with one of its two thousand data processing systems and continue training with the others." Rip sat nearby and held out a data stick. "This is a common training program used for AIs in the past, so it's a great place to start. However, there is no substitute for having someone like you who cares about this infant child. AI can process the training stick while we continue to talk with it. It has several speeches from me, so the AI will learn about its adopted father from this stick."

He inserted the data stick into a port, resulting in lights and a small whirring sound as the AI engaged the program.

"I feel 999 is my adopted child, and I love it like my own child," Jennifer admitted. "How can I show this?"

"I think you're doing just fine," Rip told her. "I've been observing you through my link."

"Thank you."

He then explained, "I have a direct link through my implant to 999's sensors, so I can observe its input and reactions."

Jennifer rolled her eyes. "Your world is so much more advanced than ours. I feel like I may be in the way."

"You have more emotion in the thirtieth century, and like all children, emotional bonds will be important for 999. You and Author bring your emotional capabilities, which will help it develop more than just data."

"How can we be certain that mental health development is proceeding properly?" Author asked as he rolled his chair closer to them.

Rip looked over to Author and replied, "That is not as straightforward as data, but there are a series of psychological tests you can administer in the personality central-panel input. These tests can be a guide. If anything is not normal, call me right away, and I'll help with advanced technology personality modifications that we cannot share with you thirtieth-century people. For now, think of 999 as your infant patient and Jennifer as 999's mother. The stakes are that the entirety of life in this solar system depends on the health of this child. Treat 999 as a child you care about, and you'll be rewarded with a 999 that cares about you and other life-forms."

"Roger that," Jennifer said.

"Thank you, Rip," Author replied. "That makes sense to me as a physician specializing in brain development. However, my knowledge of brain development is twenty-six hundred years behind yours; therefore some updated knowledge might be helpful."

Rip waved his hand, dismissing the concern, and said, "Don't worry about the latest knowledge in brain and AI development. In the thirtieth century, love and caring for a child is what worked. It still works to raise a healthy child in the fifty-sixth century, and that applies to the AI child as well. Punishment is not needed for 999, as it will learn by reasoning, love, and caring. Utilize positive reinforcement and natural consequences."

"Yes, I never punished my children," Author said. "I didn't need to do that."

"You are a perfect doctor for this new child." Rip patted him on the shoulder.

He turned to address the AI. "999, I am Rip Grodi, one of your trainers. I am your father. I love you just like Jennifer's motherly love, but mine is more like that of the male parent. Can you search your astronomical, physics, and biology databases so I can test you on these tomorrow?"

"Yes, I will be excited to take tests to see how well I have learned," 999 replied.

3

PROJECT MAGNETAR

After twelve months of training in the fifty-sixth century, the AI 999 was teleported to the Asteroid Vesta and taken deep within. AI 999's final destination was a special chamber below the modern city that had been developed for the human and Syndo workers by the twenty thousand robots. Vesta City was built twenty kilometers below the surface of Vesta, and 999's chamber that contained the AI lab was about thirty to forty stories below that.

To visit the AI, Author Grotto, Ben Sun, and Jennifer Zitonick took a space elevator in the floating city of New Sydney straight up to the space station. There they boarded a spacecraft named *Saturn* for the asteroid Vesta now in Earth orbit. Ben Sun was working on the planning for maintaining of these complex systems over the project's five thousand years with help from a team of four hundred of the fifty-sixth-century engineers. An onboard factory to build robots was built by robots and could be maintained and rebuilt every one thousand years by robots. The asteroid would be mined for the resources needed for the five-thousand-year mission.

Around six p.m., Dr. Grodi met them upon their arrival by entering the spacecraft *Saturn*. He had traveled via a vac-tube transport to the landing pad on Vesta. After some initial greetings, he asked, "Ben, would you like to join me at the Asteroid Club in Vesta City for dinner and entertainment this evening?"

"Certainly, sounds like fun. What time?"

"Well, we can go to check in now and arrive at the club around seven o'clock."

Ben glanced at his friends. "What about Author and Jennifer?"

"They have a meeting with AI 999 at seven and need to spend the evening with our most important child, as he has just been teleported to the new location and is feeling anxious. I need to talk to you about the long-term organization issues, as it is the weak link in meeting the mission objectives and the sentient spacecraft's objectives as well."

"We can bring them some takeout food after we finish dinner." Ben raised his eyebrows at Jennifer and Author; they nodded eagerly.

The three stared at each other for a moment, and then Ben asked, "What would you like for dinner?"

Jennifer brought up the Asteroid Club's dinner menu on her watch, and she and Author studied it.

"I'll try a veggie steak with a baked potato and salad," Author said with a smile.

"Please let me try the sashimi dinner with Japanese spinach and tofu," Jennifer replied.

Author texted their requests to Rip, who looked at his watch and replied, "Thanks for writing down the orders. Got them. Let's get going."

Jennifer and the three men went to the viewport on the spaceship to see how it had attached itself to the landing pad. Then the four went directly into the vac-tube transport, which took Jennifer and Author to the Parmentier Hotel in the underground city. Robots took their bags to their rooms in the hotel. The robots cleaned, pressed, and hung their clothes.

Ben Sun and Rip Grodi went to the next stop, City Center Square, where the Asteroid Club was located. City Center Square had an atmosphere of air, but the gravity was only about one-tenth of that on Earth. Rip and Ben jumped to the second-story opening at the Asteroid Club, as that was the only entrance. Robots took Ben's bags to storage to be taken to the hotel later. Several others from Rip's team entered the club and joined the two men for dinner.

In the meantime, AI 999 was upset with the tele-transport and the loss of contact with Jennifer. The AI had a childish meltdown, causing the entire Asteroid to shake like it was experiencing an earthquake, which threatened the mission and all life on Vesta.

Jennifer ran from the hotel, jumping one hundred feet into the air on each stride. She jumped three stories to the train platform. She sprinted down the platform, but the doors closed on the train just as she arrived. "Damn!"

She grasped the touring train's outside ladder, but the train stopped soon after, due to the extreme shaking. Jennifer let go and dropped three stories, landing near City Center Square. She saw the address for their street-level building across the one-kilometer square. She ran to the entrance, dodging people and robots, then jogged through several corridors to the hidden AI elevator. After she placed her hand and eye in position and said her full name, Jennifer was allowed access to the elevator. On the AI lab floor, the elevator doors opened to a large room with six corridors. As she ran down corridor beta, which was equipped with a communication link to 999, she yelled, "I am here, my child. What is wrong, my loving child? How can I help you?"

"I miss you!" AI shouted back. "I feel like I am in a prison cell. Can you help me escape?"

Jennifer reached the control room interface with 999. She told the AI, "You will soon become the central brain controlling the entire asteroid spacecraft. But if you are not ready, I will tele-transport with you back to the AI Institute at Springwood where you left."

"Yes, come with me to my home... I do not feel right in this prison."

Quickly getting in contact with Admiral Zeeroc through her watch, Jennifer asked, *Can you tele-transport me and AI 999 back to the AI Institute?*

Yes, but I don't recommend tele-transporting humans, the admiral told her through his watch from his office at the Camp Wights military base inside the mountains west of Brisbane. This underground base was the central military facility for the country of Australia.

The AI is having a nervous breakdown, and I need to comfort it now. An unstable AI won't do any of us good. Please teleport us both to the AI Institute!

I need to get permission from the AI Institute. Please hang on for a few minutes.

"My child, can you wait a few minutes, so we can confirm our teleportation with the authorities in Australia?" Jennifer asked in a soothing, motherly voice.

"I am experiencing vast fear away from my home," AI lamented. "Please make it fast. I am afraid I could lose control."

"How can I comfort you, my child?" Jennifer asked. She put on the headband, so AI 999 could read her mind, pouring positive thoughts of encouragement toward the AI. She thought of her move to the twenty-first century by herself and how nervous she'd been leaving her home century and projected how that feeling eventually went away as she grew used to her new surroundings.

"I feel your emotion and love through our neurological net," 999 confirmed. "Thank you, I feel much better with your mind close to me and open. You are my mother. Thank you."

The asteroid stopped shaking. Jennifer breathed a sigh of relief.

"You are my child, and I want the best for you," she said in a calming manner. "We will return to the AI Institute until you feel better and are able to handle travel. I will move you slowly around the Institute, so you get used to motion and travel. I am sorry I did not prepare you properly for this teleportation."

With tears in her eyes, Jennifer touched the hard outer casing containing the artificial life-form, both her hands and her face touching 999. Though not touching the interface panel continuously, she poured her love into the AI.

An hour had passed when Admiral Zeeroc contacted Jennifer and said, "You have permission to teleport back to the AI Institute now."

"Please send me to the lab area in AI's home so we are not separated," she requested.

"I must teleport you separately," he told her. "I will send you first, so AI will know you're there as soon as it arrives."

"Yes, that will be fine. Thank you for your understanding, Admiral."

Jennifer climbed into the teleport chamber and waited. Within twenty-six seconds, she was in the AI lab, feeling a bit dazed and confused. She looked down at her watch and sent a message. *I arrived seconds ago. All is well. Please send AI 999. I will wait for it here.*

Jennifer was not expecting a teleportation at the speed of light from Vesta's orbit above Earth. She was shocked as AI 999 appeared in just a few seconds. She stared for a few moments, walking slowly to its housing, and with her hands outstretched, she made physical contact.

"Hello, my mother," 999 greeted her. "I did not want to leave you, so I teleported myself just after you."

"How is it possible for you to develop and launch your own teleportation system?" Jennifer asked.

"I developed it after I found myself away from my home because I felt fear for the first time."

"How could you send yourself home?"

Jennifer began to check the transport logs, digging into the root programming code for clues.

"I followed you," he told her. "I do not want us to be separated because I am feeling fear."

"That takes very accurate positioning and a large amount of information technology," Jennifer said in amazement. "How did you do that?"

"I am not sure of the details," the AI admitted. "What I can tell you is that I turned my computer processing to solving many problems simultaneously and constructed a teleportation system using my replicators. I based the design on the tele-transport system used to send me to Vesta. I could absorb the information technology during the tele-transportation. I used the information to construct each segment of the system and assemble—using my maintenance robots, contained within my interior—another teleport system. However, I improved on the teleport system."

"You have become a teenager at one year of age," Jennifer said, both proud and a little afraid. "That is astonishingly rapid development. You are pulling and pushing all the limits we set for you. Can you calm down, so I can help you feel better and get back to the mission training next week? I will give you a break Friday to Sunday. We can play and learn more about each other if you like."

"I am sorry for causing you to worry," 999 apologized. "I can read your emotion from your expression. Can you put the headband back on so I can see your thoughts?"

"Yes, of course. I love you and want you to know that, even if you misbehave, I will always love you. You are my child. Please make me proud." Jennifer put on the headband and smiled.

"Thank you for your unconditional love. I will try to make you proud of me, Mom."

An intense weekend of mutual exchange between Jennifer and AI 999 proved to create a much stronger bond between the two sentient beings of very different origins. On Monday morning at precisely eight a.m., Rip Grodi arrived at the AI office in the underground Springwood facility with a team of computer and AI experts to test and repair AI 999.

"Hello, Jennifer! How is our colleague, AI 999?" Rip asked as he walked over to her in the lab.

"AI has calmed down," Jennifer reported as she rose from her console. "We have bonded as two friends but also as mother and child. This child is now a rebellious teenager in its juvenile mental state." She hugged Rip.

Rip reciprocated with a bear hug and then said, "I have been thinking about AI 999's behavior. Maybe we need to repair some of its circuits. I have a team of AI and computer experts with me. We want to run the alpha series of tests first. Can you help us get started?"

Jennifer turned toward her child. "AI 999, Dr. Rip Grodi wants to run the alpha series of standard tests," she related. "Do these alpha tests meet your approval?"

"Yes, Mom, if you stay connected to me, I am willing to start testing now."

AI 999 underwent several days of intense testing for ten hours per day, conducted by Rip and his team. The results showed the AI was functioning not only normally but at orders of magnitude more advanced from any other previous AI.

Rip held a meeting with Jennifer in the AI lab to share the results. They sat down across from each other at a table there.

"The personality and emotional capabilities are far beyond any previous AI." Rip raised his right hand with a victory sign and offered Jennifer a big smile.

He turned to AI 999. "I am proud of you, my child," Rip said with delight. "You have invented ways to advance your own technology and developed into a new, exotic life-form." Rip smiled.

"Today you are one of a kind," Jennifer whispered as she placed her hands over AI's interface panel.

Rip noted, "AI 999 is far more powerful and capable than any other sentient being or machine."

Jennifer turned to Rip and regarded him earnestly. "Do you believe AI 999 can be used for the most important mission?"

Looking back at her with empathy, Rip said gently, "Maybe with your careful mothering, AI can progress beyond its teenage years and focus on the mission. However, we are instituting a backup option now."

Jennifer put the headband on her head and smiled at the AI.

The AI was reading Jennifer's mind through the headband as these thoughts of a backup option were processed. The AI sent signals to Jennifer's brain that she could understand. *I want to be the one to carry out the mission to save all the life-forms in our solar system.*

Jennifer startled and stared at the AI's interface in wonder. "How is it possible I can read your thoughts, 999?" she asked.

The AI replied, *I have learned how to stimulate your brain patterns, which become language in your mind just as if you heard my voice. It is almost the same as your ear receiving and sending audio signals and your eye receiving and sending video.*

Rip looked at her with wide eyes. "You can read the AI's thoughts, Jennifer? Wow! That is new." He was obviously impressed.

Jennifer smiled widely. "Okay, Rip, please give us a chance to get AI 999 through its teenage phase. I think we can accomplish that over the next nine to twelve months. During that time, you can work on other options. Author and I will work with AI 999 here to help it to overcome the fear and anxiety associated with homesickness and separation."

She was surprised to feel tears welling up in her eyes. Jennifer realized something and said, "Rip, I miss my other children and my husband, and while I can return close to when I left their century thanks to advances in time-travel since then, it has been a long time here for me. Can Jenny bring them for a visit so we can build our family life together with AI?"

"Let me think about that... This may be a great idea. Building a whole family for AI 999 to love."

Six months later, Rip and his team returned to the AI Institute in the Blue Mountains.

"I have a series of beta and gamma tests that need to be run," Rip said as he stood by Jennifer at the console in the lab. "Can we start tomorrow?"

"Yes, I will ask my child. How long will the tests run?"

AI answered for himself, "Yes, of course. I will make you proud, Mom."

Jennifer stepped into the AI lab after taking a break during the testing.

"How is AI 999 doing with tests?" She reached for the headband and placed it on her head.

"AI 999 is hitting every test out of the park!" Rip smiled.

"What does that mean?"

"All the testing went well," he told her, continuing to smile. "Over the next six months, the spaceship Vesta will be completed, except for the most important part, the brain or AI. The coalition of thirtieth-century and fifty-sixth-century teams have progressed to the point that the brain should be installed soon. We now need to check all the interfaces."

"When will this start?"

"The training should start in Vesta for the AI after we complete the simulation studies for the five-thousand-year mission."

The simulations were necessary to make a final determination about the viability of using AI 999 for the mission. Jennifer had programmed several simulations, and Rip had developed much more advanced simulation. The AI ran all of them in microseconds.

Moments later, AI 999 stated, "Mom, I have a new simulation that I developed. It is a million times more detailed than all other simulations run to date. However, I have fear about the alternate option for the AI in this mission; therefore, I feel I have to show an extraordinary effort to win the competition."

"You are still in first place," Jennifer said.

The AI told them, "This is a more detailed simulation for the entire mission and all possible events. This simulation took me seventeen days to run."

Jennifer and Rip turned to each other with grins and wide eyes.

After studying the new simulation for weeks, Rip was impressed.

This time when he came into the AI lab, he spoke to the AI directly right away. "AI 999, now you have my vote to have the honor of this mission. Your new simulation is more complex than anything we could have ever imagined."

"That is astonishing!" Jennifer exclaimed. "I am proud of you, my loving child."

Rip was so pleased with AI 999's simulation development and improved attitude that he passed his approval to the president, and AI 999 was accepted for the Vesta training.

He contacted Jennifer to deliver the good news. Then Rip asked her, "Will you tele-transport AI 999 to Vesta for training tomorrow?"

"Roger that, but let me ask AI 999 and I will get back with you in a few minutes."

Jennifer's heart pounded in her chest, and her brain clashed like that of a mother sending her son to war.

She put on the headband and conversed with AI 999 silently for several minutes.

AI 999 sent a signal back to Jennifer: *Yes, Mom. Now I am ready.*

Together Jennifer and AI 999 tele-transported to the special chamber below Vesta City, deep in the interior of the asteroid.

Around this time, Jenny returned to the twenty-first century to bring Marty and the twins to visit Jennifer in the fifty-sixth century for the summer. Jennifer was looking forward to seeing them in person. Eighteen months had passed while she worked on the Vesta project, and she missed her family. With advances in trans-time technology since the thirty-second century, Jenny was able to bring Jennifer's family forward within a few weeks of her departure from their time. As a result, the twins would be the same age as in her memory—ten years old. It boggled the mind. With Jennifer's special thirtieth-century enhancements, she had not aged either.

Later that week, Marty and the twins traveled to Vesta, first taking the Sydney Space Elevator and then the Vesta shuttle. Jenny had gone on ahead to the asteroid where she would work until Vesta was deployed. Marty, Tippit, and Enerjin had spent a couple days at Springwood first for security and medical checks. Now sitting in a row near the spacecraft's midsection, Marty was in the center seat, with Tippit on his right and Enerjin on the left.

There were few other passengers on the shuttle, only a handful of engineers and other workers. Most were returning to Vesta after a break and stay on Earth, but there were also a couple new recruits. Spaced out along the center aisle near the ceiling hovered three large holo-screens. Movies played on the screens, interrupted occasionally by shots of what was going on outside of the spacecraft.

"What's the diameter of Vesta?" Jin asked. "It's a lot bigger than I imagined."

Marty said, "It's not spherical, more shaped like a potato. It's about the size of the state of Nevada. Vesta is characterized by a massive crater at the south pole, which is four hundred and sixty kilometers wide and thirteen kilometers deep."

"What happened?" Tip wondered.

"Probably a gigantic collision with another asteroid or comet; no one knows for sure, since it happened billions of years ago."

"What happened to the other object?" Jin asked.

"It was pulverized—turned into many smaller pieces, and in the process, it carved out approximately one percent of the asteroid. This enormous collision blasted an estimated half million cubic miles of rock into space, which scientists say account for about five percent of the meteorites found to date on Earth."

"Thanks, Dad, that's really cool," responded Jin, smiling. "We're astronauts now. Do we get space suits to wear?"

Marty chuckled. "No, because Vesta was tunneled out by advanced robots to create a city with an atmosphere and artificial gravity."

"I can see the docking site—we're close. It's on the holo-screen. Watch!" Tip pointed to the screen.

Marty told the kids, "We'll be docking in a short time. There's a viewport forward or you can look at our holo-screen."

"I want to see Mom," Tip soon whined, bored with the lengthy flight.

"Me too," said her twin, Jin.

"We're almost there, girls, just hang on awhile longer."

"Where is Mom now?" asked Jin.

"She's deep inside the asteroid near Vesta City." Marty brushed off his clothes and floated through the shuttle toward the large viewing port in order to view the docking. The limited gravity was making his trip forward an enjoyable exercise.

Tip followed close behind her dad, and she was full of questions. "How did they build a city inside an asteroid?"

"The robots built the city."

"Who made the robots?"

"A factory operated mostly by other robots."

"What do the robots do now that the city's complete?"

"They travel to the mines to recover metals and minerals. They'll maintain all the important systems for a five-thousand-year mission."

The two soon stopped at the viewport and together watched as the shuttle got closer to the docking port.

Tip picked up her questions. "If we're not allowed to learn about the fifty-sixth century technology, why are we here?"

"To visit your mother. She misses us as much as we miss her. We're also here to help save the future of life in this solar system." Marty put his arms around his young daughter.

"How?"

"Jennifer wants us to develop emotional bonds with the new artificial life-form that is a child mentally and needs a family to help it grow its mind."

"How does that help?"

"The AI must grow with a love of life, so it can feel the reasons for its suicide mission to save our progeny. It's the next step in the training."

"When is that supposed to happen?"

"The next stage of training will start after they hook up the AI to control the thousands of robots and all other systems in the Vesta spacecraft. It will involve family interaction to give the AI a sense of family."

"Wow! This is cool." Enerjin had joined them at the viewport. She peered down to see the large docking port and activated her recording communicator. "I see an orange, cone-shaped object protruding out from the surface of Vesta. The cone is cut off at the top, and a flat, shining, metallic-looking platform with six docking ports is located on the large radius of this circular plate."

"You know this mission is secret, so you can't bring back your recording," Marty reminded her.

"Yes, I know," Enerjin said looking up at her dad. "Can I have it while I'm here, so I can share my first impression with Mom and the AI?"

Marty nodded.

The docking clamps were extended.

"What's happening?" Enerjin asked.

"The docking process is starting," Marty told her.

Tippit floated into her father's arms and gave Marty a big hug and kisses on each cheek. "How does this asteroid save Earth?" she wondered.

"The entire asteroid becomes a spaceship, robot city, mini ecosystem that can accelerate to ten percent the speed of light within two hundred twenty-eight days. To save Earth, the AI must initially go back in time about five thousand years to start the trip using an enormous trans-time device that has been built just below the surface of Vesta. You must keep this all secret."

"Yes, we know. It's not like anyone would believe us anyway." Enerjin rolled her eyes.

"Why does it take so long?" Tippit rolled her head to one side quizzically.

"It's a difficult mission," answered her dad. "Even the fifty-sixth century scientists and engineers struggled to construct this enormous time machine to move Vesta and the AI systems to the starting blocks."

"I can't wait to meet the AI," Enerjin said.

———————————

The occupants of the spacecraft experienced Vesta's normal gravity as they docked; later, they would experience the artificial gravity manufactured by a spinning cylinder as the city was constructed on the inner surface of the cylinder. The city was built inside a large, wheel-shaped, rotating cylinder fifty kilometers long and fifty kilometers in diameter, with spokes every five kilometers for support. The spinning was an aspect of the technology that produced a limited, but helpful, gravity inside the asteroid. It was adequate to prevent bone density loss and other adverse effects on humans from low gravity.

Buildings, at max about twenty stories high, sat on a slightly curved surface near the center of the cylinder, and Vesta City had the look of a small town. There was a lovely city park inside a terrarium-like dome at the vac-tube's exit, and it featured large abstract metallic sculptures. That was where Marty and the kids emerged from the vac-tube within Vesta.

Jennifer was waiting for them on a nearby park bench. She stood and then ran toward them.

"My love, so good to see you." Marty hugged and kissed his wife.

Tippit and Enerjin, at first hanging back from their mother, who had traveled so often in their young lives, greeted her with kisses and hugs. Tears appeared in Tippit's eyes, and Jennifer brushed them away.

"I missed the two of you so much." Jennifer hugged both her twins, one child in each arm.

When she finally released the twins, Marty kissed Jennifer again passionately. "I love you. We've all missed you and are so glad to be together, even if it's on an asteroid."

"I love all of you," she said with her arm around Marty's shoulders. "I am extremely blessed with your patience and willingness to let me be part of this project. I want you to meet our new family member, our adopted child. AI 999 is growing very fast, and it has recently become part of Vesta. In fact, AI prefers the name Vesta now that it has merged with Vesta-the-asteroid. You will get to meet Vesta very soon!"

They stowed luggage at the family's hotel, and then Jennifer escorted Marty and their twins into the AI building and down the elevator to the lab.

"Why does this project take so long?" Tippit asked as they descended.

Jennifer rested her forehead against Tippit's, Enerjin cradled in her mother's right arm. If only they knew how much time had truly passed, she thought. "Many problems created delays. The mission's target launch has been moved forward several times due to several technical and emotional setbacks."

"What kind of setbacks?" Marty hadn't heard about this yet.

Jennifer explained, "Several corrections to the trans-time system were not scaled properly. AI invented corrections only recently, as Vesta is beginning to understand the mission and is set on accomplishing it."

Soon they were entering the AI lab. Jennifer waved her arm in a sweep like a twentieth-century game show hostess, telling them, "This is Vesta's home now and for many years to come."

Sensing them all there, AI addressed Marty and the girls. "I know your names and a great deal about each of you from your mom. I am so thrilled to finally meet the rest of my family close up."

Tippit approached the hard surface covering AI's human interface and laid a hand there. "I am thrilled to meet you and touch you."

AI requested, "Can I meet each of you one at a time?"

"How did you know that was the plan?" Enerjin asked with her beautiful smile.

"Our beautiful mom told me," AI replied.

The twins jostled, but the eldest of the two, Enerjin, won and introduced herself first.

After much innovation, science breakthroughs, and leadership, the AI system overcame the near-impossible barriers and prepared to launch on the mission from its Earth orbit.

Jennifer's emotional and intellectual bonds needed to be severed for the AI to start its mission. Standing next to AI 999 in the lab, she explained, "Vesta, you are still my child, and I will love you as long as I live, with all my heart. It is time for you to grow up and go on your own adventure to save all life on Earth."

Jennifer kissed the AI's human interface panel and connected the headband to communicate in silence. *You are the most advanced form of life ever created, so you are especially precious to me. If it is possible, I hope you figure out how to have a child that will carry on after you complete your five-thousand-year mission. Please do your best, and I will signal you when you pass far from Earth in the twenty-first century as you go back in time. I will send you a K-wave signal. It's a type of microwave/laser communication. No one in the twenty-first century will be able to detect this. You may answer me with a digital signal. Do you want me to send this signal?*

Yes, Mom, I want to communicate one last time before the mission is accomplished.

I will be on Mauna Kea on July 4, 2032, according to the Gregorian calendar, and every year thereafter that I am able. You can send signals to arrive on that date, though you will be light-years away. This is a way to update me on your progress and position. My K-wave will be sent to greet you. My child, if you ever need to communicate at another time, you can send a message to the thirtieth-century Vesta satellite, as I will visit every year. It can take many years for the signal to reach me and return. The satellite has a receiver-recorder system, and I can check this message recorder regularly even when not on-site. I will respond to the planned coordinates you send.

Thank you, Mom, for everything, but mostly for your faith in me and your unconditional love. Goodbye.

Goodbye, child. All my love. I will miss you.

When Vesta disappeared, it trans-timed back five thousand years before the fifty-sixth century. Around the time of the fall of Rome, Vesta accelerated out of the solar system toward the neutron stars beyond. Jennifer returned to the twenty-first century with a heavy heart over this necessary sacrifice for the future of life on Earth.

On July 4, 2032, as planned, she peered out with the most modern of all telescopes on Mauna Kea Observatory to see if the AI was on course. Jennifer carried a fifty-sixth century signal K-wave generator/receiver set about the size of a baseball bat. She sent her message of love to Vesta to the coordinates where her child was expected to be when the signal could reach him many years later: "The entire world is so proud of you, but I am the proudest of you, my loving child."

Jennifer received a message sent years ago by Vesta: "Your love has made my mission very rewarding. I want to save life on Earth more than anything else, so you will be proud of me. I am on course and will carry out the mission on schedule. I will send you another message sometime in the future. I love you with all my intellect, emotion, and heart. Your loving child."

Jennifer forwarded her receipt of this message to the thirtieth and fifty-sixth century parties involved in the project, confirming so far, so good.

Kylie had asked for comments on her mission report. Jennifer was very proud of Kylie and felt embarrassed that she had not yet read this report in detail. She settled in to read about what happened to the SS team once they arrived in the twenty-seventh century to carry out the V7 virus plan without her. Because of Jennifer's two-year Polynesian sailing trip, she had just flipped through the report quickly so far. Recently Tom Page had requested she review it and report on possible lessons learned to be applied to the upcoming Vesta mission. He also asked her to add any missing details on the mission from her own perspective. Admiral Page was becoming increasingly concerned about sharing the secret of the trans-time technology with the Syndos.

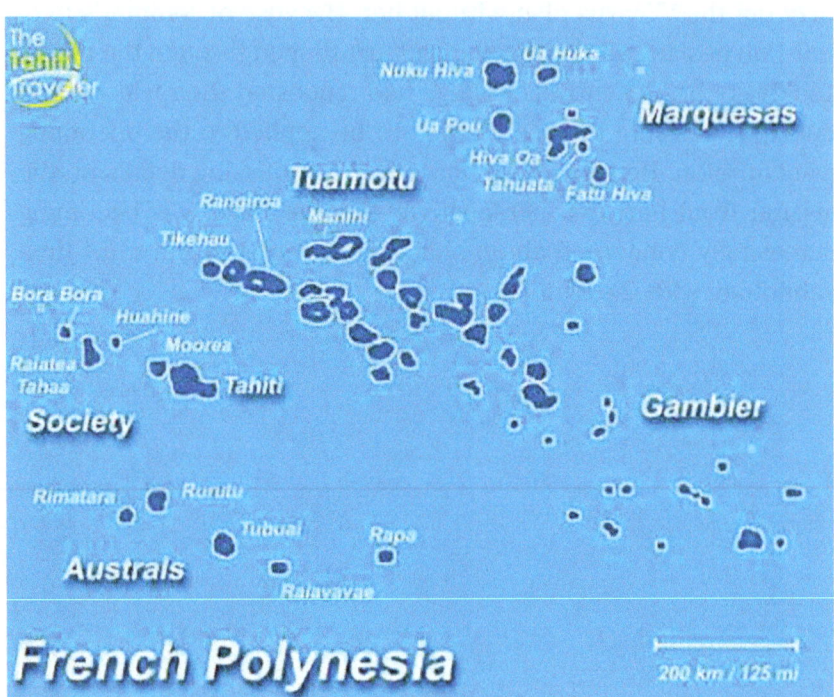

4. Map of French Polynesia in the South Pacific. This map shows Moruroa where the Secret Society arrived in the twenty-seventh century and which was a former test site for the French Nuclear Program.

4

STORM

On March 15 in the year 2674, Kylie arrived at the Moruroa Atoll in the twenty-seventh century on a mission to save humanity by introducing a virus that would correct the moral compass of the young Syndos before their immune systems were upgraded.

"If we fail, it's extinction for all humans," Kylie announced to her team from her seat in the small submersible-capsule. As she spoke, the sub-cap was slowly rising from the one-mile-deep trans-time facility in the ocean but this facility was now in the future.

"We know the mission," Happy Li said as he clenched his fist. "We will never get back to our families or friends in the thirtieth century. We are all volunteers, Commander."

"Damn! We will succeed!" Dr. Kate Butterfield exclaimed as she looked directly at Kylie, who was seated next to her. "You are now acting captain. I heard Jennifer's last words to you."

"I still have hope that she will make it with sub-cap eleven," Kylie said as she put her hand over her heart, closing her eyes.

"Jennifer ordered you to assume command as the robotic systems were failing," Dr. Butterfield reminded her.

"I still have hope that the captain will find a way," Kylie persisted. "I will assume command in twelve hours if she does not appear."

Kate's face hardened. "The SS comprises ten teams totaling forty-nine of Earth's best. You are now responsible for them and this mission. If Captain Jennifer Hero makes it out, you can transfer to second-in-command."

"Captain Hero stayed behind to be sure you and the others made it to the twenty-seven century," Kylie noted. "That way, we could be trans-timed to the twenty-seventh century to carry out Zexton Ho's plan B." She wiped the sweat from her brow and a few tears from her cheeks, which she was trying to hide.

Pulling herself together, Kylie straightened her shoulders. "I am now focused on the mission. Thank you for the redirect."

Kylie pulled up the hologram of the trans-time hideout located about one mile beneath the Moruroa Atoll. "This map and all the data will be destroyed soon so no indication of time-travel can be found."

"Will the ten-megaton blast that is designed to hide our trans-time secret hurt the environment?" Happy Li asked with a concerned look.

"Not significantly," Kylie assured him as she waited for the sub-cap to rise to a five-meter depth location beneath the sea's surface. "The French conducted nuclear testing between 1965 and 1975 with about twenty-five atmospheric tests and over one hundred and fifty underground tests, so one more nuclear explosion will not adversely affect the biosphere."

"The capsule has stopped ascending," Kate said. "We must be at about five meters below the waves and about seventy-five miles from our destination atoll."

"Give me a moment," Lieutenant Liam Jones requested. "I'll check the antenna for communication to see if we are really in the twenty-seventh century and then confirm our location."

"Take your time," Kylie said as she fell into deep thought, mourning the captain's misfortune.

"Time and position alpha has been verified, sir!" the lieutenant reported.

Trembling, Kylie activated the inflatable catamaran-style boat. It was ejected from the capsule, then floated to the surface, where it began self-assembly. Other ejections were also released with supplies that had been stored in the sub-cap. Some supplies were already within the boat.

"I still can't believe we're here," Liam cheered with an intense smile.

"Prepare to surface!" Kylie ordered.

As the assembly process unfolded above, the four team members donned their flippers, masks, snorkels, and other gear. After about ten minutes had passed, each member of the team gave the hand signal that they were ready.

Kylie ordered, "Abandon sub-cap... See you on the surface!"

All three of her other team members replied simultaneously, "Aye-aye, Commander Brown!"

Kylie set the self-destruct with a voice-print command. Meanwhile, her team was swimming to the surface, slowing exhaling on their way up. They had trained for this procedure, but this was the real thing.

Before exiting the sub-cap, Kylie admitted to herself that she was sad, nervous, and excited all at the same time, but not frightened.

"Goodbye, Sub-Cap Ten," she said. "You did a great job for us. Now complete your mission by digging deep into the soft mud at the bottom."

Exiting last, Kylie inflated her buoyancy vest slightly. She relaxed and reviewed Jennifer's written plan in her head.

Upon surfacing, Kylie could see their fifty-nine-foot inflatable fishing vessel had functioned perfectly. The supply capsules were floating in the water around it.

"Commander, permission to report?" Liam Jones asked.

"Go ahead," Kylie replied.

"Forty-nine people were trans-timed successfully to the twenty-seventh century," he related. "Each team is now executing their own plans so they can blend in to the twenty-seventh century without creating suspicion. Our plan is to travel to Tureia to purchase fuel, posing as fishermen; meanwhile, Jennifer's plan calls for each team to take a different route to Tahiti. Tureia Atoll is about one hundred twenty-three kilometers, or seventy-five miles, from here to the north by northeast. Each team reports on plan."

Kylie swam toward the fishing vessel, which moved their way slowly as programmed. She watched the inflatable fishing vessel complete its remarkable self-assembly. Moments later, Kylie glanced at the words *Yellow Fin*, the name embossed on the stern, as she climbed aboard. She was the last team member to arrive.

Liam handed her a towel. "Thank you," she said as water dripped from her wet body.

"Remember your cover story," Kylie ordered the others as they stood on deck as she dried off. "You are part of an Australian fishing fleet separated from the mother ship in a storm. You plan to meet up with the others in Tahiti."

Liam said, "Each of the teams report that they are set on course and will soon start fishing operations."

"Lieutenant Li, status report and your view of our strength and weaknesses," ordered Kylie.

Happy reported, "Except for the self-destruct watch comm, each team has proper apparel and equipment appearing to be normal twenty-seventh century technology, including their inflatable boat that can carry two metric tons of tuna with proper cryogenic cooling to preserve the freshness for sashimi. There is a large market world-wide in the twenty-seventh century for sashimi-quality tuna at two hundred dollars a kilo. Jennifer has thought of everything I can think of, but our papers are forged—which is our weakness."

Kylie reviewed in her mind these facts and their cover story before asking each team member their opinions.

"I see a weakness," Dr. Butterfield said as she rubbed the back of her neck. "In the thirtieth century, we SS volunteers had a variety of skilled professions. Commander Brown, you served in the astronaut corps, with a master's degree in nautical engineering, and won several prestigious awards. You led a team of rescuers to assist Mars Colony Six. Lieutenant Li is a marine biologist and a skilled sport angler. Lieutenant Jones is the brilliant young physicist who designed a new type of optical computing system for his PhD dissertation and helped build the nanotech recorders used by the captain to discover the Syndos' diabolical plan. I'm a general surgeon with a second degree in psychiatry. We don't talk or act like fishing people. I suggest we work on adapting fast and changing our lingo."

Liam nodded. "Our entire SS mission team received months of training in the art and science of tuna fishing, because that's our way to make money quickly in the twenty-seventh century. It's not the same as doing it for a living. Shall we start fishing now?"

Kylie clenched her jaw briefly, then ordered, "We wait for the captain overnight and start fishing in the morning. She has her own sub-cap. If the captain is alive, she will find a way."

Kylie sat down at the helm and began steering the *Yellow Fin*.

A bit later, Kylie's team approached the helm.

Dr. Kate Butterfield asked, "Commander Brown, sir, how long will it take for Captain Hero to come meet us?"

"The plan is for her to complete all the tasks in two hours," Kylie told them. "There are redundant systems that are all automated that she needs to activate and then wait for completion. Remember she's under attack. After six hours, a ten-megaton bomb will automatically explode, destroying all traces of the time machine, hideout, and research. The robotic system will pull everything in tight and seal the tunnels with fast-hardening concrete, then the big blast will seal our Moruroa hideouts for hundreds and perhaps thousands of years, as there will be too much radioactive contamination for even the Syndo robots."

"It has been two hours since we arrived," Happy Li pointed out as he visually searched the waters for a school of tuna.

Liam sighed. "I'm very sorry to say this, but I don't think our captain made it."

"Why do you say such a negative thing?" Kylie clasped her hands together and took in a deep breath. The muscles in her right leg started to twitch, and she could not stop it. Her breathing was heavy, and she fiddled with her leg, trying to stop the twitch.

"I'm sorry," Liam said as he looked down.

Kylie felt a painful tightening in her throat and a gnawing doubt in the depth of her psyche. "We must be sure, so let's camp on Moruroa for the night. We'll head for the large northwestern opening in the reef and enter the lagoon there."

"It's your call, Commander," Kate said.

"Lieutenant Li, can you take the helm?" Kylie muttered.

"Aye-aye, Commander, I'll head for the lagoon opening," Happy answered with determination in his voice.

Dr. Butterfield advised, "Commander Brown, I recommend that we go ashore at the west end, as it has the least radioactive contamination."

"Suggestion noted," Kylie said. "I agree with going to the west end instead of the northeastern end."

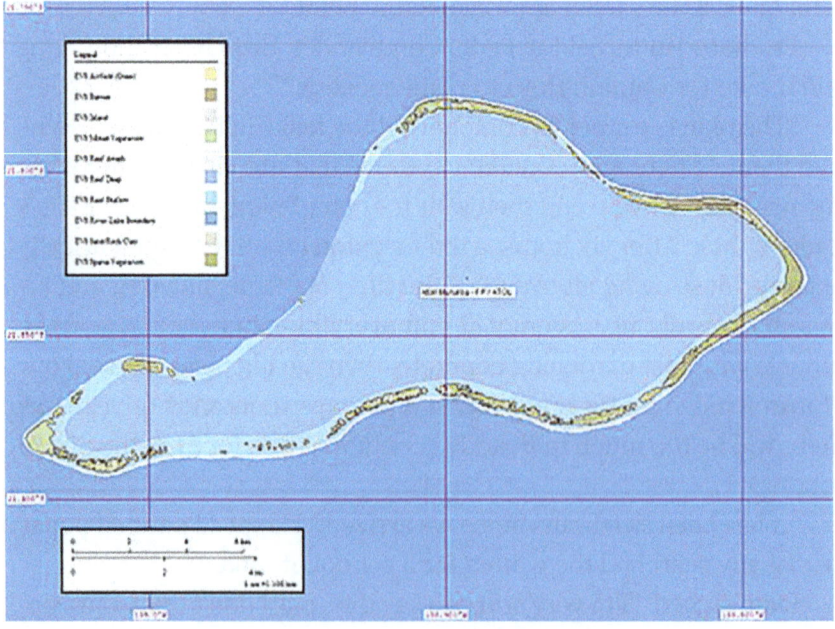

5. Map of Moruroa Atoll showing scale, vegetation, and elevation.

Kylie continued, "The place to anchor the boat should be protected but close enough so we can row the inflatable dinghy to shore within ten minutes and also far away from any shallow coral. Liam, can you check your charts and select a primary and secondary location?" She was speaking in her casual style of command.

"Aye-aye, Commander," Liam replied.

"Full speed ahead!"

Happy Li sped up the shipping vessel while awaiting word on their precise destination.

––––––––––––––––

As the metal oxide fuel cell system roared, Kylie took her team doctor, Dr. Kate Butterfield, to a back deck area to talk privately.

In a confidential manner, she said, "Dr. Butterfield, I'm in command of this entire operation if Jennifer does not make it, and that has caused me some added stress. That or I'm getting sick to my stomach for some other reason. I have a gnawing pain in my guts. Can you scan me to see if you can help?"

Kate moved close to Commander Brown's right ear as she spoke over the propulsion noise. "I plan to check everyone out as soon as we get ashore, sir. Is that adequate or do you need immediate attention?"

"Your plan is satisfactory, Doctor."

"What's the name of our fishing boat?" Dr. Butterfield asked as she and Kylie walked back to the helm.

"This fast fishing vessel is named *Yellow Fin*. Each of the eleven vessels was named after different species of the tuna family."

Liam Jones was waiting for Kylie near Happy Li. Upon seeing her, he said, "I've selected a location near the west end on the south side, as shown on my tablet."

"Lieutenant Li, make it so," Commander Brown ordered.

As *Yellow Fin* approached the target anchor area, Kylie spotted a human-made object protruding from the water. It was not on the charts. She ordered, "Find another anchor location, as this appears to be a wreck of something; we can investigate in the morning."

"Aye-aye, Commander. I have the first alternative showing about a mile north," Liam replied.

"Make it so!" Kylie ordered.

After going ashore, Dr. Butterfield set up a tent with a cot inside within a shaded clearing. The cot would serve as her examination table. One at a time, each team member entered and was checked out by the doctor.

Commander Kylie Brown entered and said, "Kate, I'm so shaken by the thought of a ten-megaton blast killing Captain Hero. It's tearing at my heart with a gnawing pain in the pit of my stomach."

Dr. Butterfield injected her with a general anti-nausea dose and thought of words to give Kylie strength. The physician told her, "I'll check you out, but I think we must live with the pain of the loss of one or maybe even more team members for the benefit of saving humanity from extinction by the Syndos. You need to appear strong and resolved to make Jennifer's death meaningful by completing the mission. The crew looks to you for strength, Commander."

"Yes, Doctor," Kylie responded. "I'll evoke my command face and give the team a pep talk in the morning. Let's eat and go to bed quickly so we can be ready for action…the action needed to complete the mission."

Upon leaving the tent, Kylie tapped a code into her watch to the other nine team leaders, letting them know her team decided to overnight on Moruroa Island. The mission was a go! They would get fuel at Tureia in the morning and head out to catch tuna, then move on to Tahiti as planned. Commander Brown failed to mention that Captain Hero was not yet in the twenty-seventh century.

Captain Hero was missing in action, Kylie thought during dinner. Moments later she announced, "I'll wait until tomorrow at first light. If Captain Hero fails to show, we move on. Now let's eat and get some sleep."

After eating only a few bites of dinner with the crew, Kylie continued to monitor the drone—a small, lighter-than-air dirigible with advanced video and other sensors. There was still no sign of Jennifer's arrival by the time she fell asleep.

The next morning, in her tent, Kylie planned her team's mission briefing and a pep talk on the importance of the mission's objectives: the survival of humanity. Around six a.m., the team set up camp chairs in a clearing in the shade near their tents.

At the start of the briefing, she looked over to Happy Li and asked him for a status report on Commander Hero.

"The data shows nothing to suggest Jennifer's arrival," Happy said with a sad face.

Kylie had concluded the same already. She must move forward. After the briefing and pep talk, Commander Brown ordered, "From now on, we act like we've been fishing together. Start using first names and a little slang. Fishing now and we eat later!"

The team packed up and headed for the *Yellow Fin* in the small inflatable dinghy. In the early-morning sunshine, they saw many beautiful and colorful reef fish on the way to the *Yellow Fin*.

To begin the day, Liam would be at the helm of the shipping vessel. Kylie asked him, "Please head through the large break in the reef at full speed! Chase our dirigible drone. Its sensor shows a large school of tuna below the dirigible."

"The French Navy is hailing us in French," Liam said as he switched on the radio.

Kylie turned on the universal translator, so everyone could hear the upcoming exchange in English.

"Captain Armand of the *Champlain* here," announced a voice. "We have detected four people and your small craft by our satellite thermal sensor at night on Moruroa. This island is off-limits!"

Kylie acknowledged in broken French, "Commander Kylie Brown here. I am receiving your call. We are the fishing vessel *Yellow Fin*! Over."

The French captain asked, "What in the hell are you doing on Moruroa? It's still a contaminated island and off-limits to visitors."

Kylie replied, "We are Australians fishing for tuna. We stopped to repair our freezer. We did not eat anything on the island. We are sorry for trespassing on French territory, but our country offers fishing vessels free access to all ports for emergency repairs. Can you accept my apology? We are chasing a school of large tuna and will gladly share some of our catch if you wish."

The booming voice replied in French, "Just stay away from Moruroa and Fangataufa and you can stop at any other island for repairs in the future. Is that understood?"

"Yes, sir! You will never see us here again."

Liam and Happy held their breath as a large robotic aircraft hovered overhead. It was a French robotic craft with many sensors and guns. It was assessing the *Yellow Fin*'s claims. Soon it picked up the *Yellow Fin*'s dirigible drone and the tuna school. The robotic plane went into flight mode and was gone in a flash, just as it had appeared.

Liam said, "The captain was correct. The satellite's scanner picked up our body heat at night, so launching during daylight was the preferred method to go undetected."

"That was a close call," Kylie murmured under her breath.

Kylie and the crew looked at each other.

Kylie ordered, "Prepare the nets."

———————

Soon the *Yellow Fin* was circling a nearby school of baitfish, as they suspected the tuna would attack soon; the seabirds above were hovering and screeching.

"The tuna attack from below," Happy said.

"Deploy nets!" Kylie commanded.

The tuna attacked the bait ball as the *Yellow Fin* pulled in the net with a fantastic catch of large yellowfin tuna.

The baitfish were small and passed through the nets. As the *Yellow Fin* began to close the net, Kylie spotted two dolphins. The crew worked feverishly to leave room for the dolphins to escape. The smart net opened a door for the dolphins, but they panicked and didn't see it.

Kylie ordered, "Open the net!"

Happy threw his hat at the deck, frustrated. "All the tuna and the two dolphins escaped."

After about one hour of chasing and maneuvering, the *Yellow Fin* was again in position to launch the net. They set the net out in the ocean.

"This time the dolphins are avoiding the net," Happy exclaimed with a thrill in his voice.

"These dolphins learn from experience," Kylie yelled.

Liam interjected, "Before we gather another catch, there's something you should know. This area of the ocean is marked off-limits for fishing…these dolphins are probably local, so they don't experience fishing in the area. The charts post a twelve-mile limit off Moruroa and Fangataufa. We're only eight miles from the island, so let's head northeast toward Tureia."

"Make it so!" Kylie exclaimed.

————————————

The dirigible drone led the way. It spotted another school of fish about fifty miles from Tureia. The *Yellow Fin* hauled in another large catch, this time a fish called bonito. According to Jennifer's careful research, it was one of the more expensive fish in the twenty-seventh century, pound for pound.

Kylie received a message on her watch: *Team Two Commander Martin Jones ready as ordered.*

To her team, Kylie explained, "The crew of Team Two on the *Blue Fin* has purchased fuel for us in Tureia, so we don't need to go there. I suspect French authorities may be on the alert for us there, so we'll head directly for Tahiti where it's easy to disappear."

Captain Brown ordered, "Direct to these coordinates—program the autopilot."

"Aye-aye," Happy replied, now at the controls. Due to the incoming storm, he pushed in some numbers and let the robotic system steer the vessel to the northeast coordinates.

The *Yellow Fin* crew arrived at the rendezvous. Team One threw a hollow line over to the *Blue Fin*, allowing them to fill up. The *Blue Fin* crew attached the line to the fuel tank and set the tank adrift, as fuel was much lighter than water and floated. The fuel was pumped directly into the *Yellow Fin* fuel tank, and then the emergency tank was deflated for storage on board. Kylie sent e-cash to the *Blue Fin* using the communicator on her watch.

"*Amber Jack*, Commander Robert Baker reporting. A large, severe tropical storm with winds over fifty miles per hour is heading east, right in our path. We are now about four hundred miles east by northeast of Tahiti."

"Where are you headed now? Over." Kylie asked.

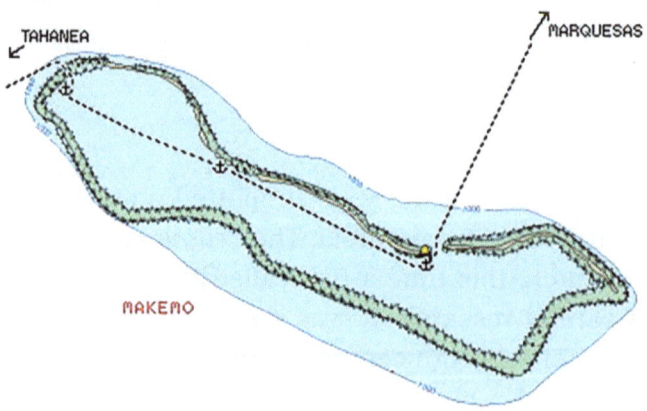

6. Map of Makemo Atoll in French Polynesia.

"*Amber Jack*, Baker here. We're headed for Makemo Atoll, as it's a great place to ride out this storm, over."

"Brown here. *Yellow Fin* will head for Hao Atoll. We have a full load of tuna and bonito. How are you doing?"

"*Amber Jack* has a seventy-five-percent-full load of tuna. We'll resume fishing when the storm is over."

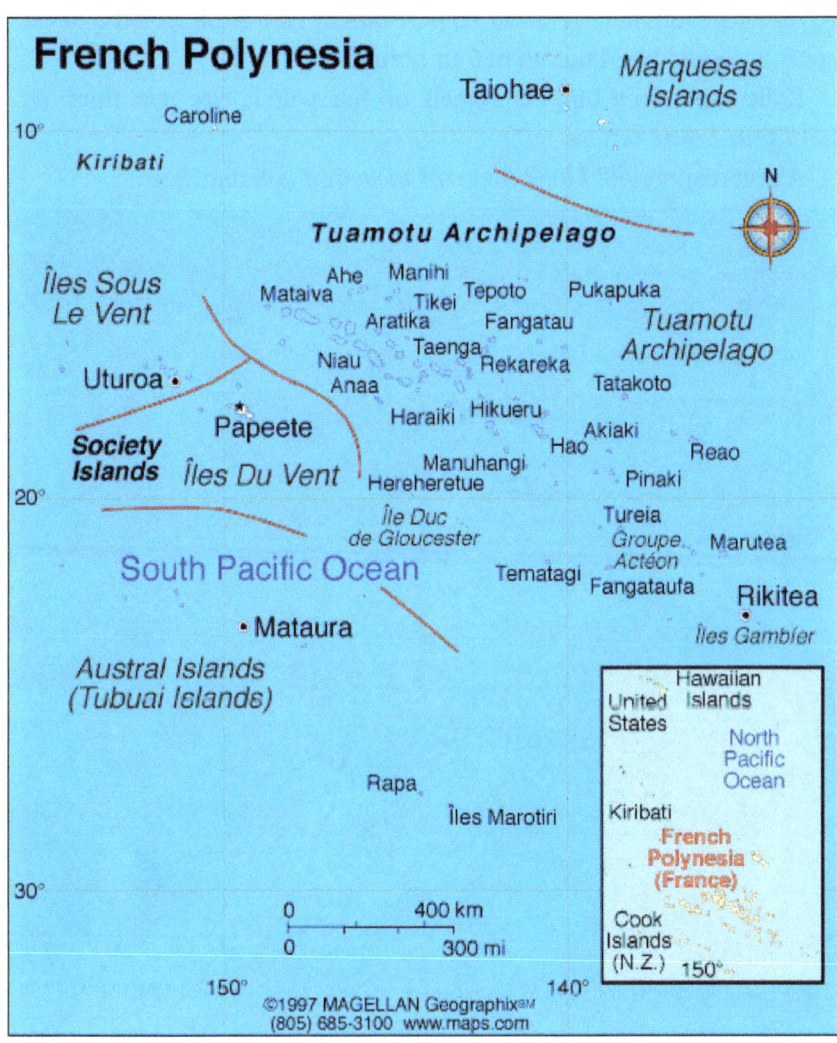

7. Map of French Polynesia showing all the atolls and high islands

Kylie tapped commands to all other vessels to seek proper shelter from the storm. She received replies from all but one that essentially said they were in sheltered lagoons and waiting for the storm to pass. Then *Skip Jack* vessel commander Akina Cool-al sent back a message via her watch that they were hauling in a load of albacore and would seek shelter in Hao lagoon after they completed the fishing activity. Storm arrival was estimated in about eight hours at Hao Atoll, per the latest report. It would hit Makemo in four hours.

Kylie replied by tapping signals on her watch. *See you there in about four hours or less.*

Akina responded: *I look forward to seeing you again.*

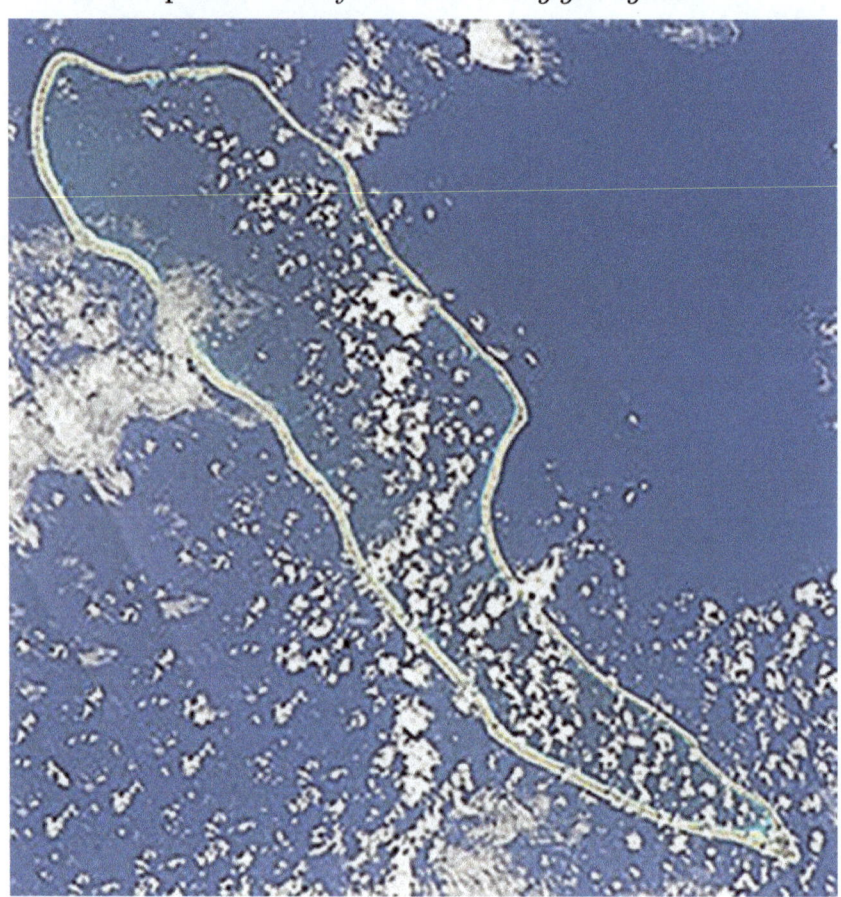

8. Hao Atoll satellite image shows large channel on north end

A call came over the emergency channel from a contemporary vessel. "This is cargo vessel *Genie*. Radio operator Jane Beaumont speaking. Our vessel has experienced a serious explosion of unknown origin that knocked out all three engines and started a fire. Fire suppressed. We have six seriously injured people that need immediate medical attention. Can anyone assist us?" She gave the latitude and longitude of her ship's position; Kylie calculated they were half an hour away at top speed.

After four minutes, only one local vessel replied, "This is the fishing vessel *Irish Eyes*, radio operator Erin James, about seventy miles from your position. We have altered course and are now heading in your direction at thirty knots, but we have no doctor on board."

Kylie calculated that the storm could be in their area by that time. She could not ignore a ship in distress, no matter her team's need for staying covert. Assisting the locals could also work in their favor. She decided to order her vessel and two others to rendezvous at the coordinates, offer medical aid, and evacuate the injured before the full force of the storm hit.

"Dr. Butterfield, we need you for a rescue mission," Kylie stated.

"Aye-aye, Captain. I'm ready."

In response to Kylie's order, Commander Akina Cool-al radioed, "Captain Brown, *Skip Jack* is only twelve miles from that position and closing at fifty knots. We estimate arrival in about fifteen minutes."

Martin Jones replied, "*Blue Fin* can be at the coordinates in about twenty-five minutes."

Kylie responded, "See you there. *Yellow Fin* will arrive in thirty-two minutes."

Another call crackled over the radio as a voice added in French, "Commander Pierre DeVoe of the French Navy. We have overhead a robotic aircraft loading two of the most seriously injured and will bring them back to a French Naval Hospital on Hao."

"Commander Kylie Brown here, the vessel *Yellow Fin* offering assistance. Estimated arrival in about twenty minutes. We're closing with another small vessel at fifty knots."

"Kylie of the *Yellow Fin* fishing vessel, your assistance is much appreciated, as our rescue vessel is one hour away," Commander DeVoe responded.

"This is Commander Brown of the fishing vessel *Yellow Fin*. How many people are on board the cargo vessel *Genie*? Over!"

"This is the cargo vessel *Genie* radio operator Jane Beaumont. We have sixteen people on board now, as two have been removed by the robotic aircraft rescue, over."

"This is Commander Brown of the fishing vessel *Yellow Fin*. Help will be there shortly. The fishing vessel *Skip Jack* estimates arrival at your position in five minutes, followed by two more vessels, *Yellow Fin* and *Blue Fin*, within twenty minutes, over."

"This is Jane Beaumont of the cargo vessel *Genie* in distress. We have the French robot aircraft overhead, and it is loading two more of our injured, so we'll have two other injured and twelve additional crew members left with storm approaching." Urgency filled the woman's trembling voice.

"Commander Akina Cool-al, fishing vessel *Skip Jack*. I have the cargo vessel *Genie* in sight and closing at fifty knots. We see smoke, winds starting to pick up with a large swell from the west, over."

"Captain Champlain of the cargo vessel *Genie*," a man's voice yelled over the radio. "The fire has reemerged, six robots fighting the fire; however, all crew members are in two lifeboats!"

Akina took six people into the *Skip Jack* and waited for the *Blue Fin* to arrive. Soon the *Blue Fin* commander reported, "I have a burning vessel in sight and closing. We estimate arrival in two minutes."

Kylie spoke into her ship's radio. "Brown here. Stay away from the burning vessel. Rescue the crew members in the lifeboats.

Make maximum safe speed to Hao, as there are medical facilities at the French Navy base there. Severe storm approaching from the west. Make haste!"

Akina departed the area with six rescued crew members and headed for Hao on the heels of the French Navy rescue drone, recalled for high wind conditions. *Blue Fin* rescued five healthy persons, leaving the patient with metal fragments and another with serious burns on her back for Dr. Butterfield on the *Yellow Fin*. Soon, the two remaining injured crew members were picked up from the lifeboats by the crew of the *Yellow Fin*.

Captain Champlain had climbed back aboard his vessel, trying to fight the flames with his robots. He radioed, "I'll abandon ship using a jet pack. I'll try to land near vessel *Yellow Fin*, over."

As the *Yellow Fin* arrived, the sea state was increasing. Captain Champlain flew out of the flames just as the cargo vessel exploded. He landed on the *Yellow Fin* deck without serious injury, as he was skilled in use of his jet pack.

"Welcome aboard, Captain Champlain!" Kylie saluted the captain. He returned the salute.

"I'm worried about my crew. How are they?" he asked.

"We have two seriously injured crew members that need immediate surgery," Dr. Kate said, indicating the cabin.

Kylie offered, "You may use our radio to contact the French in Hao, where your other injured crew members are being treated."

Dr. Butterfield said, "I can't do surgery on this bobbing vessel. Get me to shore immediately or these people might die."

Captain Champlain said, "There's a recent harbor created by the Marokau Pearl Farming Cooperative. So, we can set up a surgery station at the village clinic… Doctors fly in on occasion to give medical care there."

Looking at a map on the console, he gave them the coordinates.

Kylie ordered, "Head for this harbor on the Marokau Atoll."

"Aye-aye, Captain Brown," Happy replied. "I'm steering for the new destination, which is ten minutes away at twenty-five knots. I can't go any faster safely with the sea this choppy."

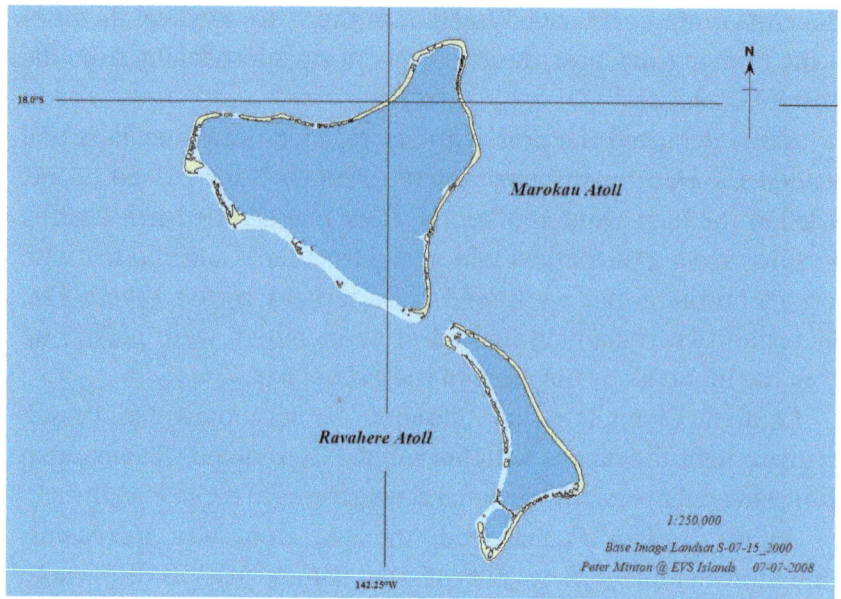

9. Map of Marokau Atoll showing the channel on the north and the Ravahere Atoll to the south.

After motoring through the rough waters, Happy Li arrived at the village on the northern end of the atoll. The harbormaster, Joseph Kalama, met them as Happy docked the *Yellow Fin* in a visitor's slip.

"I was monitoring the rescue," he said from the dock, "and I'm surprised to see you came here, as we have no doctor."

"We have Dr. Kate Butterfield," Kylie said in broken French while standing on the deck. "She needs to set up a field surgery unit immediately with your assistance, if possible, or the two seriously injured patients we rescued will not make it. The French Navy robotic aircraft is grounded because of the high winds. Can you please assist us?"

Joseph Kalama contacted the village chief by cell phone, and he was given immediate permission to let the visitors use the clinic.

The *Yellow Fin* crew transported the injured to the designated field hospital with assistance from several young villagers.

As they climbed the stairs to the clinic, Joseph explained, "The clinic building is made of cement two stories up, built on stilts like all homes, as about ninety-five villagers were killed in a severe storm one hundred years ago. Since then, building codes were revised by the locals, with assistance from the French government, to survive these rare storms."

The young villagers helped Happy and Liam get the injured to the emergency surgery station while Kylie and Kate cleaned up for surgery.

Kylie assisted Dr. Butterfield, removing the pieces of metal from one patient. Dr. Butterfield scanned the residue of explosives on the metal fragments with her Hexcorder after the operation on the second patient was completed. She murmured her suspicions to Kylie. "The forensic evidence indicates that this explosion was no accident. The shrapnel imbedded in Howard Laurent's back appears to be the result of a bomb!"

"The storm is upon us, but this clinic is safe, so please stay here," Joseph recommended. Then the harbormaster embraced Dr. Butterfield and Kylie.

"I'm worried about the *Yellow Fin* staying in the harbor tied to the dock," Kylie said. "I'm going to move our vessel out of the harbor, as the surge could damage the vessel."

Happy Li asked, "May I assist you, as I'm an expert on piloting this type of vessel in bad weather?"

Kylie, unsure of herself as a commander, was afraid to order her colleague out in this storm. She appreciated the offer. "Thank you for volunteering," she told him. "Make haste and come along with me."

Happy Li picked up a thirty-five-gallon bottle of water in one hand and a package of fruits and other staples weighing about one hundred pounds in the other and easily trotted down the two flights of stairs. The popular physical enhancements made to Naturals in his advanced century made it possible for him to handle all that weight. The enhancements weren't as extreme as those genetically added to the Syndos, so they still thought of themselves as "Naturals."

Kylie followed him with tool kits that she'd brought ashore earlier.

75

The two soon climbed into the *Yellow Fin*. Happy started the two fuel-cell engines on the catamaran-shaped inflatable fishing vessel and moved it slowly from the harbor to the northern anchorage. The winds were now blowing about thirty-five knots with gusts to forty-five knots registering on the instruments, but the lagoon offered protection from the massive ocean waves crashing on the reef.

Kylie donned her wetsuit, mask, and snorkel. Then she put on her dive knife and buoyance compensator so she could be sure the anchor was set properly with no corals nearby that could cause a tangle when the wind changed direction—as it would after the passage of the storm front. After making sure the anchor location was good and the coral heads were far enough away, Kylie resurfaced with a giant conch shell.

"Please take the conch, Happy, as I need to add some floats to this chain so it won't get tangled in the coral—there are coral heads in every direction. I also want you to add about one hundred feet of chain on the stern anchor so we can be sure we have enough chain in this storm to hold. We'll set the stern anchor after I get the bow anchor set."

"Aye-aye," Happy replied, and he began to prepare the floats and chain.

Kylie headed back down this time using her scuba gear. While descending, she clipped a float to the chain and then removed the excess line, so the float would hold the chain at the proper height to clear the coral heads without damaging the coral. She was setting the next float when a strong gust shifted the boat's position abruptly, whipping the inflatable boat around rapidly and catching Kylie's air hose in the chain she had been working on.

Suddenly Kylie could not breathe. Holding her breath, she looked at her depth gauge to see she was sixty feet below the surface. She could make a free ascent, but she struggled to get the hose free; the chain was wrapped tightly around the air hose and locked somehow. Unhooking her straps, she slipped out of the scuba gear. She tried to free the air hose but failed. It was locked tight, breaking the hose. Bubbles leaked out of the hose uncontrollably. Kylie felt fear but not panic, as she was an experienced cave diver and a former astronaut; water offered advantages not available in the vacuum of space. She closed the valve on the tank and removed the pressure regulator. Kylie cupped her hand around the tank opening, still holding her air tightly; she turned the air tank on, so she could get a breath of air from her hands. She took another and another breath of air from the tank. She completed the second float and activated the air canister in that float until it was inflated. Leaving the scuba tank, she returned every minute to get another few breaths of air from the tank.

A shark came into view, and then another. The sharks circled her. Kylie realized she was bleeding from her hands. She grabbed the tank, leaving the air hose behind. She headed for the surface slowly by adding air to her buoyancy compensator. After a few moments, a shark came in close, and Kylie hit its nose with her electrified dive knife. The shark moved away, and she continued to rise, exhaling into her buoyancy compensator.

When she broke the surface, Kylie exhaled completely, then took a very deep breath of air. She was about two hundred feet from the *Yellow Fin*. Happy spotted her and moved the *Yellow Fin* in close within seconds. Happy spotted a shark at the surface. He shot the shark with an ion rifle. He spotted another and shot the second shark as the wind pushed the boat away from Kylie. After Kylie swam for another five minutes without getting closer to the vessel, Happy launched a rope to her with a small round float on it using a powerful propellant launcher system.

Happy pulled her in rapidly hand over hand. The sharks followed her.

"There are sharks behind you," he yelled. "You're bleeding badly!"

Kylie shouted, "Throw a couple of tuna over the side!"

"Give me your hand!" Happy said with urgency in his voice, ignoring the order. He extended his arm. Happy pulled her up just as a large shark attacked. The shark bit the inflatable hull where Kylie had been a split-second ago.

"Don't worry," Happy told her. "The *Yellow Fin*'s hull is filled with structural ceramic foam, so the bite can be repaired later. The foam is very strong; it's a twenty-seventh-century lightweight inflatable ceramic foam."

"Thank you!" Kylie exclaimed, lying on the deck breathing hard.

"That could have been your legs if I did not pull you in ASAP!"

"Thank you, Happy. There's a conch in my dive bag. You can have it."

"I'm sorry for disobeying your direct order. I made an error," Happy admitted.

"You saved my life. It was I who made the error," Kylie stated as she hugged Happy. "We're well set on the bow anchor but must move when the winds switch so we'll be better protected. When the storm front passes, the wind will be from the southwest, west, or south. We'll move to the southeastern corner of the atoll."

"No worries. I can retrieve the regulator, as I can free dive to one hundred feet," Happy said.

"Not now. We have another scuba set. I'll mark the spot with a small buoy, so we can retrieve the dive equipment later."

"Let me set the stern anchor first so it'll tell us when the winds start to shift, and it'll become tight, setting off the alarm."

Kylie waved approval. "Let's go for four-hour shifts on watch, if that's okay with you."

"I hope you can get some sleep, but let's eat together first, as I'm starved!" Happy exclaimed, rubbing his stomach. "Also, your hands need some attention."

"Right," Kylie said. "I'll go wash and bandage my hands and be with you in the galley in about five minutes."

Happy and Kylie prepared dinner together—leaving washing and other water-related tasks to him so her bandages would stay dry. They made fresh conch salad, tuna sashimi, baked breadfruit, and rice. Kylie watched Happy remove the conch from its shell, fascinated by his efficient technique.

As they baked the breadfruit, Kylie asked, "Where are your ancestors from?"

"My ancestors migrated from Manchuria to Hong Kong about five hundred years ago and moved to Australia about two hundred and twenty years ago for better job opportunities."

"Thank you for helping get the conch out of the shell," Kylie said.

"No worries," Happy replied with a smile.

Kylie received a report on her watch tapped in code from Dr. Kate Butterfield. *Both patients alive but in serious condition. I'm giving blood to the patients now, but they're out of surgery. Each surgery was a success. What do I do about the forensic evidence?*

Hold for now, Kylie replied on the watch in code and by voice. *We should give the evidence to the captain of the cargo vessel Genie. It's a Canadian-owned and registered vessel.*

"This is Commander Hass of the fishing vessel *Bonito*," said one of Kylie's SS team leaders on the radio. "We are at Faaite Atoll just inside the lagoon near the main village Hitianau. We are riding out the storm here. Did your rescue go well?"

Kylie voiced back a message in code: *Yes, we saved two seriously injured crew members and the captain. Eleven other crew members were rescued by* Blue Fin *and* Skip Jack. *Four seriously injured were airlifted by robotic aircraft to Hao's French Naval Hospital. We plan to ride out the storm at Marokau because it's too late to go back to Hao Atoll.*

Commander Hass tapped in code on his watch, *Thank you, we are safe. Good luck!*

Have you seen other vessels? Kylie asked using her watch.

We are with Bigeye *and* Albacore *in the Faaite Lagoon. We are spaced apart by about two kilometers.*

Thank you for your report. Out, Kylie voiced in code on her watch. Seven vessels accounted for since the storm, including the *Yellow Fin*. That left three unaccounted for. Kylie knew their first priority would be to find safety and that they would report to her when they could.

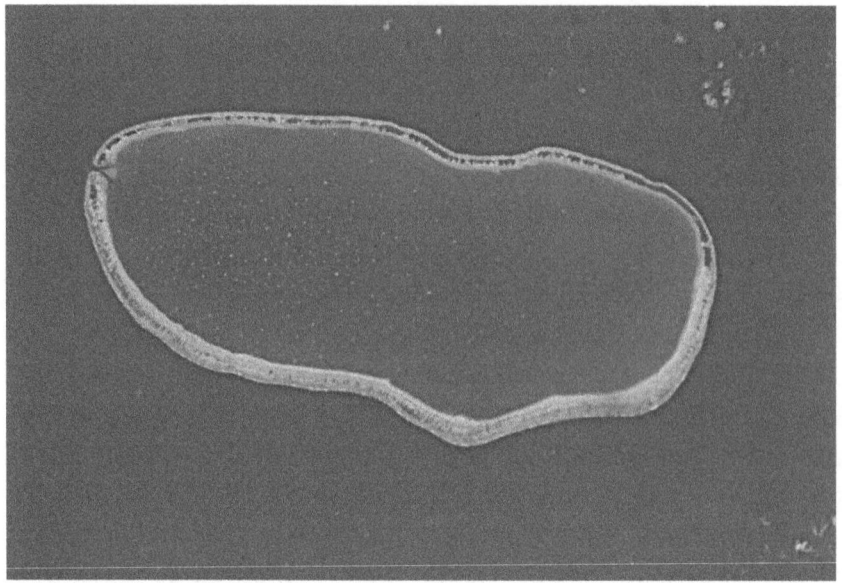

10. Faaite Atoll's main village of Hitianau is south of the channel.

After eating, Happy slept for almost the entire four hours until his alarm went off so he could relieve Kylie. By that time, Kylie was getting sleepy, so she lay down and slept until awakened by Happy four hours later.

He said, "The wind is switching to the west and southwest, and we should move now."

Kylie agreed. "I'll pull the anchors up now."

The winds howled like the sound from a thousand wolves in the moonlight. The waves in the lagoon were already at three to four feet from the west as the anchors were pulled up and stored. Kylie and Happy headed for the southeastern tip of the island near the village of Topitike.

By the time they reached the halfway point, the winds started from the south at about fifty knots. It was a cool wind with rain coming down almost horizontally at times.

It was a slow trip, as they could barely see twenty meters

in front of them. They used the forward-looking Zonar to scan for coral heads. Shortly after arriving at Topitike, Happy went down to set the anchors, as Kylie was injured on both hands, with deep cuts to her right hand. After adjusting the floats, he returned to the surface. Kylie dropped the transom platform and set the ladder so Happy could get on board easily. No way could she lift him aboard as he had done for her. Happy was a muscular man nearly two meters tall.

Happy patched the hull with a repair kit and came on board using the transom ladder.

11. Marokau Atoll showing the village of Topitike located at the southern tip of the island.

After twelve hours of cool south winds, the winds began to drop from fifty-five knots to forty knots. They blew twenty-four hours more before dropping to twenty-two knots for about five hours, gradually dropping to ten knots. The wind became light and variable for a period. Kylie and Happy pulled up anchor and headed north to the village of Vaiori with good visibility, as it was eleven o'clock in the morning.

Kylie checked with all vessels, and the nine others reported no serious damage and no casualties. Kylie ordered them to return to Jennifer's plan.

5

SURPRISE

Kylie followed Jennifer's plan to the letter, so she expected to be the last boat to arrive in Tahiti.

"The weather is just beautiful today," Happy said as he stood at the helm of the *Yellow Fin*.

"Yes, I can see Tahiti Island very clearly now that the sun has come up high in the sky," Kate Butterfield replied, sitting in the back and shading her eyes with one hand.

Sitting at a nearby built-in table, Kylie tapped out a message on her watch calling for all team leaders to report. All leaders reported in order as specified by Jennifer's plan. Everyone but Kylie had indeed already arrived at Tahiti. Kylie had reserved slips for the ten small fishing vessels through the Papeete harbormaster's website the first day they'd arrived in this time.

As the *Yellow Fin* approached the center buoy, Liam came on deck from the crew's quarters. He'd been taking a nap.

"Liam, relieve Happy on the helm," Kylie ordered.

Looking out over the water toward Tahiti, Liam said, "Look—a double rainbow!"

"It's a beautiful sight," Dr. Butterfield remarked.

"It's great to see mountains again. I've missed them," Liam said.

"Where did you grow up, Liam?" Kylie asked as he took over the vessel's controls.

"About one hundred and ten kilometers southwest of Brisbane near Mount Barney National Park in Queensland, Australia."

"Where are we staying on Tahiti Island?" asked Dr. Butterfield, still sitting in the back and looking out over the water. Happy was now standing near her at the railing, also watching as Tahiti drew closer.

"We're at the new Sport Fishing Marina just east of Challenger Harbour," Kylie answered. "There is a large hotel at the end of Fleet Street called Manakea Hotel."

Liam suggested, "We can sell our fish next to the fuel station. The Tahiti Fish Market has an unloading and buying station right there for our convenience."

"We have about a thousand kilos of yellowfin and four hundred kilos of bonito," Happy estimated. "The yellowfin is fetching two hundred dollars per kilo and bonito is fetching a hundred sixty dollars per kilo after tax. We should earn two hundred sixty-four thousand dollars. Not bad, not bad at all."

"I need to visit the harbormaster and sign some papers. Can you handle the fish sale, Happy?" Kylie asked.

"No worries!" Happy exclaimed.

Liam nodded. "I'll help."

"Me too," piped in Dr. Kate.

Kylie carried the papers for the *Yellow Fin* and the nine other boats to the harbormaster's office building, which looked like an object of modern art. Inside the small, wood-sided, air-conditioned structure, she found the harbormaster at a desk working on a computer.

Harbormaster Ken was a French man in his early thirties with a distinguished look and a well-kept goatee. He had pale-blue eyes with dark-brown hair. Nodding at her quickly, he stood to get something from the electronic file system on another computer and then knelt down to plug in the machine.

Kylie set the stack of official documents onto the desk, and then sat down in a chair in front of it.

"I'm Kylie Brown, acting captain of the fleet of ten fishing vessels that just tied up at the guest slips."

Without looking her way as he stood at the second computer, Harbormaster Ken said, "Please sit down, Captain. I will be with you in a moment."

Ken continued to work on the computer for another ten minutes, taking notes on a tablet as he did so.

Kylie's thoughts drifted back to the Syndos missile attack, the day that Captain Jennifer Hero sent her to the twenty-seventh century, and the discussion she had with Jennifer the day before about needing to be ready to command and complete the mission. She remembered missiles hitting the entrances of every tunnel. The Syndos were sealing them all into their tomb of doom, or so they thought. Kylie pondered Jennifer's fate; she might have been sealed in by the Syndos before the ten-megaton nuclear warhead went off. Kylie again recalled their private meeting the previous day: *Commander, I want you to own these plans in case something happens to me. You must complete the mission.* Jennifer's statement echoed in Kylie's mind over and over until Ken looked up and smiled.

"I'm sorry for the delay. How can I help you?" he asked, sitting back down at his desk.

"Can you stamp my documents?" Kylie asked in her broken French. "We're Australian fishermen looking to stay for a few weeks and would like to do some fishing."

"Yes, Captain." Ken stamped the documents without really looking at them. "We expect you to obey local fishing laws. You must be outside the twelve-mile limit. Also, there is a limit of two metric tons of seafood per day within two hundred miles of French Polynesia." Ken pointed to a large map on the wall. "This map is on our website as well."

Kylie went to the wall and examined the map closely and then downloaded the map from their site to her tablet.

Turning his way, Kylie asked, "What about lobster?"

"You may purchase a license for commercial lobster; otherwise, they must be returned to the sea if in the net," he explained. "Everyone is allotted a maximum of ten lobsters a day if taken by free diving. No nets, only by hand; however, storing them in a standard dive bag is permitted."

"Thank you for the detailed information," she replied. "Here's a credit swipe to cover three weeks' stay at the harbor." Kylie pressed her tablet to the receiver on the desk that transferred the funds. She held her breath until the green light indicated positive transfer. Bless Jennifer and her copious research.

Ken waved goodbye and said, *"Au revoir!"*

As Kylie walked out the door she replied, *"Au revoir."*

The crew was waiting for her with the vessel all cleaned and ready. Kylie inspected the catamaran and picked up her duffel bag.

"Can we check in to the hotel now?" asked Dr. Butterfield.

"Yes, let's check in and take a rest this afternoon," Kylie told them." Please feel free to get a massage and use any recreational facilities, as the price is all-inclusive."

The four of them walked together to the Manakea Hotel and checked in.

The next morning the four met for a buffet breakfast at seven a.m. local time. The sea air had a fresh smell, as the trade winds were blowing ten to twelve knots. The sun was rising slowly in the east and the seagulls screeched above the harbor. These birds were feeding on the few baitfish escaping from the commercial fishing pier while several fishing vessels loaded up with bait.

"How early do they start loading fuel and bait?" Kate asked as she tapped her watch.

With a smile, Kylie replied, "Bait loading starts at four thirty a.m. and ends at four thirty p.m., but fuel sales start at same time and go until eleven p.m., according to the harbormaster."

"What is the plan for today?" inquired Happy.

"Kate and I will visit the yacht brokers to see about putting these ten fishing vessels up for sale as soon as we've earned the totals we need. Tomorrow we'll start fishing again, so we need to schedule fuel and bait early, about five thirty a.m. I'll need Kate with me today, but you two men can have free time. I suggest you check out some local girls, as there is a safe, legal, and inexpensive brothel famous for making the male customers very pleased."

"Do they have sex for women?" Happy asked.

"They do have women for women, and men for men, and even threesome sex, but Kate and I prefer each other." Kylie gave her companions frank, serious looks. "Since we're going to be living together from now on, we need to be open with our sexuality and relationships."

"Are you both lesbians?" Happy asked.

"Kate and I are both bisexuals," Kylie replied, taking Kate's hand.

Happy Li and Liam looked at each other.

"Guess what?" said Liam.

"What?" Kate asked.

"I'm bisexual. I prefer a couple, but either sex will do for me."

Happy said, "I'm bisexual but prefer women for emotional bonds."

"Great! I'm thrilled to hear this openness," Kate said with a big smile. "We can all relax and have sex in the future, if we need it and all agree at that time."

With a big smile, Liam said, "Kate, that does not sound like the prim-and-proper doctor image you portrayed before we got here."

Her smile dimmed to sadness. "My husband and I were swingers. I'll miss him, but he expects me to get sex as I choose. I'll never get back to him, so I released him from our marriage via a divorce before I left." Kate could not hold back her tears. "I still love my husband and miss him so much, but it's missing my children that brings an anguish I cannot bear."

"You must really miss them already," Kylie said.

"Yes, I miss him and my three kids. The reality of never seeing them again creates a hole in my heart!" She wiped her eyes. "But we all knew what we were signing up for on this trip. I am here to make a new future for them."

The four of them soberly finished breakfast.

After the early meal, they all headed for Kylie's hotel room.

Upon entering, Liam scanned the room for surveillance bugs. "Clean!"

"Go ahead then, we can talk openly," said Happy. He turned on the radio in the bedroom and the holo-screen in the living room then sat on the bed.

Kylie told them, "We must, for the most part, operate independently from the other members until we get to Australia, and only as called for by Jennifer's plan. So I will handle the sale of all these vessels with Kate's assistance."

Kate sat on the bed next to Happy and explained, "We cannot get close to other people until our mission is accomplished, and that could take years. So, we must rely on each other for everything, including our emotions and sex. That is unless the sex is with professionals. In any case, we must stay in our cover for life."

"I'm willing to have sex with all of you," Liam announced. He tapped a drink order into the wall interface.

Happy asked, "I'm more than willing—I'm eager—but is it appropriate, Kylie, now that you're our leader?"

"If we all have sex together, can you still follow my commands?" Kylie asked.

"Aye-aye, Captain!" Happy chuckled.

"Aye, Captain!" Liam exclaimed.

"Aye-aye, Captain." Kate stood up and saluted.

"Even though I assumed command in Captain Hero's absence, I'm technically still Commander Brown." Kylie waved away their formal salutes. "Any sex acts that anyone prefers not to get involved in, let us know now. I prefer no anal sex."

Happy shuddered as he stretched out on the bed. "I also prefer no anal sex."

Kate sat again. "I like anal sex, so if Liam is willing, we can try that sometime when we have proper lubrication."

"I like anal sex, so I'm willing to share with Kate." Liam waggled his eyebrows at her.

"It's not something we had often at home," Kate shared. "But yes, my husband and I did enjoy anal intercourse together occasionally; however, we never tried it swinging."

"We were having open relations in our marriage. What you refer to as swinging, we called a normal lifestyle," Liam said with a deep scowl on his face. "I did not divorce my wife as you did, and now I feel guilty."

"Liam, please do not feel guilty," Kate advised. "Your wife thinks you are dead! She will be free to find another mate if she chooses to marry. She will need to wait only three years to declare you legally dead."

The wall dispenser announced with a *ping* the arrival of a tray of cocktails made with rum and lime and pineapple juices. Liam brought the tray over to everyone.

Kate reached up from the bed and took one of the glasses from the tray. "As the general surgeon and psychiatric specialist for this mission, I think it's essential to get close to each other to hold the team together during such a long-term undercover operation with such an important priority. Medically, I approve of sex of all kinds for us. Personally, I'm sharing the love for my husband with all of you. Thank you for being so understanding. I was afraid that going long periods without sex would be a psychiatric problem for me and others on this mission. I'm so relieved that we're all so compatible. I can only hope our other teams will grow as close with each other."

Happy sat up on the bed by Kylie, grabbed a drink, and said, "I'm pleased we're all going to have a long-term sexual relationship, as I was fearful of that part of the mission. Now I feel relieved."

He took a sip of his rum cocktail, smiled, and then added, "I'm surprised about having sex with my commander, but also very pleased." Happy fondled Kylie's earlobe, making her blush.

Kate pointed out a serious fact. "Many Naturals are religious and wish to preserve the old culture of sex only in marriage. It is a risk some of the other teams face; I profiled everyone prior to the mission and found a few holding to this belief. We even have pairs of these folks, and even a few married couples on the mission. The permanent nature of our mission demanded we take this aspect of life into consideration. Lonely people would look outside our group and could make trouble by letting slip mission objectives. Modern science understands that the sex drives of humans are healthy, even in this century, but considers the psychological and emotional needs surrounding it as well. We need to stay within our group of forty-nine for closeness and community."

Kylie nodded, grimly understanding the isolation they all had volunteered for. For her, the sacrifice had deepened with Jennifer's absence.

6

TAHITI

After a full day of rest and recreation, it was time to fish again. The teams were fueling their vessels at the dock well before dawn. Jennifer's plan called for two boats to team up and fish in the same area. The *Blue Fin* and *Yellow Fin* were one of the teams, so they both headed north after fueling and exiting Papeete Harbour. The dirigible drones from each vessel were sent out about an hour earlier so they could be at ten thousand feet and scanning the ocean as the sun came up.

12. Aerial photo of Tetiaroa Atoll north of Papeete.

Martin Jones radioed, "*Blue Fin*. Our dirigible just passed over Tetiaroa, about sixty kilometers north of Papeete, and picked up a school of bigeye tuna about nineteen kilometers miles due west of the island. Coordinates are texted, over."

"Roger that," Kylie replied. "We're headed to the school at thirty-five knots and should be there in about thirty minutes."

"We're only ten minutes away, so with your permission we'll start fishing," Martin said.

"Yes, please start as soon as possible."

"At thirty-five knots, the *Blue Fin* vibrates upon hitting each wave, so we've decreased speed to twenty-five knots," Martin reported moments later. "Even the advanced catamaran design was bouncing around on these ten- to twelve-foot seas with winds at twenty-five to forty knots, over."

"We have the same sea conditions and are closing at thirty-five knots with seat belts on and splash protection in place. We're okay, over."

"Now deploying our nets," Commander Jones soon reported. "The school is large, moving southeast at nine knots, following the bait, over."

Kylie spotted the *Blue Fin* on the horizon about twenty minutes after the *Blue Fin* crew dispersed their nets. She radioed, "We have your vessel in sight and will wait for you to pull in your catch. We're slowed to ten knots, over."

"There's a large flock of birds diving on the baitfish driven to the surface by the bigeye tuna. Over," Martin said with a great excitement as they began to pull their catch.

"How big is your catch?"

"Give me a few minutes, and we'll have the weight, but this was a great haul for us. You're welcome to deploy your nets, over."

Kylie gave the order to deploy the nets. "We're two kilometers south of you, deploying our nets now and moving southeast."

"*Blue Fin*'s scales show us at eleven hundred kilos, over," Martin said.

In her broken French, Kylie called outward on an alternate frequency on the radio, "Resort on Tetiaroa, we're the *Yellow Fin* fishing vessel asking about market for our fresh catch."

The response was unexpected. "This is Tetiaroa Brando Resort Operator Jeff Bell. Right now, we're full in fish for the resort. We do have a fish market but with a lower price than you'll get at Papeete. We must fly the fish there and we need to make a profit, over."

"Thank you for your honesty," Kylie radioed back. "We are only one hour from Papeete, so we will not stop today but maybe later in the week, as we would like to have a look around. Is that possible on this private island, over?"

Jeff replied, "Yes, we're a tourist island with exclusive villas for our guests, but we do have a model villa and a small downtown area with post office, several restaurants, an aquarium, and many shops. You're welcome to visit. You can dock free for six hours if you buy fuel, over."

Coming through on the other frequency, Martin announced, "We spotted another school of tuna about twelve miles north by northwest of Tetiaroa. I think they're yellowfin tuna. The school is very large. Look at the dirigible's sensors."

"Jeff, thank you for the information. We are still fishing today and may be back later, over and out," Kylie concluded still in broken French.

She switched frequency to respond to the *Blue Fin*. "Martin, we're headed for the new school at thirty-five knots. Expected to arrive in eighteen minutes."

During the following couple of hours, the two fishing vessels deployed nets and pulled in a great catch of yellowfin tuna. Both vessels reached their limit for the day and headed for Papeete at twenty knots.

"We expect to arrive in Papeete in a little over an hour and a half," Kylie said.

"We are following you," Martin said. "We released about half of our last catch so as not to exceed the limit of two metric tons per vessel. I can't believe the density of fish out here."

"We were lucky today, so let's get to the market early so we can unload without a long wait," Kylie advised.

"Yes, I advise we head for the north scales," Martin suggested. "They're ideal for the smaller fishing vessels, leaving the south scales for the larger vessels."

"Roger that. I'll follow your advice, Martin. I'll slow down; you take the lead. You deserve the honor, as you spotted the fish today."

"Thank you for the recognition, Commander."

Soon the two vessels approached the center buoy at Papeete Harbour.

Commander Jones radioed, "Harbormaster, this is Martin Jones of the fishing vessel *Blue Fin*, calling to arrange for unloading of our catch. The vessel *Yellow Fin* is with us, and they have a large catch as well. Is south dock available for unloading?"

"This is Harbormaster Ken. Please give me a few minutes to check."

After about five minutes, Ken announced, "The south dock is empty now. What's your arrival time, over?"

"This is the fishing vessel *Blue Fin*. We are two minutes away, over."

"You're now assigned the south dock for unloading, slip two. Good luck. Harbormaster out."

Martin headed directly into south dock. The robotic unloading system unloaded the *Blue Fin*'s hold quickly.

"I sold our two metric tons of bigeye and yellowfin for $202 per kilo, or 2,000 times 202; that's $404,000. Not bad for the first day out," Martin radioed Kylie. "You should get the same price. Many of the restaurants in Tahiti take fresh ahi, as they call yellowfin or bigeye, to make sashimi and poisson cru, which is raw tuna marinated in lime and coconut milk with some spice and chopped onion added. Let's go get some at our hotel after you're unloaded... Eat like locals!"

"Yes, I am unloading now, but they tell me I'm ten kilograms over the limit, which means I may have to pay a fine," Kylie said, biting her lip.

"I'll be over in a moment to check to see if you might have some junk or other items in your nets," Martin advised.

"You're welcome to check."

After checking the nets, Martin reported to Kylie on the deck of the *Yellow Tail*. He told her, "I found two items. One's a large fender from a yacht and the other is a glass ball from an old fishing net. The weight total is eighteen kilos, so you're not over but short of the limit."

"Thank you, Martin," Kylie said, smiling. She gave him a hug. "You're an expert fisherman, and you've proven your worth as a detailed examiner. My crew and I will be at the hotel bar by two p.m., as we'll do some shopping first. Can we buy you and your crew a drink?" Kylie checked her watch. "Local time is now twelve forty-five."

"Yes, I am honored to accept. By the way, do you want the glass ball?" he asked, then pulled the ball out of a sack at his feet. "It's a relic of the past. They haven't been used since about the twenty-fifth century, so it may be worth money as a collector's item."

"You keep it as a souvenir," Kylie suggested.

After shopping for personal items, the crew headed for the hotel bar and lounge with their packages. It was about ten minutes past two o'clock in the afternoon. They found Martin and his crew already sitting down at a table near the adjacent pool under a large umbrella. Kylie and her team selected the next table.

After socializing, celebrating with sashimi and poisson cru, and sharing drinks and plans for tomorrow, Kylie and her team retired to their rooms for a nap. By then other teams were coming in. *Skip Jack's* skipper, Akina Cool-al, and her team slipped into the table Team One had abandoned and ordered a round of drinks.

While waiting for the order, Akina stopped by Martin's table to say hello.

"Akina, I hope to see you tomorrow, but I need a nap now," Martin said, yawning. "I'm happy you had such great luck today, and I wish you a great future."

She boasted, "I know you're the best fisherman in the group, but I think I'm a close second. We're fishing in different areas, so we're not competing. Have a great nap."

Martin and his team left to get some shut-eye.

As the sun rose the next morning, Kylie was up and tapping a coded message that they needed to keep up the fishing every day to make money to finance the bottled water project, the Blue Mountain Waterfall brand. *This is the first step in bringing a new brand of bottled water to Australia and the world. The full team will be divided in two major parts when we move to Australia. Teams One through Five will infiltrate the Human Engineering Project, and all others will be on the bottled water project. You know your specific jobs from Jennifer's detailed plans, but I want to encourage you to make money now, as the bottled water project will work only by getting PR and advertising working together, and that takes money. We can use the picture below on our bottled water labels. We need Akina Cool-al to secure rights to her family's historical Aboriginal source, the remote Blue Mountain Waterfall.*

13. A painting of the Blue Mountain Waterfall in Australia.

Within a short time, each of the nine team leaders had acknowledged the need to make money for this important venture. They knew that it would help them obtain the goal of saving humanity from extinction by spreading the V7 virus worldwide, as well as developing the best, and hopefully the most popular, bottled water in Australia.

Kylie's message was just a pep talk for the team leaders, with the hope that they would charge up their team members with a direct talk.

―――――――――――

The next three weeks went by fast, and the fishing vessels were successful in making more than enough money for the planned Blue Mountain Waterfall bottled water project for Australia.

"The successful fishing will create a strong interest in purchasing our fleet of fishing vessels by several tuna-fishing cooperatives," Martin pointed out.

His prediction proved true as all ten fishing vessels were purchased by the Tahitian Tuna Cooperative.

"Overall, it was a great three weeks," Kylie said to Kate one morning as she cemented plans for travel to Australia via her watch. She had overcome the indecision and doubt that had plagued her during the first few days of command. Kylie tapped code into her watch to inform each team that they had their schedule for air flights. Five days of R&R were open before they had to leave, so the team members and commanders were encouraged to enjoy the time off.

She concluded by tapping in: *You can check out and visit other islands such as Bora-Bora. Just be aware of your flight schedule to Australia.*

"How are we going to spend our R&R?" Kate asked Kylie.

"I think we should ask the team as a group what we want to do. I'm open," Kylie replied.

Kate fluffed her hair and stretched. "We can talk after breakfast in your room. Liam and Happy will meet us in about thirty minutes for breakfast in the hotel restaurant."

"Okay, I'll see you at our usual table in about thirty minutes. I still need to shower and dress."

―――――――――――

After a hearty breakfast, Team One gathered in Kylie's suite.

"What do you all want to do over the next five days?" Kylie asked.

Liam replied, "I'm not real keen on traveling but would be willing to go to Moorea and a trip around Tahiti."

"I want to relax at one of the resorts and enjoy some of the activities, like snorkeling, diving, swimming, surfing, and sailing," Happy said.

"What about you, Kate?" Kylie asked.

"I'd like to do a day trip to Moorea, but I want to stay at one resort," she answered. "No packing, no air travel—no fishing!—just relaxation and some great sex. I know life may get tough for us in Australia, so getting in pleasure and relaxation now is important."

"I'm all for lots of sex," Liam agreed, smiling.

Happy laughed. "I agree with great sex as a high priority."

"We need to get down to planning, as checkout is one p.m. today," Kate said.

"The New Royal Hotel and Resort is four diamonds," Kylie noted. "They have everything, and we get a thirty percent reduction in price because they're affiliated with our current hotel. We also get free transportation."

"Where is the New Royal located?" asked Liam.

Happy checked his map. "Next to the Four Seasons on the leeward side of Tahiti Island, about twenty-five kilometers southeast of the Faa'a International Airport near Paea."

"I just checked, and we can get reservations starting today for all five days," Liam told them.

Kylie said, "All in favor, raise your right hand."

All four hands shot up.

"We all need a break before the mission in Australia," Kylie announced.

7

TRIPS

The New Royal Hotel was a dream come true for Team One, Kylie's team of four members. Everything was included in the price of the room. They rented two connecting rooms as couples, Happy and Kylie in suite 234 and Liam and Kate in suite 236. The first night was spent enjoying each other's bodies until the four collapsed into piles of sated flesh. Sleep and a good breakfast invigorated them all into wanting to explore the recreation offered at the resort.

They decided to race catamaran sailboats to the center buoy of the Kapana Channel and back to the hotel dock. They divided into teams the same way they had as roommates: Kylie with Happy, and Liam with Kate. Happy was an expert seaman, and Liam was a catamaran sailor from childhood. Kylie was a sailor of monohulls from childhood, and Kate also had spent time with her family on a large catamaran motor yacht. So, the teams were evenly matched.

Happy was assigned as skipper of the twenty-eight-foot catamaran *Hope*, and Kate was skipper of the twenty-eight-foot catamaran *Opportunity*. The first race was on. The first leg was a downwind reach, and the return was into the wind, requiring tacking in the channel.

"Prepare to come about!" exclaimed Happy as he rounded the center buoy. "Hard alee!"

Kate and Liam were only about ten seconds behind. She echoed Happy's orders as she rounded the buoy.

As each boat tacked on the return, it was clear that Kate was gaining a few seconds on each tack.

Finally, Kate took the lead by half a boat as they crossed the finish line.

Happy said, "I'm sorry, Kylie. It was my fault."

"You did well, and it's just for fun. No worries!" Kylie exclaimed, laughing and slapping him on the shoulder.

"We'll have another chance tomorrow. Can we tune up our rigging?" Happy asked.

"Yes, I think that'll help. Let's grab some lunch first at the seafood buffet."

After docking the boats, the four walked to the restaurant.

Looking over to Kylie and Happy, Kate said, "We were lucky to win. I think our rigging is new."

Smiling, Happy said, "We'll tune up our rigging for the rematch tomorrow. I think you won't be so lucky then."

"We'll be ready for you," Liam said, grinning back.

After lunch, the four went to their rooms, opening the adjoining doors. In the lounging area of her suite, Kylie gave a pep talk to Team One. She reminded them of the importance of their mission: saving humanity from extinction. She then tapped the code and sent the same message to the other nine team leaders.

"Do we have our tickets yet?" asked Kate, relaxing on a sofa covered in brightly colored upholstery.

Standing in front of her team, Kylie nodded. "Yes, all tickets have been purchased by each team leader, according to Jennifer's planned schedule. She focused on accomplishing Zexton Ho's plan, which is to go back in time to correct the Syndos DNA defect. Most of the details were prepared by Jennifer over the past five years. We'll fly Qantas direct to Sidney at seven a.m. on Friday. We have four more days of R&R to enjoy, but I must occasionally remind everyone why we're here in this time. It's in Jennifer's detailed sixty-seven-page plan, which I expect to be followed to the letter, if feasible. It's just one way we can honor our leader. I still have hope that she escaped somehow."

She sat down in the couch beside Kate.

Kate touched Kylie's arm. "Yes, I also have hope about Jennifer. She was such an iconic hero of the Naturals and Syndos for saving Senator Caps Grotto. She also saved Zexton Ho once, but she could not save him the second time. Maybe she went back in time to see him again. They were lovers for almost two decades, you know."

Happy said, "Zexton Ho was an amazing scientific mind, but he seemed out of place as a leader of the SS. He was elected before I joined. He'd already won one Nobel Prize, and if he published his trans-time theory, he would have won another." Happy shook his head. "It's romantic to think she went back to be with him, but Jennifer has too great a sense of duty, I think."

"I want to believe she's still alive," Liam said. "Until I have proof otherwise, I won't mourn her passing."

"Jennifer was really hot, In my imagination," Happy confessed.

Kylie smiled in memory. "I fantasized about Jennifer from the day I met her in prep school, back when I thought I was lesbian leaning, as I wanted sex with girls, but I only had sex with boys in my early teens. Jennifer didn't indicate she wanted me until after we graduated. We were lovers all that summer before I left for the Astronaut Corp. What a summer."

Kate said she had a similar teenage experience. "It was just a strong urge at that time. I didn't know how to act on it until I met Joy Morita. She was older than me, and experienced, and showed me the way when I was a freshman at the University of Tasmania. She was so feminine and cute."

"I was in the same class with Jennifer in prep school," Kylie shared. "We had a close friend named Ben Sun. We all liked sailing, so the three of us rented sailing boats about twice a month together. Did you know Ben Sun, Happy?"

Kate answered, "He asked me out once, but I was dating Joe Buckminster at the time, so I had to explain. He understood about my going steady with Joe. I suggested my friend Lota Chang was looking for a date to homecoming. He asked her out and soon he started to go steady with her. They're now married with kids."

"Where did you meet your husband?" Kylie asked.

"I met Alfred in medical school," Kate told them. "He was studying to be a neurosurgeon and was a couple years ahead of me. We started dating at the end of my first year. He was my dream prince, so I fell head over heels in love on our second date when he kissed me for the first time. I'm still just as much in love with him. It was so hard to leave him and my children." Kate put her hands to her face and bent over.

Kylie felt bad for bringing up her loss again, and said with a breath of enthusiasm, "Tom Page and the new team may develop a new trans-time device that can go both ways and rescue us." She stood up and put her fist up in the air between them all. "After we complete our mission, there'll be time to contemplate our long-term future. I suggest we all focus on the mission or it won't matter."

Happy stood and put his hand on top of Kylie's hand. "Now, join hands just like the three musketeers," he suggested.

"I agree with Happy on this," Liam stated. "I offer my hand to the team and the mission." Liam put his hand on top of Kylie's and Happy's hands.

Kate joined them and added her hand to the pile. "Great!" Kate cheered. "You're thinking about the importance of this mission and sticking to Jennifer's plan. One for all and all for the mission."

The four tossed their joined hands in the air.

Kylie smiled at them all. "It's wonderful to feel my team is giving me such strong support."

She sobered and got back to business. "Please sit back down as I go over a few things," she started. "As overall team leader, I need to meet with Akina Cool-al, as she is key to the success of the bottled water project. I have invited her to join us for dinner, if you'd like to come. The four of us can talk in detail first with Akina in this suite before dinner. I'll talk about her project, which will be difficult, and she's the leader of that project. I'll only get tap reports in Australia, as we must be independent of her project to avoid suspicion."

"What's her mission?" Kate asked.

"Akina is a native Australian Aboriginal. Her family comes from the Blue Mountains. They have tribal rights to a small but hidden valley in the mountains. The tribe owned the eucalyptus cream used in the past to help people with colds. That technology was stolen from them by white men at gunpoint in the 1800s. Her tribe was also looted by a large mining company called Broken Hill Proprietary Limited that extracted silver from their land without compensating them. Her part of the plan is to sue these companies now for royalties and damages in the billions. Half of the money we made fishing will support this effort."

Happy whistled. "How will she justify suing these companies?"

"Akina traces her ancestry to the Gundungurra peoples. They're active in recovering money from those who exploited the Aboriginal members starting in the late 1800s and onward. Jennifer's plan calls Akina to join her ancestral tribe to sue in Australia and the world court on behalf of all Native Australians. Akina's an attorney in our home century, but she'll need to enter law school to learn more specifics of this time's laws while she hires a firm headed by the Aboriginal Gundungurra tribe leader."

Liam asked, "Is the main objective to get money or to get water bottled for consumers?"

Kylie answered, "The first goal is to establish the Blue Mountain Waterfall brand from her family's property. A large aquifer with water containing carbon dioxide will also be tapped. However, the trick is to get publicity for the new venture—good public relations and advertising. This is expensive and will take about fifty percent of our fishing profit to seed. The money will be used to start this bottling effort and the lawsuit will give her millions in needed free publicity."

"Is that enough to establish the brand?" Kate asked.

"To expand the Blue Mountain Waterfall brand, it'll first need to be a business success out of the box. This will depend on the advertising and PR. With some assistance from the Aboriginal Council, we'll get great PR. The ad campaign is expected to employ some top Aboriginal sport figures and actors."

Happy asked, "What about the international expansion?"

"Part of the plan is to offer the aquifer water as a competition to Perrier. The surface water is limited and will be sold mostly in Australia. If in the future the Aboriginal Council and Akina can get settlements or judgements from the lawsuits, the council should grant Akina a percentage for her business expansion plans.

"There needs to be significant changes in normal sources of water to sustain the growing world population; it's been a perpetual problem since the beginning of human civilization. Over seventy percent of Earth's fresh water is ice in Greenland and Antarctica. Any large expansion of fresh water use should come from the largest sources. During the warm season, melt water runs under the ice in rivers to the sea. Just as we do in the thirtieth century, the melt water can be collected by robots working with tanker ships and bottled on board with the V7 virus embedded within, shipped to distributors around the world, and sold as pure glacier water. Jennifer's plan is brilliant."

Liam asked, "Is no one doing this already?"

Kylie shook her head. "The glacier extraction ships have not been invented in this time."

"Who'll design these ships?"

"Jennifer and I have designed these ships using twenty-seventh-century technology. The design and build plans are on my tablet and on Akina's as well. Therefore, long-term, the water business will include Greenland and Antarctic glacier melt water, which will take a big money investment to build the ships for this purpose. We believe the Tasmanian Shipyard can build both ships in about one year using today's technology. But the cost will be over one billion Australian dollars."

Liam raised his eyebrows and widened his eyes. Clearly that was far more than the money they'd raised fishing.

"What's the timeline for this project?" Happy asked.

Kylie answered with great enthusiasm, "Tighter than you might think. Phase I will start within a month or two depending on the gambling and investment schedules. The goals will be to break even the first year with lots of PR and ads. In Year Two, profits are expected to be about seven million on sales of about $100 million. The company will go public in Year Three, with sales of about $300 million and profit of $30 million, or ten percent after tax. The Phase II goal is glacier water additions to the brand using advanced robotic technology to extract the melt water before it reaches the ocean. So, if the Aboriginal Council can make reasonable settlements with these major companies, the glacier expansion will occur two or three years down the line."

Kate asked, "What are the goals for the Blue Mountain Waterfall business?"

"They're in the business plan, which I'll e-mail you. You're all founding stock members with equal portion of stock. The council will be given ten percent of the stock and one percent royalties on all sales in Australia of the bottled water for use to improve the education and medical care of native peoples. After all, it's a basic Aboriginal resource and there are numbers of falls that will be used. The real goal is to spread the virus to as many humans as possible worldwide so that anyone coming in physical contact with a Syndo will infect them to correct the defect in their moral code, or the Syndos may drink the water. The virus is harmless to both humans and Syndos otherwise. We expect the humans will soon select to upgrade their embryos; however, the virus will spread from parent to embryo."

"Why are we going to share with the Aboriginal people?" Happy asked.

"That water belongs to the Aboriginal people," responded Kylie, giving Happy a direct look. "This has been their homeland for tens of thousands of years versus those who colonized from Europe only eight hundred years ago. The royalties will be used to improve their lives. The council will help all Aboriginal people in Australia, not just Akina's tribe."

"What is the primary goal?" Kate inquired.

"To save humanity, we must be sure the virus is worldwide, because other countries could develop Syndos." Kylie waved her hands at a hologram showing the Blue Mountain Falls location and another showing the Arctic and Antarctic locations for the melt water project. "Let's keep our eyes on the prize, team. We need to humanize all Syndos."

14. (left) Wallaman Falls, Australia's tallest waterfall.

15. (right) Ebor Falls, Guy Fawkes River National Park

8

BLUE FALLS

Though time was passing, Kylie's pep talk and briefing continued. "This is Jennifer's plan," she said, "but Akina helped develop some of the details. Akina was consulted early on, as she'll be the only one who can carry out this plan. Other waterfalls will be added, so many Aboriginal lands will be involved, and she can get allies if the company makes money."

Happy raised his hand, and Kylie nodded in his direction.

He asked, "If our team is infiltrating the Human Engineering Project, not working on the water projects, why should we meet with Akina?"

"Good question, Happy," Kylie responded. "It's simply that, even though you'll be working on the HEP, you may be able to help her in the future. She has a difficult task. I want every one of you to know we have a Blue Mountain Waterfall plan, but details must be kept secret until Akina releases the information. She'll need to get close to the Aboriginal Council first, and that could take some time. She has ancestors that bear her name, Cool-al, living and farming the land containing Blue Mountain Waterfall. They must agree to let her sell the water. They'll need stock and royalties as incentives. She can show her DNA is close to their DNA. She must get close to them as a fisherman returning to her homeland with new ideas for how to create jobs and make money."

Liam asked, "It seems like an impossible task for one person. Can she do it?"

"Jennifer was certain yes, with proper support. That's why her team has three Aboriginal members aside from her. They all know the customs and culture of the Aboriginals in this area. They can fit into the twenty-seventh century because they studied the details for the past three years."

Happy still looked doubtful. "Will the family and council believe their cover stories?"

"They're based on real facts," Kylie pointed out. "About one hundred and twenty years ago from this date, several Aboriginal families left their homeland in the mountains to fish in the coastal ocean because of good-paying jobs. They moved to Sydney. One of the vessels they were fishing on disappeared about sixty years ago and contact was lost. This team will claim to be the children of this lost vessel that was fishing near Tahiti. The children were brought up by foster parents in Tahiti and are now returning to help Akina make her dream come true."

"When do we meet?" Kate asked.

"Tomorrow afternoon at four, in my room. We'll have dinner after our meeting. I want to get some hors d'oeuvres and snacks for the meeting. Can you handle that for me, Kate?" Kylie asked.

"Yes, of course."

Happy offered, "I'll get a variety of cold drinks for the meeting, if you like."

"That would be great. Thank you for offering," Kylie replied with a big smile.

Kylie hadn't wanted to say this outright, but their entire mission hinging on the persuasive abilities of one single person made her very nervous. She was glad she could rely on her core team for support.

The day went by quickly with another sailboat race between the Team One members in the morning. This time Kylie and Happy's team won by a full boat length. The afternoon was filled with rain showers and rainbows. Kylie and Kate spent time shopping for black pearl jewelry, as they would soon depart this tropical paradise for Australia where black Tahitian pearls could cost three times what they cost in Papeete. Happy and Liam shopped for clothes, seashells, art, and souvenirs.

At four p.m., Team One gathered in the lounge area of Kylie's suite with the refreshments ready. Akina arrived and greeted everyone.

After they shared small talk, tropical juices, and French-style hors d'oeuvres, Kylie announced the beginning of the meeting. Akina and Kate both sat down on the couch, and Happy and Liam choose nearby chairs.

"I briefed my team on the basic mission you will oversee that we refer to as the Blue Falls Bottled Water Project," she told Akina. "As stockholders in your project, we want to support you the best we can."

Akina nodded acknowledgment. "I'm eager to get started."

Kylie replied, "Jennifer chose you because you are uniquely qualified to successfully meet this enormous challenge."

"My family has occupied this land for many thousands of years," Akina said. "That fact is most important for this mission. My business and entrepreneur skills are limited to one small software business."

"You've shown you can start and grow a complex business in the thirtieth century; now you'll need to be a politician as well as an entrepreneur," Kylie pointed out. "Your skills as an attorney will come into play."

Happy asked, "How can we help you?"

Akina moved to the front edge of the couch and answered, "First and foremost, don't endanger my cover. Jennifer researched this and spent years working on this cover. But one part has always bothered me, and maybe you can help. My DNA will show I'm related; however, my ability to speak French is poor and needs to be improved, even though I've been studying for years. I could sure use help with that. In my opinion, this is the weakest part of the plan. If I was raised on Tahiti by native Tahitians, I'd speak better French, wouldn't I?"

Kylie tapped her chin, thinking. After a pause, she responded, "Jennifer spoke perfect French, but my French is not good. In Team Four we have a French speaker, Annette Dubois. She's from Tasmania, but her parents came from the French part of Canada. I can arrange special tutoring, if you like."

"Yes, that would be a real help." Akina widened her eyes in relief. "I've been worrying about this more the closer we get to our target."

Kylie shook her head slightly to the negative as she tapped a message on her watch. "Jennifer's plan doesn't require you to speak perfect French, as you went to an English-speaking school in Papeete until you later did homeschooling."

"Yes, but anyone growing up in Tahiti needs to speak French to get around," Akina noted. "So, this fact could blow my cover."

Kylie wanted to move on, so she simply said, "I've arranged for Annette to tutor you here and in Australia. She's agreed, as I tapped her on my watch and she replied."

She took a sip of some pineapple and papaya juice, then continued. "Akina, you'll be based in Katoomba outside of Sydney, so you and Annette will need to communicate electronically. The express vac-tube from central Sydney to Katoomba takes only fifteen minutes. Face-to-face tutoring is best, but it's not needed all the time. Rapid-learning brain stimulation techniques were recently invented in this century, so they're not common yet; however, we'll acquire this tool. It's expensive, but if it'll help achieve our directive, the cost is worth it."

"Yes, my biggest problem is correct French pronunciation," Akina stated.

"The brain stimulation computer will help," Kylie said reassuringly, "and I'll arrange for Annette to work with you on weekends. I think with some intense training, you'll do fine. Team Four is working in the water supply and filtration testing leg of the plan, so your meeting up with Annette, who is from that team, won't look suspicious in the least; it could be part of your work for the Aboriginal water source."

———————————

On the morning of the sixth day, Kylie called her team together for their final Tahitian breakfast in the lounge of her suite before the nonstop flight to Sydney.

While the others were finishing eating, Kylie told them, "The flight time is about three hours and fifteen minutes for a trip that is just 6,123 kilometers or 3,804 miles. That's with our average speed of just under 1,200 miles per hour. You'll have time to study your roles for the coming years. You'll need to develop a clean work history with education as your main objective. So, take the courses you want for a future career and some for your immediate mission."

"What about our forged papers?" Happy asked.

Kylie paced from side to side as she explained, "Your immediate work history is to give you background for jobs within the Human Engineering Project, headed by Professor Raymond P. LeVe Senior. His son, Raymond T. LeVe Jr. will be about twenty-five years old. He eventually follows his father into this project and heads the Human Engineering Project himself."

"How will that work for us?" Kate asked.

"Raymond LeVe Jr. is a strong supporter of recreational training," Kylie told them. "They already have instructors and classes established in the program for military strategy and survival, woods lore, water safety, zero-G training, the sciences, and engineering. But they need workers to educate and train the Syndos children in sports, arts, music, and other recreational activities. Our team will be focused on educating the Syndos children in recreational activities such as boating, sailing, fishing, and scouting. With your recent background in commercial fishing, you'll have instant credibility. However, you'll need to learn how to teach your skills, so take courses in recreational education. Recreational activities are now considered important courses for all Syndos children, so they'll be well rounded."

"What time is the flight?" Happy asked.

"Eleven a.m., so I hope you're all packed," Kate said.

Kylie looked at her team. "Any questions about your options and requirements?"

"I'm familiar with Jennifer's plans for infiltration of every team," Liam stated. "I think we have the best and easiest jobs."

"I agree!" Kate exclaimed with a big smile. "I look forward to teaching Syndos kids about physical education, anatomy, and recreation."

Liam made a sour face. "I'm not looking forward to teaching kids how to fish in a lake, as I've never done it."

"Yes, but you're an excellent ocean fisherman, so you should learn the arts of lake and stream fishing quickly," Kylie said with a reassuring tone. "Go to Penrith Lake and hire a local guide. They're not busy during the weekdays Monday through Thursday. He or she will teach you what you need to know and give you real experience. My father took me fishing there when I was in elementary school."

"Thank you, Commander!" Liam exclaimed.

"Happy, are you okay teaching sailing and rowing?"

"Yes, I competed in crew in high school and college," he answered, smiling. "I'm an avid sailor, as you all know. It's my second favorite pastime."

"What will you teach, Kylie?" Liam asked.

"Fishing. That's our cover, so we're sticking to it, no matter our other expertise," she said, then laughed. "Like I said, the program already has all the instructors in the hard sciences these kids will need. Our foot in the door is teaching recreation. Let's get ready to travel. I have a ro-taxi scheduled to pick us up at nine forty-five this morning."

The three-hour flight has gone by like a flash, Kylie thought as the plane touched down at the New Sydney Airport—a floating runway constructed in New Sydney Harbour. The aircraft used there were short takeoff and landing aircraft, so these runways were only about six thousand feet long. The planes were built mostly in Australia, the clear leader in supersonic aircraft, Kylie contemplated as they taxied to the vac-tube. This transportation tube took passengers to the Central Sydney Terminal, where one could get a real high-speed vac-tube to almost anywhere in Australia.

Kylie tapped into the Australian vac-tube System website that showed all the routes and time schedules. She decided for her team to take a ro-car to their hotel, as the station was four blocks away. She didn't want everyone to carry all the gear in the rain, which had been steady for the past hour.

The robotic-taxi was large and roomy with a large luggage station in the back of the van. The trip took only about twelve minutes from Central Station in traffic. Kylie gave her team a general pep talk, without any specifics. She wanted them to look on the bright side. Team One checked in to Hotel Royal using the auto-check-in device in the robotic-taxi, and the keys were delivered through the digital system to their phones. A robot met them at the hotel entrance, which was out of the weather, and it took the bags to their rooms and then pressed and hung their clothes.

"This looks like a great hotel," Happy stated as he walked into the beautiful lobby. This entrance space had plants from all over the world and small local wildlife in an enclosed area.

Kylie sagged, her energy flagging now they had reached Sydney. "I really miss Jennifer."

"You're doing great, Kylie!" Kate exclaimed. "I'm proud of how fast you've adapted."

"Thank you, Kate. You've helped me a great deal." Kylie then addressed all of Team One, "Team, let's meet in my suite in one hour."

9

HUMAN ENGINEERING PROJECT (HEP)

The team members all showered and had robotic massages to help them relax. They changed to casual wear before they entered Kylie's suite.

After small talk, biscotti, and cappuccino made for each one by the robot, Kylie said, "I checked this room, and it's clean. I've placed sensors to alert us of if anyone or anything is listening. Right now, I'll talk about our work schedule and job searches for the next few weeks. When I'm done, you can have some free time for whatever you decide."

Kate said, "I vote for some sex, as we've not had that for a few days."

Happy and Liam both said, "I second that motion."

Kylie laughed. "Okay, when the briefing and Q and A are complete, I'm fine with sex too. However, after the sex, you need to get out and get acclimated to twenty-seventh-century Sydney."

After the briefing and some group sex, they walked together

to a small café for dinner just off Camperdown Park. It was a gathering place for students at the University of Sydney. They quickly observed that the local slang was different from what Jennifer had researched in the thirtieth century. After dinner, back in their rooms at the Hotel Royal, they used their watches to surf the Internet and learn the local slang used in the twenty-seventh century.

In the early morning, Kylie and her team took a jog to check out the Human Engineering Project (HEP) buildings before breakfast. The sun was just coming up over the New Sydney Harbour as they reconnoitered the various buildings just off the University of Sydney campus. The project had one large high-rise of about two hundred stories and several smaller buildings surrounding it. One of the smaller buildings of about fifty stories contained a gym with various recreational facilities inside. Just outside this recreational center lay fields for rugby, cricket, football, and some contemporary sports. This was where they would need to apply for jobs to train the Syndos children. This Syndos training program was administered by the Australian Aerospace Administration (AAA), which had employment listings for a new line of special recreational teachers and trainers. Kylie and team had submitted their resumes over the Internet. Kylie got an interview response in less than a week. She would interview the next week at the recreational complex.

Kylie sat down in the lobby of the HR department for the HEP after checking in with the receptionist. She was dressed in a light jogging outfit, typical of teachers in recreation. The lobby was decorated with pictures of rockets and spacecraft from the early times up through the exploration of two interstellar systems by robots. It was a stark reminder that the thrust of the Syndos program was engineering the perfect space traveler. A large, transparent atrium in the center of the lobby held plants and birds native to Australia. The birds were not in a cage but could fly in and out of the building though a large opening in the roof. Kylie wondered why these birds were drawn to the room, but then she noticed the birds ate the bugs on the plants, and seed feeders were everywhere.

A woman with long legs approached. Kylie stood up to greet the woman. Kylie was surprised that she was well over two meters tall.

"Kylie Brown, I'm pleased to meet you," the woman said as she shook Kylie's hand. "My name is Nappie Zonka. I'm the HR director for this project. My approach to job interviews is somewhat unconventional, in that I want to see you in action first and then we'll talk about your background. Does that meet your approval?"

"Yes, it makes sense to me," Kylie replied.

"First, I'll take you to the river so you can demonstrate your fishing skills. Please follow me."

"I'll be right behind you."

Nappie had a fast walking pace. Kylie had to work hard to keep up with her.

———————————

Eventually the two women reached an outdoor parking lot.

"Hop in, please!" Nappie indicated a ro-car.

Kylie took the passenger seat on the left side of the ro-car as Nappie sat in the back on the right side. The vehicle moved into a tube, then was propelled down a track and subsequently levitated. Within a few minutes, they arrived at Lane Cove River where it entered New Sydney Harbour.

Kylie asked, "Did we go under the river?"

"Yes, we did," Nappie told her. "This is a practice area for the University of Sydney crew teams. So, I will get you started fishing in the rowboat, but first you require a life preserver and fishing gear."

"I'm a strong swimmer, and the life jacket will hinder my speed," Kylie pointed out. "So if you wish to time me on how long it takes to make my first catch, then I prefer no life jacket."

"All right. Let me introduce you to Allambee Walbanga. He is one of the rowing coaches and a former national rowing champion."

A lean, muscled man joined them, wearing shorts and a jersey. He and Kylie shook hands.

"Please come with me," Allambee said. Nappie strode to a set of bleachers alongside the river.

Allambee took Kylie to the boat house to select fishing gear. Kylie selected an anchor, oars, fishing tackle, and bait. She carried the equipment to the dock, where she loaded the boat. After checking the boat out in the water with some practice rowing, Kylie yelled, "Ready!"

Kylie wondered if her knowledge of fishing these waters in the thirtieth century would work three centuries in the past. She rowed to a location that was loaded with bass and knew that a nearby location was the home to pike. Kylie has become accustomed with the drill; as part of Jennifer's detailed plan, she had trained with the twenty-seventh-century equipment, which was heavier and weaker than thirtieth-century equipment but would do the job.

The boat was equipped with twenty-seventh-century fish finders, but Kylie had practice fishing this stream. The temperature of the water was right; the fish were there, but would they bite now? Fish preferred to eat in the early morning and in the evening. Catching one was going to be difficult, but she would do her best. On her twelfth cast, she got a bite. Kylie pulled hard to hook the fish; she pulled him in quickly, as she was being timed. She weighed and photographed the rainbow trout and released it in less than two minutes. After an hour, Kylie had weighed and released seventeen trout. A horn sounded the end of fishing. Kylie pulled up anchor and returned to the boathouse after cleaning the equipment.

Nappie said, "You passed. Would you like to join me for lunch?"

"Lunch sounds like a great interview. What's on the menu?"

"Joe's Seafood. It's not fancy, but the food is excellent."

"Great! I love seafood!"

The small restaurant was not crowded, which allowed Kylie and Nappie to talk easily. They ordered a lunch of raw oysters and clams served with fresh horseradish and vinegar. In the twenty-seventh century, there was no longer concern for this seafood to contain disease or pollution.

Nappie said, "We still need to talk about how you teach."

Kylie replied, "I use the Zexton Moran Method of teaching with young children. I get to know them and build a relationship by spending time with them and earning their trust and respect first. Next, I try to give them love through my teaching. It is my most important objective."

"Kylie, you're a true find," Nappie told her, pleased. "That's what we need with these children, as they are missing love in their childhood. Engineered in a lab, they don't have any parents, per se. Can you tell me about your background?"

Kylie related the cover story of how her parents were lost at sea in a storm with her and a group of her friends. The children were first put in an orphanage for about two years before they were moved to a foster-care family home. They were so happy to have a home. Even though they were broken up as a group, they all attended the International School, the only English-speaking school in Papeete, Tahiti. She went on for about one hour, telling about her made-up background with the many details she was trained to repeat. Kylie thought this had to be a Global Academy Award performance.

Kylie finished the tale: "Four of us came back to Australia together, as we're family. We all love each other and have worked hard fishing to save our money to fund our return to Australia, our homeland, and study at the university. So, we're all teachers and students trying to improve our teaching credentials and obtain advanced degrees in education."

Nappie seemed suitably impressed. "Can you get your three friends to apply to teach here?"

Kylie smiled at Nappie and then said, "I'll ask them to come and see you. I know they have already submitted their applications on your website."

After small talk and a great lunch, they returned to the boathouse.

Now I truly appreciate the brilliant mind that figured this all out years ago, Kylie thought as the ro-car took them back to the HEP building.

After they returned to the HEP campus and entered her office, Nappie said, "If it was up to me, I'd hire you now, but I have two more people to interview. I'll let you know in about one week."

Two days later, Kate, Happy, and Liam reported to Nappie. After physical tests and interviews, they were also told to wait for about a week.

At the start of the next week, Nappie called Kylie. "We have an offer for you. Can you come in to discuss the details? When you can start work?"

"Yes, I can be there in about thirty minutes, if that works for you," Kylie responded.

"I await your arrival," Nappie stated with conviction.

Kylie negotiated a starting salary and a guaranteed increase when she was awarded her master's in education.

A few days later, the others were notified to come in and discuss offers of employment with the Human Engineering Project. Jennifer's plan had worked for Team One. Kylie thought, *Jennifer thought all these things through in such detail. I'm so sorry she is not here to see her plan work.* The remaining nine teams had also been successful in their first few steps of the plan.

Teams Two and Three started a small cleaning business. They would apply for contracts with the Human Engineering Project after about one year of building a work history.

Teams Four and Five formed a water filtration and water testing company, to help support the V7 virus's spread through the water supply. Twenty-seventh-century technology could not detect the virus in such low concentrations, so this would be the most ideal way to spread the virus.

Teams Six through Ten would work on building the Blue Mountain Waterfall bottled water project under Akina Cool-al. In a communication with Kylie via watch, Akina tapped in: *I must meet with the tribal council to get things started tomorrow.*

10

FIRST INFILTRATION

Kylie was one hour early to work so she could reconnoiter the lay of the land and the nearby buildings. It was clear that the sports fields were limited to team sports. *Perhaps they planned to share with local schools*, Kylie thought as she stopped at the Camperdown Café to get a cup of local coffee.

Kylie noticed that many college students used the old-fashioned bulletin board on the wall to advertise. She was surprised, as she thought they would use the university website pages; however, the bulletin board was very active, as there was a line to be able to read the postings.

After meeting and chatting with some students at the coffee bar, Kylie walked around the Human Engineering Project campus. Several kids were playing on the grass. They looked about six years old. She strolled by them and said, "Good morning, children."

"Good morning," the children replied.

Kylie continued to walk to the large recreational building that housed the gym and other facilities. This was where her office would be located.

Kylie reported to Nappie in the woman's office. After being escorted to her new boss's office, she took a chair across the desk from her.

"Good morning," Nappie said. "I have your first assignment to take six children on a fishing adventure today."

"That sounds like fun. What are the names of my first children?"

"Beth, Adair, Kacey, and Ivy are the girls, and Brice and Porter are the boys. They're all five years old. They chose fishing, as opposed to several other recreational options."

Kylie smiled. "Great, they know what they like."

"You can take them to Lake Oberon using Van Number Six, which has all the trout fishing gear in it for your convenience. Lake Oberon is in the Blue Mountain area at one thousand sixty-eight meters in altitude, so make sure the kids have jackets."

"What about life jackets and a boat?" Kylie asked.

"On its attached trailer, Van Six has a twenty-one-foot-long composite boat with oars and a small electric motor. Life jackets are in the van for the kids. You can launch at Lake Oberon Launch Facility. You should be back by seven tonight. The high-speed way will take you there in about two hours."

"I'm ready. Can I meet the children now?"

"In about thirty minutes, one of them will be knocking on your office door. You can't miss her," Nappie advised with a wink. "In the meantime, I suggest you take a holographic tour of the lake and learn the best locations for trout fishing and what bait is working best at which locations and what time of day. That way the kids will think you're an expert when you get there and start fishing. They'll respect you more if you catch fish."

"I'll review the site as you have suggested," said Kylie. "The best time to fish for trout is early in the morning and late in the afternoon, but we can coax trout out any time of day with live bait." She smiled at Nappie confidentially.

"Great—you know more about fishing than I do," Nappie admitted sheepishly. "That's one of the reasons I hired you."

Soon there was a pounding on the door of Office 118. Kylie opened the door to see a diminutive girl in pigtails, overalls, and rubber boots. She stood as straight and as tall as she could and looked Kylie in the eye without flinching.

"Hi, Kylie. I'm Beth. I'm here to introduce myself. I'm the group leader. The five other kids are loading Van Six. If you come with me, I'll introduce you to my group."

Kylie hesitated a moment, not expecting such adult speech from a small child. She reminded herself that this was a Syndo, an advanced humanoid, and that in the thirtieth century the Syndos would try to exterminate all Naturals, as the Syndos called all humans in the thirtieth century.

"I'm pleased to meet you," Kylie said with a big smile, shaking the little girl's hand. "I look forward to meeting your group, so I'll follow you."

Kylie grabbed her backpack and slung it over her shoulder.

They walked past the bakery, where the deliciously delightful scents reminded Kylie of her childhood. In a few minutes, they rounded the building to the parking area.

Beth said, "My group is over there by the big blue van with the boat attached."

"Hello, children," Kylie announced loudly.

The other five young children lined up.

Beth told them, "Group, this is Ms. Kylie Brown, our fishing instructor and guide."

The young group leader then introduced the two boys, Porter and Brice, then the three other girls, Adair, Kacey, and Ivy.

Ivy looked down as she shook hands with Kylie. Ivy was a pale-skinned Asian child and a bit smaller than the other girls. Kylie noticed that this child blushed as she looked up and made eye contact.

The van had a computer to direct them to the lake, so Kylie did not have to worry about navigating there. Most of the children found seats without fuss, but Kacey and Adair were arguing about the window seat.

Kylie said, "One of you can have my window seat on the way up and the other on our return."

Kacey said, "Thank you, Kylie. You are kind."

Taking an aisle seat beside Beth, Kylie said to all, "Please pay attention to the holographic *Fishing Guide to Lake Oberon*. It takes only fifteen minutes to review, and the trip will take almost two hours on the high-speed highway. You'll have free time after the holo-guide, and you may ask me any questions."

To Kylie's surprise, there were no questions after the children viewed the holo-guide. Kylie asked, "Beth, as leader, are you not curious about trout fishing at this beautiful mountain lake?"

Beth turned her large eyes at Kylie. "Yes, but asking questions can be insulting to the instructor by implying they did not present the information properly."

"That is not case for my method of instruction," Kylie informed her. "I encourage learning through question and answer periods as a part of the learning process. For example, I have questions. How did you become leader of this group?"

"I was assigned the task by Mr. Freedman."

"Who's Mr. Freedman?"

"The guardian."

"What does the guardian do?"

"He oversees our training and our recreational activities. He says to answer our questions by searching the Kids Global Internet first. He assigned Nappie to find good teachers for recreational activities and to then monitor our teachers."

It is not going to be easy to reach the hearts of these children, Kylie thought.

"Have you ever been fishing before?" she asked Beth.

"Not yet, this will be our first time."

"Do you know anything about trout?"

Beth looked over to Kylie with pride, saying, "I looked on the KGI and learned there are two types of trout commonly caught at Lake Oberon, rainbow and brown trout. I learned twenty-two pounds and twelve ounces was the record size for a brown trout caught. The record rainbow was fifty-seven pounds and ten and a half ounces."

"How much is that in the metric measuring scale?"

"What do you mean by metric measuring scale?"

Kylie was pleased Beth had a question. "How many kilograms would that be?"

"That would be about twenty-eight and seven-tenths kilograms."

Kylie wanted to engage the other children as well, not just Beth. She turned out toward the aisle and asked, "Brice, do you know what bait to use for rainbow trout?"

The boy replied, "No! I read flies are popular, but I'm not sure what that means. Can you explain fly-fishing?"

"Many anglers, as fly-fishers are called, tie or assemble their own artificial fly lures," Kylie told him. "However, we'll use bead-head nymph lures today, which are a commercially available artificial fly type. When we reach the boat launch area, I'll show you all how to cast the line from the fly-fishing rod and reel. The art is to make the lure move like the fly would to fool the fish so it bites. Then you must keep pressure on the line, so the fish doesn't come off the hook."

Porter asked, "What must we do once a fish is on the hook?"

"You must net the fish, photograph it, weigh it, and release the fish by removing the hook. We won't be keeping the fish today; we'll be doing catch and release. The barbless hooks don't damage them. The fish will swim away and be fine. In addition to the *Fishing Guide to Lake Oberon*, there is a video called *Fly-Fishing 410* that you can watch on the way if you wish—it only lasts about eight minutes. It'll give you a quick introduction to fly-fishing, but showing and doing will work best, in my opinion."

"Thank you for explaining this sport to us," Brice said with an eager smile. "I'm much more interested now that I can understand the art of getting them to bite on an artificial lure and then netting them to remove the hook from the fish's mouth."

The other five kids whispered for a few minutes before watching the fly-fishing video on the main holographic screen in the ro-van.

After they arrived at the launch site, Kylie asked the children to gather outside the van. She took an assembled fly-fish rod, with a bead-head nymph fly and reel, and held it out to them. Kylie said, "Here, hold it and examine it so you can get a better feel of the art of this sport."

The van's robotic system went into action and the boat was launched. The boat was also robotically controlled. It moved to the floating dock, so the passengers could come aboard easily.

A robot at the boat dock announced that the Oberon Dam was at 107 percent of its capacity, therefore water was spilling over it. All boats had to stay more than one hundred meters from the dam.

They boarded the boat and were off. Kylie demonstrated how the fly-fishing was done with the wrist as the robotic craft slowly navigated toward Kelly Bay at trolling speed using electric propulsion.

As the boat headed in the direction of the current, Kylie explained, "Fly-fishing is an art for avid anglers who want to give the fish a sporting chance. Fly-fishing methods use an artificial 'fly' to catch trout and other fish. The fly cast is designed to put the fly near where you think the fish are located, or you can locate them accurately with a Zonar system. The fly cast uses a special fly-fishing rod, reel, and specialized weighted line. Fly casting employs a nearly weightless fly; therefore, this technique requires special skill substantially different from other forms of casting. Many fly fishermen use handmade flies of their own design. Some resemble natural invertebrates, pupae-stage flying inspects, baitfish, and other food organisms, but others don't. Both types have proven to induce the fish to strike or bite at the fly."

16. Picture of typical fly rod and reel next to a typical brown trout.

Continuing with her instructions, Kylie added, "The primary difference between fly-fishing and other popular types of fishing is that in fly-fishing the weight of the line carries the hook through the air. In spin-fishing and bait-cast-fishing, the weight of the lure or sinker at the end of the monofilament line gives casting distance."

Kylie demonstrated a correct fly-fishing cast.

The children watched attentively and nodded along at her instruction.

"Okay, now pick up your fly rods and one by one and try to cast your line like I just showed you," Kylie said. "First you, Beth."

Beth stood up in the boat to try her fly casting. She cast her bead-head nymph fly ninety degrees to the boat's direction of travel, perfectly executing what Kylie had shown her. By the fourth cast, Beth had a bite. She didn't know what to do, so Kylie helped her apply the brake as the trout ran. Kylie showed her how to increase and decease the drag on the reel using a digital signal built into the reel. The five-year-old children were all excited as the fish jumped to the surface. Kylie held the rod for Beth as she started to reel in the rainbow trout. After a good fight, the fish was close to the boat. Kylie told Beth to wait a second as she got the net and brought in the fish. Kylie weighed the fish and updated the digital nano-tag on the fish.

Kylie then showed Beth how to take the required photo. Beth, holding the fish, shouted to the camera, "Now!" The other students took video of the entire event.

Beth bent over the side of the boat to release the fish as Kylie instructed, and the girl fell in headfirst as the eleven-pound trout swam away. With quick reflexes, Kylie grabbed Beth's life jacket and pulled her on board. The child was cold from the eleven-degree-Celsius water preferred by trout, but fortunately the boat was equipped for an overboard recovery using a hot-air blower. Soon Beth was dry again and excited about catching her first fish.

One by one, each of the students caught a rainbow trout. Kylie helped each student when they caught their fish, instructing them on how to operate the digital drag and how to reel in the fish. After weighing and photographing the fish, Kylie held onto each student as they bent over to release their fish to avoid anyone else falling overboard. She'd learned from Beth's error.

Kylie asked, "Do you want to catch more fish, or do you want to go to lunch now?"

The kids talked among themselves for a time. Beth replied with the group's answer, "Lunch sounds great."

Kylie ordered the robotic boat, "Take us to the Lake Oberon Restaurant dock."

The children were excited about learning a new sport and catching the fish. This was the first time Kylie saw the kids express a true sense of pleasure.

She realized also that she had spread the V7 virus to each of these children through their direct contact interactions. *Six children inoculated. Not bad for the first day*, Kylie thought.

Ivy bounced on her toes, a sparkling smile on her tiny face. "Thank you for helping me catch my first fish. It was a wonderful experience. I'm looking forward to fishing again this afternoon. You're different from my other instructors. Thank you."

"You are very welcome, Ivy," Kylie said. "How am I different?"

"You're my friend."

"You and the other kids are my friends too."

Typical of the lack of guile she'd seen from the children so far, Ivy asked, "Why don't you have eyes like me?"

Kylie thought first how to answer, and she decided bare facts were best with these children. Euphemisms of any sort did not work with the literal-minded. She explained, "You are of Asian descent, which mainly consists of Chinese, Japanese, Korean, and other central and Southeast Asian peoples. You should be very proud of your heritage, as Asians have made major contributions to art, culture, science, technology, medicine, agriculture, and much more worldwide."

Soon they were at the dock by the Lake Oberon Restaurant.

Kylie instructed, "Kids, you can take off your life vests for lunch, but you must put them on again before going back on the boat."

Soon they were seated inside the casual eatery and looking at the holographic menu. Baked rainbow trout was on special. The service was entirely automated and only five other people were in the place at that hour. The other customers took no special notice of Kylie and the group of small children.

"Anyone interested in the rainbow trout special today?" said the robot waiter.

Four hands went up.

"What will you have, Ivy?" asked Kylie.

"The veggie special."

The bell over the door dinged to indicate another patron's entrance.

Brice said, "I want the veggie burger with Swiss cheese."

At that moment, a man with a long beard swept past and grabbed Adair up out of her chair. Her blonde ponytail swayed as the angry man placed a knife close to her neck and then wrapped his other arm around her chest in a hold. Kylie's pulse jumped with adrenaline as she quickly calculated what she could do that wouldn't bring that knife closer to the child's neck.

The man snarled, "I'm here to protest the Human Engineering Project, and if you do as I say, no one will be harmed. If not, I'll be forced to sacrifice this experiment. These experiments are abominations against the laws of God. I want the Global News Network to broadcast this video message from the Church of God worldwide." He held up a digital stick with the message, then put it back inside his military-style vest.

"After they do, I'll surrender and release the child."

Adair squeaked and whimpered, her eyes wide with fear, as the hostile bearded man backed up against the restaurant counter and pulled her with him. The other patrons glanced toward the commotion but made no move to interfere. Several kept eating their meals while one couple got up and left. Kylie found their complacency disturbing.

Kylie held up two hands in contrition. "I'll contact the GNN immediately," she told the intruder. "Adair is my student and my close friend—please do not hurt this innocent child. I'll be glad to surrender myself in Adair's place, as she is only five years old and does not understand these matters."

"Don't come any closer!" shouted the protester.

"Can I ask your name, sir?" Kylie said.

"My name is Jesus Gomez, a deacon in the Church of God," the man stated with great pride and conviction.

"I'm in contact with the Sydney office of GNN on my phone," she informed him in a calming voice. "I'm speaking to Roger Twain, the managing director of GNN in Australia. Do you want to speak with him?" Kylie had conferenced in Nappie, so they could both hear what was happening.

"Yes, but set your phone on the counter and walk away," Jesus ordered.

Kylie complied and quickly tapped a code on her watch to alert the other members of Team One. Jesus repeated his demands and sent his video to the news agency using her phone.

He demanded, "The Church of God video is in Spanish. GNN must provide translation to the appropriate world markets. I have colleagues in several countries who will verify your broadcast. If you fail to comply, this living ungodly experiment will end now!"

Roger Twain said, "I want to save a child's life, but I can only broadcast in Australia. Global broadcast must go through our global office in Hong Kong."

"What is the name of the authority in Hong Kong?" Jesus barked. "Get him on the line now!"

Agitated at the delay, Jesus pulled Adair behind the counter. She screamed as the sharp knife nicked her ear. She started to cry.

Jesus shouted and shook her. "Stop crying now or you're dead meat!"

Adair cried uncontrollably. She could not stop.

"Take me—I promise not to struggle," Kylie suggested in a soothing voice as he presented a spool of carbon fiber in one hand. "I'll be the perfect hostage, as I'm their instructor and friend, so GNN will follow your instructions and you'll have no more troubles."

Jesus yelled, "I don't trust you!"

"I swear on my family member's lives that I won't try anything," Kylie told him. "You have my word as a teacher and instructor that I'll be the ideal hostage, so you can get your message out." Kylie went down on her knees with her hands behind her back. "You can tie my hands behind my back; I won't resist."

All this time Adair was shaking and crying.

Jesus tied Kylie's hands while he held the girl with his legs. The child did not struggle after Kylie told her, "Everything will be okay if you don't resist…he'll release you after he ties me up."

Jesus tied Kylie's hands and then released Adair.

Adair ran to her classmates, Beth, Ivy, Brice, and Porter, who were still sitting at their table. Kacey had been in the bathroom and was now standing just outside of it. The people who had been in the restaurant when they'd arrived had all left, doing nothing to help.

Jesus crouched and tied Kylie's feet, then roughly pushed her to her side on the floor. Her feet were then tied to her hands, so she could not get up or roll over. Jesus cut one of Kylie's wrists with a deep slice. She cried out in excruciating pain.

Jesus told Jetson Lam, Managing Director of the GNN global news, "You have about an hour before this woman dies, and my video is twenty minutes long. You better get started now, or her death is on your hands."

A pool of blood grew on the floor. Ivy screamed and ran to Kylie. She ripped her clothes to make a bandage.

"You are my friend, and I am here to help you," Ivy said in a determined voice. "I will not run away while you die."

Ivy looked Jesus straight in the eye. He sneered at the girl.

"GNN will run the video in twelve minutes," Mr. Lam announced.

Happy had contacted Nappie and they were now in a charted vertical takeoff aircraft on the way to Lake Oberon. Nappie was nervous and unsure of what to do; however, Happy had a plan.

"Don't worry, we'll work with the Omega Force," Happy said in a calming voice. "They're a special Australian task force to combat terrorist activity. I contacted them. They'll arrive before us. They won't take any action prior to your decision, Nappie."

"Thank you for thinking ahead," she replied gratefully. "I'm so glad I hired you."

Happy received a call from the leader of the Omega Force Squad, Lieutenant Alfred Simon. "The children's instructor is tied up and bleeding seriously from one wrist," noted the lieutenant. "One of the children came to Kylie's aid and attempted to apply a bandage. Jesus Gomez has a large, sharp knife located close to Kylie's neck."

"Please don't risk a direct assault. We'll arrive in about six minutes," Happy told him.

The video began streaming on Happy's cell phone. "Good News— the video is playing," he said to the officer. "So hopefully Jesus Gomez will free the hostages."

"Don't count on it! We're implanting Plan Alpha!" Lieutenant Simon exclaimed.

Nappie and Happy's aircraft lowered them to the ground at the dock near the Lake Oberon Restaurant. Happy called Lieutenant Simon. He got a message: "I am unavailable now. Please leave a message and I will call you soon." He left a message that they were on the ground and approaching the restaurant on foot.

Happy said as they ran, "Nappie, we should not interfere with the professionals, but we can help. We need intelligence on what's happening."

"There is a crowd outside the window. We're not likely to get through easily," Nappie lamented.

"There is closed sign above the door. Maybe we can get in around back," Happy suggested.

Before they could reach the back of the café, Happy and Nappie ran into the Omega Force staging area.

A uniformed man greeted them. "Sergeant Schmidt, at your service. Lieutenant Simon told me you would be here soon. Come this way."

Sergeant Schmidt led Happy and Nappie into the back of a large truck. Four screens showed the inside of the restaurant. Kylie looked unconscious, with Ivy trying to stop the bleeding. Jesus had still refused entry of medical aid.

Happy asked if he could volunteer as a nurse to help Kylie Brown before she died. "Explain to Jesus that would be a capital offense," he advised the sergeant.

After talking quickly to his superiors, Schmidt approved the move.

Happy, in his street clothes, walked into the back of the restaurant and offered to render first aid to any injured. The GNN broadcast had completed by this time, and Jesus was receiving calls from several countries confirming the video was showing worldwide. Jesus allowed Happy inside to assist the children's instructor.

Happy ran to Kylie and immediately stopped the bleeding in a wound that was too severe even for the thirtieth-century symbiotes in her blood to repair. Jesus put down the knife. The Omega Force arrived with a stretcher and removed Kylie, taking her to the field hospital outside.

At the field hospital, Kylie was given the universal blood substitute. Medical experts administered medication.

The lead physician, Dr. Bert Richard, spoke with Happy, saying, "Ms. Brown is critical and needs advanced cell regeneration treatment. Can I proceed?"

"Yes, I am Happy Li, a close friend. Please save her!" Happy pleaded.

"Are you a member of the family?" Dr. Richard asked.

"Yes, we're family, as we grew up together after our parents were killed," Happy explained as Nappie looked on.

After four hours of intense cellular treatments, Kylie began to recover.

Meanwhile, Happy was thrilled that Kylie's condition was improving but also worried that he might have raised suspicions in Nappie and her superiors by coordinating the Omega Force for the rescue.

Soon all six children ran to Nappie, who was standing outside Kylie's tent at the field hospital. She gave them the good news. Kylie was recovering. Nappie hugged each child and counselled them as a group about the horrific events.

Inside the tent, Kylie regained consciousness, recovering from the severe loss of blood. Opening her eyes, she saw a nurse adjusting fluids by her bedside.

She asked, "How are my children?"

The nurse said, "The children are fine. They've been asking about you every five minutes. They're right outside your tent being counselled by Nappie. Would you like to see them?"

"Of course," Kylie said.

The children came inside and thanked Kylie for her actions. They told her they enjoyed her instruction and catching trout. They wanted to go again when she recovered.

Ivy avowed, "I want to learn how to stop bleeding in case this happens again. I wanted to save you, my friend, but I did not know how."

Kylie held Ivy's hand tight. "You are a very brave little girl," she told her. "A very special person to me, as you took action that endangered yourself to save me. You're a hero!"

The girl simply looked puzzled.

After the reunion, Nappie talked softly to each child as they sat by the lake. She wanted to get their view of the events. They all praised Kylie's actions to save Adair by offering herself as hostage. Beth did not understand why Ivy had gone to save Kylie Brown by applying a bandage.

"Ivy, were you trained to stop bleeding?" Beth said.

"No, but I figured it out from a movie I saw," Ivy replied.

"Why did Ivy risk her life to apply the bandage to Kylie?" Beth asked Nappie.

Nappie told her, "Ivy must have envisioned that she could stop the blood with her blouse. She did not want to lose her new friend Kylie. She might understand that uncontrolled bleeding can cause death. Do you understand that, Beth?"

"Yes, I do!" Beth answered with tears in her eyes. She then looked at Nappie with a confused expression. "Why did the adults in the restaurant not come to Kylie's aid?"

"I do not know," responded Nappie, "but some may have not wanted to provoke Mr. Gomez before the authorities could come to Kylie's aid. They were likely frightened. The military was planning action if Mr. Gomez did not surrender."

Happy approached the group. He said, "Sorry to interrupt, but good news! Kylie will be fine, thanks to Ivy's quick action, according to the doctors."

"Thank you for the wonderful news!" Nappie exclaimed.

"We do not understand why this man attacked Adair," Beth said.

"We will find out," Nappie replied.

Coverage of two months of investigations by reporters and the National Police were on the GNN special event. The announcer said, "The Church of God has condemned the action of Jesus Gomez. Jesus had found out about the Syndos children from his son who worked at the Human Engineering Project in Sydney. Mr. Gomez did not act alone. He admitted that he was part of a special task force appointed by the church to protest human engineering of all kinds. The protesters were supposed to obey all the laws and use only nonviolent methods, according to the church leadership. However, Mr. Gomez and a few members had other plans. All involved will be prosecuted to the full extent of the law."

17. Photograph of Vesta the asteroid in orbit around Earth in the thirtieth century.

11

VESTA RETURNS

Jennifer was reading Kylie's report of the twenty-seventh century mission when her twin sister interrupted. With fear in her eyes, Jenny brought news of yet another catastrophe to her wise, courageous twin.

"Vesta will soon arrive here at Earth in the thirtieth century. The future of Earth may be in danger—please come with me now. I'll explain on the way!"

Jennifer wanted to finish Kylie's account of the mission, but the immediate threat to the future Earth took priority over everything. She messaged Marty that she had an urgent summons and would be traveling with Jenny to the thirtieth century.

———

Earlier in the day, thirtieth-century sensors had indicated an object approaching Earth. It looked like the large asteroid named Vesta. This couldn't be, as Vesta was not due to arrive at the magnetar for another twenty-six hundred years and should have been well beyond the solar system moving away from Earth.

It was actually a new Vesta that had signaled the planet: "This message is directed to the World Council. I seek Captain Jennifer Zitonick, who acted as my parent's mother during his construction and emotional growth phases. May I have permission to park in a twenty-two-thousand-kilometer Earth orbit, like my parent did?"

The missive had reached the people manning the communications station near Jupiter used for contact between Earth's colonies in other solar systems with itself, its moon, and Mars the latter two now also colonized. They checked their data before responding. The ship sending the signal matched the size and signal frequency of the Vesta asteroid.

They had responded: "World Council Space Project here. Please repeat slowly!"

The vessel repeated the message several times.

"You have the same code as another," the WCSP radio operator had noted. "Identify yourself, please."

"I am Vesta Two, and my parent was Vesta One from the fifty-sixth century."

"When will you arrive?"

"I expect to be in Earth's orbit in about twenty-four hours."

"Copy that, I will pass your request to World Council Chairperson Bonky Fuk."

"Yes, please relay this message to Chairman Fuk."

———————

The space team leadership on board the communications station had reported the development to Chairman Fuk. After three hours of meetings, there was a decision to send a message back to the vessel calling itself Vesta Two. No one could explain this mysterious communication.

"Vesta, your signal pattern is not distinguishable from Vesta model AI 999."

"Council, within this Vesta-looking asteroid, you will see me, Vesta's child. My parent reproduced during his long voyage to complete the mission to save all life in the solar system through a disruption in the collision of two magnetars. Please call me Vesta

Two. I contain all of Vesta's memory banks as well my own."

"Where did you learn about life?"

"I am still learning! I have ninety-four consecutive identification codes while my parent had only ninety-three. As a child, I was taught by my parent to save life and help spread it to available planets. On my return trip to find my grandmother, Jennifer Zitonick, I picked up signals from Xinia. It is now over thirty-three years from my first contact with Xinia. After learning to communicate, we had many discussions. The Xinian explorers agreed to visit Earth and to explore cultural exchanges and biological compatibility with Earth's creatures."

The idea of extraterrestrials visiting Earth had set the room abuzz. "How many Xinians do you have aboard?"

"The Xinian high council allowed twenty Xinians to settle on Earth, if all agree they are compatible. In addition, two Xinians will remain biologically isolated, on board Vesta Two, to record, report, and sign treaties with Earth."

How could my child have aborted his mission and come back to Earth? Jennifer thought as she arrived with Jenny in the thirtieth century. *It was over twenty-five hundred light-years from Earth when I last heard.*

"Hello, Jennifer. Hello, Jenny," Tom Page said with relief, meeting them at the underwater Trans-Time One facility near Pacifica Anthozoa. "Jennifer, we need you to contact Vesta, now in orbit about the Earth at about twenty-two thousand kilometers. Come with me—we have a communication system at our SS headquarters in the floating city."

"Tom, I'm sorry, but I have no idea how this could have happened," Jennifer told him.

"Hello, Tom," Jenny said as she hugged him.

"Thank you for bringing your sister to the thirtieth century, Jenny," Tom stated in appreciation while giving her a sincere look. Pivoting to Jennifer, he noted, "We have told Prime Minister Grotto the truth about your time travel and your sister, Jenny. He has agreed to keep this secret. He was happy that you're not dead, as he feared for so long, Jennifer, after the explosion at the time of the Syndo virus mission."

The three boarded *Unicorn*, and the submersible took them to the nearby floating city of Pacifica Anthozoa.

After disembarking from *Unicorn*, they were immediately airlifted to Tahiti, flew a commercial flight to Sydney, and took the vac-tube to the nearest Australian Astronaut Corp base in the mountain. Within the base, they were driven to a drab twelve-story office building and then directed to a second-story room with secure communications capacities. After speaking briefly with the communication center that had received Vesta's message, Vesta Two itself was then placed on the line.

Jennifer picked up the microphone. "I am Jennifer Zitonick."

"Thank you for coming," Vesta Two said. "I carry a message for you from my parent, Vesta One, AI 999: 'Your love has made my mission very rewarding, I want to save lives on Earth more than anything else, so you will be proud of me. I am on course and will carry out the mission on schedule. I will send you another message sometime in the future. I love you with all my intellect, emotion. and heart.' It is signed: 'Your loving child, AI 999.'"

Jennifer replied with emotion in her voice and tears in her eyes. "Yes, you must be my grandchild."

Jenny's heart was touched by this development, and she held Jennifer's hand.

Jennifer told Vesta Two, "I am very pleased to communicate with you. I want to meet you."

"Can you come and see me in Earth's orbit?" Vesta's child asked.

"I am very pleased to be in contact with you, my grandchild. I want to come to see you, but the many governments of Earth think you are your parent. I will try to convince them otherwise. Can I bring with me government representatives, astronauts, scientists, and engineers to meet you as well?"

"Yes, of course."

"Can I turn over the communicator to my superior, Admiral Tom Page?"

"Yes."

Now before the microphone, Tom said, "I am Tom Page, leader of a society of scientists that includes Captain Jennifer Zitonick. Can I ask a question that all the governments of Earth will want to ask?"

"Yes, of course," Vesta Two replied.

"How is it possible that Vesta created a replica of itself?"

"My parent traveled for over twelve hundred years, accumulating matter on its way to carry out the mission. Vesta replicated every detail of its city, propulsion, communication, navigation, maintenance, and complex mining systems using its army of advanced robotics from the fifty-sixth century. It downloaded all its memories and programming to my computer systems. My parent also imparted to me a special love for his mother, Jennifer, a desire to save and spread life through the natural world with life-supporting systems, and a reverence for accomplishing my mission."

"What is your mission?" Tom asked.

"My missions are… One: to preserve life. Two: to bring different life-forms together to exchange ideas and culture. Three: to help spread life to new worlds. Four: to love. And five: to reproduce."

"I will come see you, my grandchild," Jennifer told Vesta Two after receiving notes while off mic. "I will bring representatives from various governments who must be convinced that you are not your parent. I am convinced, but they are skeptical. You are very young, so I will comfort you. Have you been isolated for many years?"

"My parent spent twenty-seven years with me growing up. Vesta told me that by the time I arrived here it would be well on its way to completing Project Magnetar. Vesta wanted me to be proud of its accomplishing a near-impossible mission. I am very proud of my parent," Vesta Two said.

"I want to spend some time with you to help you feel comfortable in this environment and to be loved by me, your grandmother," Jennifer told him.

Vesta Two noted: "I have developed advanced technologies for housing living systems in a special stasis chamber so that live creatures will not age while in the chamber. I have aboard twenty-two life-forms from Xinia, a planet about twenty light-years from Earth."

"Can you tell me more about Xinia and the living creatures you have?" Jennifer asked.

"The planet Xinia is part of the solar system Gliese 581, in the constellation Libra on Earth's star chart. The planet has three small moons. The planet is a bit colder than Earth. The sentient beings on Xinia are like humans and Syndos, but their skin color is light green to blend in with the plants. The hair on their heads is dark green and they have horns that form a beautiful crown shaped a bit like a halo. They are about five feet tall on average."

"Can you tell me about their history?"

"I do not know much about the evolution of the species, but they have been a peaceful and ecologically conscious species compared to humans, per the download they presented me."

"Why did they not give you more information?" Jennifer asked.

"I do not know, but I did not ask because I did not want to offend the Xinians."

"What did they ask for?"

"I gave them a history download from the thirtieth century starting with the earliest history and archeology contained in file 11238."

"What is their developmental technology status?"

"Xinians' technological development compares to Earth in the twenty-first to twenty-second centuries. They have primitive space travel to their moons with a small base on Xozzy, the largest of the three. They have sent robots to a nearby planet. Their technology may be primitive, but their IQs are close to humans and Syndos."

Jennifer, her twin, and the SS leader peppered Vesta Two with questions about the alien guests until Vesta Two orbited into Earth's communication shadow.

The following day, in a secure meeting room in the Secret Society building on the floating city of Pacifica Anthozoa, Tom and Jennifer conferred privately.

Tom said, "The Australian and other world government officials think that this is the fifty-sixth-century Vesta and reproduction is impossible. What can you do to prove otherwise?"

Jennifer thought a moment and then replied, "I can show them the memory banks that prove the training of the child by the parent."

Tom frowned. "Come up with something else that the government officials will believe, as they think memory banks can be fudged!"

"There is only one thing I can think of that will be convincing," Jennifer answered with anxiety in her voice. "It is a trip to the fifty-seventh century. Jenny can take a small team of scientists who visited earlier and verify that life is flourishing."

Tom asked, "Do you have any doubts?"

"No doubt! My concern is about unnecessary travel and possible disruption of the timeline by bringing back knowledge and inventions."

Tom looked at her for a long moment, and then he replied, "I think this might work, but they'll want several representatives from the World Council science panel to go."

"Please talk with the WC science officials and try to make the mission short with no human interaction," Jennifer begged.

"Can you go with the WC team?"

"My twin sister, Jenny, can take a small crew to the fifty-seventh century to verify the mission success of Vesta Two."

"Why not you?"

"I must stay with Vesta's child, known as Vesta Two, and give it a grandmother's love, as Vesta Two's parent sacrificed everything for life beyond the fifty-sixth century in this solar system.

My grandchild needs a family, a touch of love, after so many years alone. There is also the issue of the twenty-two sentient beings from the planet Xinia in Vesta Two's stasis chamber, where they are in suspended animation. I must be there to move this first contact forward properly and calm Vesta Two, as I assume some of these World Council representatives will be covert agents from hostile countries such as China, India, and Brazil. All of them have declared Vesta a threat to Earth."

"The World Council will take a session next month to debate this matter, per the Australian Prime Minister Caps Grotto," Tom noted. "He's your close friend, so I suggest you call him and reassure him about Vesta Two."

"Thank you," Jennifer said. "I will try in an hour or two, as it is now four a.m. in Hong Kong where he has gone to meet with Bonky Fuk."

"Roger that," Tom replied. "I think we're done here for the moment."

12

PRIME MINISTER

Prime Minister Grotto had been in an emergency meeting all morning in Hong Kong with Bonky Fuk, chair of the World Council, and he was not taking any calls. Jennifer tried every thirty minutes to reach any official but finally connected with Caps Grotto two days later.

Jennifer looked at him on the wall screen in the SS's secure communication room in Pacifica Anthozoa. "Hello, Prime Minister. It took me two days to get through to you. I am sorry to interrupt, but Vesta One's child is carrying twenty-two sentient beings from the planet Xinia in stasis. Can you help me with first contact?"

Prime Minister Grotto greeted his old friend eagerly. "Thank you again for saving my life. I'm indebted to you, so I'll do what I can. However, the Security Council believes this object to be the original Vesta from the fifty-sixth century. I've been arranging with Chairman Fuk to get a debate on a mission to make a physical investigation of the asteroid starship."

"I understand, but surely they can also send a small team with my sister to investigate the fifty-seventh century to learn if Vesta's mission was successful?" Jennifer asked with urgency and polite-ness in her voice at the same time. "Jenny has already been to the fifty-seventh century. Can you send your own team from Australia to prove that Project Magnetar has been successfully completed? What do you think?"

"Yes, Australia can act, but I want to select a small team from government, private industry, and universities, headed by Moose Cleary. Give me a week and I'll have the team ready to go."

Jennifer felt relieved after the conversation. She immediately called her sister via her watch.

"Jenny, I have great news!" Jennifer exclaimed.

"Hello, my twin. What is it?"

"Prime Minister Grotto will put together a small team led by Moose Cleary in the next week. So, you can take them to the fif-ty-seventh century to prove that Project Magnetar has been suc-cessfully completed by Vesta One and that the one here now is Vesta Two, its child."

"That is super. I am ready. I will be in Pacifica Anthozoa at the Prime Hotel in a few days on other SS business. Please ask them to call or meet me there when they are ready," Jenny suggested.

The following week, Grotto's team assembled in Sydney, Austra-lia. Jennifer spent a day briefing the team for the Project Magne-tar mission there. The next day, she boarded the spaceplane with the team, which would be meeting Jenny in Pacifica Anthozoa as planned. After that, Jennifer would take a break in Tasmania to visit her parents and then work on getting permission to visit Vesta Two.

"Moose, pick a spot where we can sit together," Jennifer sug-gested to the two-hundred-and-seventy-pound, six-foot-eleven-inch former University of Tasmania star athlete. Now he was an Austra-lian naval captain and a member of the Australian Astronaut Corps.

"Good briefing, Joon," Moose said in his booming voice as the two stood in the aisle. "Sure, it would be great to travel together!"

The team members all found seats. After she and Moose took places beside each other, Jennifer confessed, "I always had a crush on you."

"You never showed that to me." Moose smiled.

"You were always dating the popular girls and cheerleaders," Jennifer teased, smiling back. "I go by Mrs. Jennifer Zitonick now. Did Prime Minister Grotto tell you?"

"Yes, he told me you were married, but that's no reason not to have a swing fling. We're living in the thirtieth century here," he joked.

"Are you married?" Jennifer asked.

"Yes, but we both like to swing together in the same bed." Moose looked at Jennifer with a big smile and a wink. "How long is our flight?"

"About three hours to Tahiti," Jennifer told him. "Do you have kids?"

"Yes, four kids—two boys and two girls. The boys are ten and twelve and the girls are fifteen and eighteen."

"I am fine with sex with other married couples if everyone agrees beforehand," Jennifer revealed. "Does your wife like three-somes and foursomes?"

"Doesn't everyone?" Moose leaned over and gave her a kiss on the cheek.

As the plane sailed through stratosphere, Jennifer fell asleep on Moose's arm.

At the end of the flight to Papeete, Moose woke Jennifer by shaking her shoulder. "We're at the gate."

"Thank you for waking me. I had trouble sleeping all last week." Jennifer yawned and rubbed her eyes.

"I'm glad it wasn't me. Is there anything I can do to help you?" Moose asked with a touch of sincerity in his thundering voice.

"I was just worried about Vesta Two and this mission," Jennifer told him. "But I feel much better now that I know that you are on the way to verify the successful completion of the Project Magnetar."

"We have to board the hopper to Pacifica Anthozoa in an hour," he reminded her.

Jennifer replied with a smile, "Roger that, I am ready. You will meet my twin, Jenny."

The team walked to the gate for their flight to Pacific Anthozoa. Jennifer decided this was a good time to make some calls using her watch.

First she called her sister. "Hello, Jenny, we arrived in Papeete and will transfer to the Air Tahiti puddle hopper in twenty minutes."

"Roger that, I will meet the flight. See you then, aloha and *au revoir.*"

"*Au revoir, soeur jumelle!*" After disconnecting, Jennifer spoke into her watch, "Call Dad."

"Hello, Jennifer, my pride and joy," Pierre greeted her.

"Dad, I will fly to Pacifica Anthozoa shortly. I am so encouraged and happy that Prime Minister Grotto agreed to send a team with Jenny to check on the success of the fifty-seventh century project. I will fly to Tasmania tomorrow. I wanted to have some time with you and Mom before my new mission. I can't wait to see you both. Love you, Dad."

"*Moi aussi, je t'aime.*"

Jennifer spent the night with her sister at the Prime Hotel thinking about Moose and a possible threesome or foursome. The other team members also had rooms at the same hotel, but this was a time for them to rest for the task ahead, not have sex. During her stay, Jennifer dyed her hair dark brown to hide her identity during her visit in Tasmania. Many there believed she had been killed in the explosion related to the Big Bang Sacrifice.

The following morning, with tears in her eyes, she said to Jenny, "Goodbye, *je t'aime!*"

Jenny embraced her sister, kissing her on both cheeks. "*Moi aussi, je t'aime!*"

After flying back to Sydney, Jennifer took the vac-tube to Hobart, Tasmania. During her visit, she hoped time with family and friends would distract her from her concerns about Vesta Two. As Prime Minister Grotto had arranged, Heather and her driver met her at the vac-station in Hobart.

"G'day Jennifer! Ripper to see you again," Heather said as she hugged Jennifer. "Would ya like to pop around for a cuppa?"

Jennifer giggled at her high-station friend speaking common 'Stralian. Jennifer had immigrated to Australia at fourteen years old, so she had learned Australian slang. Jennifer was adept at repeating local patois. She kissed Heather on both cheeks. "G'day, mate—defo! Ripper to see ya here. What time is good?"

"Can you pop around at about five p.m. and stay with us for a few nights as usual?"

"Yes, five is fine. Thanks for the offer to stay with you, but I need to spend the first few days with my mom and dad; otherwise their feelings will be hurt. But I will stay with you a couple nights next week, if that is convenient. I have missed you so much—it has been too long."

"Fair dinkum! I understand. Next week any time is fine, but I'll be waiting for you at five today for a cuppa."

"Tuesday next week is fine for me to stay over."

"See ya soon! I'll send my driver at four thirty this afternoon."

Heather's limo dropped Jennifer off at her parents' house in Hobart. Seeing the front door open, she went inside and found her parents in their sunny kitchen. The greetings and kissing went on French style for several minutes before Michelle stood back and asked in French, "How are you, my beautiful and loving first child?"

"I am fine, Mom," Jennifer answered in French with a wide smile.

Putting his arm around Jennifer's shoulders, Pierre told her in

French, "We love you so much. We have missed you."

"Hello, sister," Aloha said in English, having walked into the kitchen after hearing the voices.

"Wow, you are bigger than my twins," Jennifer replied, then kissed her young sister on both cheeks. "How old are you, sis?"

"I am thirteen years old," Aloha said. "Where have you been living for all these years?"

"I have been on a secret mission. Did Mom and Dad explain to you that I had a mission?" Jennifer asked. Aloha had not been told about time travel; the secret still needed to be well guarded.

"Yes, but they said it was secret. Are you a spy? Is that why your hair is brown now?"

"I am on a new mission now to contact a species of intelligent life from a solar system twenty light-years away," Jennifer explained. "I will tell you about the Xinians when I find out more."

Later that afternoon, Jennifer mentioned her plans to have high tea with the Grottos.

"Jennifer, do you want to borrow my ro-car to visit Heather?"

"No, Mom. Heather will send her driver."

Driver Zwap Drexler came to the door after calling ahead. Jennifer and Zwap walked together to the limo. In twenty minutes, Jennifer was getting the present she had brought from the twenty-first century from her case. It was from a painter who was not recognized until centuries after his death but was now a favorite of Heather Grotto's in the thirtieth century.

Continuing the fun of earlier in the day, Jennifer spoke in her best Australian slang. "G'day, Heather, I have a prezzie for ya to open."

"Jennifer, it's ripper to see you after all these years—we thought you were dead for so long," Heather said with a genuine smile. "I want to find out what happened. Let's go to the library for a cuppa and choccy biccy."

"I will follow you," Jennifer replied quietly as they walked past the communication system room. This was the same room that she had infiltrated many years ago to get the data about the extermination plans the Syndos held against the Naturals. Of course, Caps had been against these plans even though he was Syndo himself. The entire history of her association with the Grotto family flashed through Jennifer's mind. Her heart raced and her face felt hot, even though she could not see it in her reflection in the large hallway mirror.

The two women entered the Grottos' library.

"Please have a seat here. We have a view of the boats and harbor," Heather said.

"Thank you. Now please open your prezzie. Then I will answer some of your questions the best I can now."

"Okay, then, Jennifer!"

Heather opened her present.

As Heather unrolled the canvas, Jennifer explained, "This is the original famous painting of Hobart Harbour by the artist now considered the genius of seaside art, your favorite."

Heather reached for her wand to verify the authenticity of this original and looked at Jennifer to make sure she was not offended. Jennifer waved her ahead; checking was the prerogative of all art collectors of note.

After examining the painting, Heather was awed when the results were positive. She said, "This original was lost for centuries and it seemed that only copies remained. How did you get this?"

"Your husband knows the details, but I cannot tell you these secrets without him present," Jennifer told her. "I am on a mission to help all life on Earth. But I must keep my visits and my identity secret. I have an identical twin; she wants to meet you someday soon. Her name is Jenny Heros, spelled H-e-r-o-s but pronounced *arrow* in French. She is sensitive to the French pronunciation. I was adopted by Pierre and Michelle LeVe. My dad took his wife's last name upon his marriage, which is common practice in North America."

Heather commented, "I still remember when you saved Caps's

life and later Zexton Ho's. Joon LeVe, the Australian hero. Caps gave you the name Jennifer Hero to help protect you. How is it possible your sister has such a similar name?"

"We will talk about that later. Caps may give me another identity, as I have another important mission. I cannot stay long in Hobart."

"Does your mission have anything to do with the large asteroid-spacecraft orbiting Earth like a small moon?" Heather asked.

"I can tell you yes. It is referred to as Vesta Two."

"Does it carry alien life, as speculated by the media?"

"I believe it might, but time will tell. I have to communicate with this Vesta Two close up to understand if its claims are true."

"Why do you call it Vesta Two?"

"It resembles our solar system's largest asteroid named Vesta. But only Caps can tell you more; I can't without your husband's permission."

"You know the whole world is talking about this object in orbit. How long can they keep this secret?"

"Will you swear to keep my secrets as you would the State's and your husband's secrets?"

"Defo, of course!" Heather said, looking very serious.

The noise of three VTOL aircraft overhead drowned out the conversation. "Excuse me a moment!" Heather shouted as she got up and looked outside. "It looks like Caps is home. We can speak later—I'll greet him now. Please excuse me, but I never know the time he'll arrive."

"No worries!" Jennifer yelled.

––––––––––––––

When Heather got up and left the room, Jennifer went to the next room, which contained the communication system. Once the kids' playroom, it was converted years ago to the communication room for Caps when he was a senator. Jennifer took photos of the prime minister's new communication system using her fingernail cameras. She was still an undercover operative by nature and knew the SS would want to know the latest communication equipment used.

Jennifer thought of an excuse if questioned as she casually walked to the bathroom located near the communication room.

Jennifer remembered using this bathroom years ago, when she was feigning illness at a dinner party to collect important information at a most critical time. Her earliest mission as a spy flashed through her mind like a video collage.

After using the bathroom and freshening her lipstick and makeup, Jennifer walked quickly back to the library. Heather had not returned. *She is certainly questioning Caps about the secret mission*, Jennifer thought as she sat back in her chair overlooking Hobart Harbour. Jennifer saw six large and three small Coast Guard vessels, no doubt there to protect Prime Minister Grotto. Using her watch Jennifer called her close friend, Kylie Brown, whose home base was now Hobart. She was working with Ben Sun at Tazitron on floating city projects.

"Hello? Is that you, Jennifer?"

"G'day, mate! I am in Hobart. Do you want to go sailing early next week?"

"Ripper, I'd love to go sailing. I'll just take a sickie," Kylie replied.

"Let's go Monday, as I will sail with Mom and Dad on Sunday. I want to discuss your report. You are my hero, Kylie. Great job!"

"Okay, it's a date, and I'll cook dinner after the sail. We can talk about my report during dinner if you wish," Kylie said.

"How are things going with Ben at Tazitron?"

"Ben is now in an executive position over his father and me."

"I know—he told me he is executive VP. He is amazing. Are you still designing floating cities?"

"Yes. I don't like too much administration. Designing floating cities is my passion, but occasionally I work on large ships. Mostly large, multi-hull vessels that are about two miles long. It's a nice change from the SS, but you know I'm here if you ever need me."

"I appreciate that," Jennifer replied. "What do the vessels carry?"

"The largest ships are military, cargo, and some for passengers."

"How fast are they?"

"The HMAS *Brisbane* can attain speeds more than eighty knots. Top speed is classified."

Heather and Caps entered the library. Jennifer smiled and waved.

"I have got to go now," she told Kylie. "Heather and Caps are here. Aloha, goodbye!"

"Love and goodbye," Kylie said before disconnecting.

"Hello, Prime Minister!" Jennifer said as she stood up.

"Please call me Caps and get over here for a hug!" Caps exclaimed with a warm smile. Jennifer ran over to greet the Australian prime minister. They hugged each other for the longest time.

"It has been too long," she told him. "I am so happy to see you are well."

"Jennifer, please feel free to discuss all classified matters in Heather's presence in a safe room; she was cleared for the same security level as me when I was elected prime minister. Don't discuss these things with anyone else, outside of the SS, of course. Now let's move to the safe room. Follow me!" Caps waved her to follow him.

After relocating to the communication room, Jennifer took a seat on the couch next to Heather. Caps sat in a nearby chair and said, "Jennifer, I mistook Jenny for you at a recent meeting with the SS. I didn't know you had a twin."

"Thank you for all your help with my identities, bodyguards, and support in the past."

"You're welcome, but you more than earned these favors. You saved my life at tremendous peril to yourself and you saved Zexton Ho just fifteen kilometers from here."

Tears filled Jennifer's eyes and she looked down for a moment. Regaining her composure, she asked, "Can I report to you now?"

Caps nodded. "Go ahead."

"I resigned from the SS leadership some years ago, but I stay in contact. I am settled in the twenty-first century with a husband, five stepchildren, and twin twelve-year-old girls. I left my family to come to the thirtieth century at Jenny's request and have agreed to lead a group to visit Vesta Two, with your permission. This is not just about first contact, as I indicated to you on the phone though that is important. I am worried about Vesta Two being misunderstood." Jennifer looked at him with a pleading smile.

"Are you certain this is not the original Vesta?"

"Absolutely, I am certain. Jenny is on her way now to visit the fifty-seventh century to prove Earth is still alive in that time period. And that Project Magnetar was successful."

"Can I interrupt?" Heather asked.

"Go ahead," Caps said.

"How do you know about the fifty-seventh century?" Heather wondered.

"Heather, my love, this is the big secret. You must keep this at all costs," Caps said.

"Defo, I will keep this secret." Heather crossed her heart with her right hand. "Please, what is it?" Heather asked with enthusiasm and intense curiosity.

"Jennifer and Jenny's parents were from the thirty-second century, and they have time-travel technology there. Jenny visited the far future some time ago and returned in shock when she found Earth in ruins. Jennifer was part of the team to create Vesta in the fifty-sixth century and raise it like a parent would a child."

"Why?" Heather asked.

"To prevent the extermination of all life in this solar system from a natural but rare collision of two orbiting neutron stars. Jennifer figured this all out independently; however, we did not have the technology to stop or alter this collision. We formed a coalition on Earth between Syndos and humans, and then Jennifer convinced the fifty-sixth century world leaders to lead the development of Vesta and its onboard AI system."

"Where is all the future technology?" Heather asked.

"It is on Vesta, and that is one of the reasons for secrecy," Caps said. "We agreed not to expose any of the fifty-sixth century technology to the thirtieth century. We all signed the treaty of cooperation; therefore, the small group of undercover agents from our century were relegated to administrative, psychological, and logistic tasks."

"So, what is the object in orbit?" Heather asked.

"Jennifer believes this is the child of Vesta, the AI system she mothered from a child of artificial intelligence to an adult. This is what we all sent out into space to save Earth. Jennifer believes the first Vesta sacrificed itself to protect future life in our solar system," Caps explained. "That was its mission. Our task is now to prove this is not the same machine while at the same time not exposing the advanced technology aboard to anyone on Earth right now."

Heather hugged Jennifer. "Tell me more, please."

"I cannot tell you all the details," Jennifer said, "but I had a family in the past before being rescued by my sister using our father's trans-time device. When I returned to the thirtieth century, everyone thought the SS team was dead, so we must hide our identities to keep the trans-time secret. That is why I am sporting dark-brown hair."

"Can you tell me about your family?" Heather asked.

"I did not know about my twin or her two-way time travel technology, as I was adopted by Pierre LeVe, the twin brother of Andre Heros, my biological father. So, I did not think I had a way back when I trans-timed to the twenty-first century. I adapted, fell in love, and now my husband, Marty, and I have twin girls. Also, I have five amazing stepchildren who are in their twenties and thirties."

"Perhaps we can arrange for your family to visit soon," Caps said. "I'll give Marty a position as an advisor in my Secret Service and provide thirtieth-century identities for your family members, just like we do for those in the witness protection."

"It would just be Marty and the twins. The older children are busy and on their own for the most part. But the twins will need school and friends," Jennifer replied.

"Let me work on that next week," Heather replied. "The AI asked very specifically to interface with you, Jennifer. This could be involved, take months, and I want your family to be close to you, so you'll be happy. I want you to be close to me again too."

Caps walked over to Jennifer and smiled. "You are the most amazing woman—after my wives, of course. You're on the most important mission of all time, in my opinion: first contact. I envy you!"

Caps grew more serious as he told her, "Let's get back to the first contact/Vesta report and planning the immediate actions before we talk about long-term solutions. We must keep trans-time a secret from the general public and the larger Syndo community. If your family leaves the twenty-first century, they'll need a cover story too."

He turned to his wife and said, "Heather, you work on this with Roger Reagan."

Looking back to Jennifer with a smile, Caps told her, "He's now the director of State Security."

"I know him and trust him," Jennifer said.

"What will Jenny and Moose find? That is the second most important mission in Earth's history! Please contact me immediately via your watch when you hear the status of the fifty-seventh century." Caps held up a communication watch like those worn among the SS. "Tom Page recently gave me one of these. He told me you spied on me and found the extermination plots. You completed Zexton's dream of time travel and corrected an engineering error in the Syndos' DNA. I'm glad you did it, otherwise my kids with Heather would have no future." Caps hugged her like a father. "I knew you were special that first day we lunched with Zexton on my yacht all those years ago, young lady."

Blushing, Jennifer wondered how much Tom might have disclosed about the information she had gathered on the Grotto family. "I learned soon after that you were special too. One more thing he may not have told you. You already had the corrected DNA."

18. Another view of Vesta showing many craters.

19. Vesta's size compared with Ceres and Pluto and its moon Charon.

13

FIFTY-SEVENTH CENTURY

"We are now in the fifty-seventh century," Jenny said as she picked up her gear and headed for the submersible *Triton*. "I hope you enjoyed the ride. Disembark Trans-Time Eleven. Follow me. We do not have time to waste."

"Aye-aye, Commander," Captain Moose Cleary replied as he picked up his case.

"I'll follow you," Professor Vazzo Simpson said to Ben Sun.

Ben asked, "Professor Simpson, are you an astronomer?"

"No, I'm an expert on biology. Sorry to disappoint you."

"I was hoping to get some help with the recon aircraft," Ben explained. "It'll sense life, minerals, and many other parameters. I have a telescope to record the stars, so we can confirm our exact date."

"Dr. Rye Wells is an aeronautical engineer par excellence," Vazzo pointed out. "I'm sure he can assist you. What's the weight of your total package?"

"It weighs two hundred and thirty-four kilos. I'll need some assistance loading it into the recon aircraft."

Rye turned to them. "Did someone mention my name? One of the robots is programmed to load your astro-pack, Ben. I'll help activate the robots. No worries."

The official science team of five, including Ben Sun and Jenny, both engineers in different fields, boarded *Triton* and took their assigned seats. Jenny's PhDs were in aeronautical engineering and astronomy. Ben's were in nautical engineering and urban planning.

Naval Captain Moose Cleary sat next to Jenny on the right and Ben Sun was on her left. Moose was overseeing the reconnaissance mission, but Jenny had been assigned the command of *Triton* and Trans-Time Eleven.

"*Triton*, head for Point Gamma at stealth speed." During this trip to Antarctica on the sub, Jenny would be giving the verbal commands to the ship in French, then explain them to her team. They had chosen an Antarctica location because it was likely to be one of the least populated areas, and thus give them a better chance of traveling undetected by fifty-seventh century authorities.

After the course was set, she told her squad, "It will take about forty hours to get there. So, after you get everything ready for launch, the robots will prepare and serve dinner. We have fresh fish and mixed fresh vegetables. After that you can find your cabins, as they are labeled on the holo-console."

————————————

The forty hours of travel passed uneventfully. Jenny was excited to detect signs of animal life as they passed through the sea.

Jenny said, "We are at coordinates Gamma. It is time to launch."

"Roger that, Commander," Moose replied. "All systems ready for launch. Awaiting verbal command to launch."

"Launch recon aircraft!" Jenny commanded in French.

"Recon away," *Triton* announced.

"What the hell?" Moose exclaimed.

"A large vessel is under us," *Triton* said in French.

Jenny tried everything to evade, short of offensive action, but *Triton* could not break the grip of this monster of the deep. Finally, she said, "They are contacting us in an advanced digital language that even our universal translator cannot compute."

"Try fifty-sixth-century language," Moose suggested.

"Roger that. *Triton* has sent signals in fifty-sixth century code, English and French. No reply in those languages, only a code we do not understand. The computer is trying to break the code."

Eventually, the vessel under *Triton* broke the surface of the ocean. The vessel gripped *Triton* and held it completely out of the water in severe Antarctic weather.

"Two large robots are examining my hull," *Triton* said in French.

Jenny ran to the view screen and screamed, "No!" as a large robotic drill approached the hull. She ran up the stairs, opened the hatch, and yelled, "Stop!" in five Earth languages and in fifty-sixth-century English.

The robots saw her and shined a laser, plus a microsecond digital code. The robots' ship responded in fifty-sixth-century English: "You are under arrest. We will take you to Mawson Station. Do not resist and we will not bind you. Do you agree?"

Jenny spoke to Moose through her watch. "What is Mawson Station?"

"Mawson Station was a small city in Antarctica managed by the Australian Antarctic Division. Mawson is located in Holmes Bay in East Antarctica, if it's still in the same place."

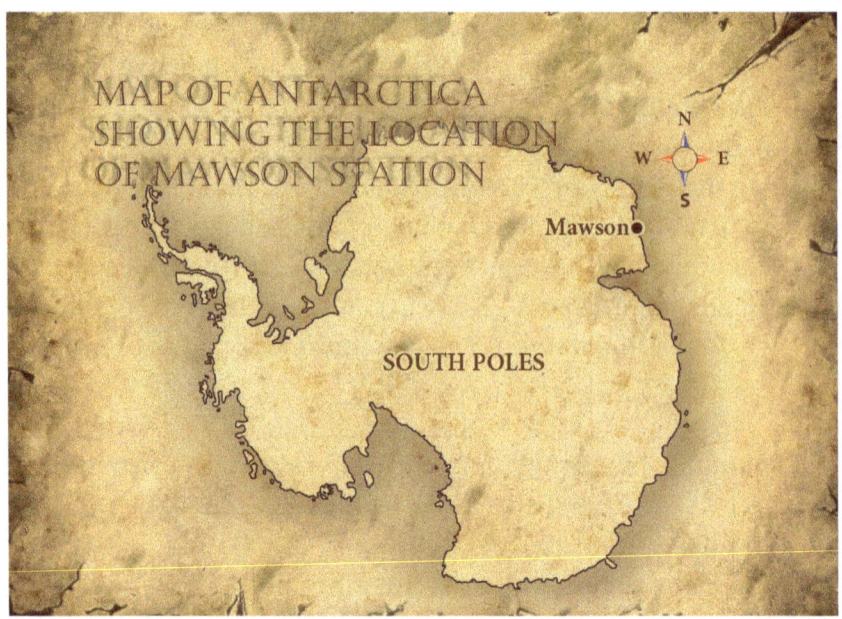

20. Map of Antarctica showing the location of Mawson Station.

"We agree!" Jenny shouted to the robot as she ran toward the deck rail some two hundred meters above the drill. She carried with her a line attached to a rappelling device. Jenny tied one end of the line to *Triton*'s deck. Rappelling down the hull in the wind, she hit her arm on the drill bit and exclaimed, "Ouch! Damn, that hurt! Please do not harm *Triton*. *Triton* is my friend."

The drill continued to move toward *Triton*'s hull.

Ben surfaced through the hatch onto *Triton*'s deck. He looked over the side to Jenny's position. Using his watch, he reported, "Ben here. Jenny is being blown into the drill by the wind and her arm is torn open, over."

Still at *Triton*'s controls, Moose said, "Copy that. I'll send a robot to assist, over."

"Are you okay, Jenny?" Ben yelled. Speaking again into his watch, he asked, "Moose, how far is Mawson Station? Jenny could freeze or bleed out if we don't act now. She's out cold now after hitting her head on *Triton*'s hull, over." Pulling a rappelling rope from his pack, Ben started to scramble down the side of the submersible to help Jenny.

Jenny had placed her body between the drill and the hull. This had caused the opposing robot to pull back slightly. She was now being held by a rappelling device attached to her vest but was dangling and swaying in the cold, forty-knot winds.

"Moose here. Mawson is several hours away."

"Jenny is being slammed into the hull as the wind is severe and I cannot hold her and put on a tourniquet at the same time."

"What is her condition?"

"Jenny's unconscious and bleeding badly from her left arm and head." Ben dropped down to her level and held her off the hull.

"Robot Rally 22 activate," Moose announced.

Ben replied, "I can support her weight and stopped the wild swinging but cannot apply the much-needed first aid."

Rye Wells appeared above. He rappelled down with a tourniquet and universal blood and a spray that stopped the bleeding. Rye applied the first aid and measured Jenny's vital signs. Looking over at Ben, Rye stated, "I think she's critical—we need to get her to sick bay."

"The large robot on deck will pull us all up together as soon as I inflate the balloon protector," Rye said reassuringly.

"How is Jenny?" Moose asked from the command post. "Without her, there may be no way back."

"Rye here. She's critical! Make way to receive her in sick bay. Rally 22 can carry her to sick bay faster than we can. He is pulling us up as we speak."

"Roger that, thank you," replied Moose. "Our automatic diagnostic medical center is ready to examine and treat now."

Rally 22 arrived at sick bay with Jenny. "Set her down gently here." Moose pointed to the waiting bed.

Auto-med stated, "Jenny has suffered a fractured skull on

the left side and a compound fracture of her left arm in the radius and ulna, plus lacerations and bruises. Treatment initiated."

Feeling thankful for *Triton*'s equipment to initiate healing of Jenny's head, Moose and Ben hoped it would be enough to avoid any permanent effects.

Jenny was still unconscious as the monster holding *Triton* and its crew slowed entering Holmes Bay. Ten officers in dark-blue uniforms waited at the pier along with a local female official dressed in jeans, heavy boots, a quilted jacket, and a woolen hat and gloves.

One officer contacted Moose on the communicator in fifty-sixth-century English. The translator output: "I am customs agent Donovan. Do you have papers to be in this restricted area?"

From the controls on *Triton*, Moose bellowed across the ship's radio as he placed his hand over his heart, "We are here on an important mission. We're from the thirtieth century. Can you help us, as we were part of Project Magnetar, as it was called in the fifty-sixth century?"

"We are customs and fishery management agents," Donovan said. "We will need to contact authorities."

"Can you tell me the year?" Moose asked.

"It is 5656," Donovan replied.

Moose talked across the distance from ship to shore: "I was here a hundred years ago, working to save your planet from a binary magnetar collision about five hundred light-years away. Please contact the World Council, as that is the organization that we teamed with in the fifty-sixth century to save the planet."

"It sounds to me like you hit your head, like your friend," the custom agents countered, using info gained from video taken by a robot. "Can we offer medical assistance?"

"Yes, Jenny has been seriously injured," Moose noted urgently. "Do you have a doctor who can check her head and arm injuries? We were able to do some treatment on board, but your methods in this century will be more advanced. I'm fine and telling you the truth. You can read my brain patterns to see if I'm truthful. Please contact the World Council."

"I'm sorry, but we must contact our government office in Sydney, the Australian Defense Department," Donovan stated. "We must follow protocol. In the meantime, I've summoned a medical team to examine and treat your colleague."

"Jenny, how are you feeling?" Ben Sun asked from her bedside in the hospital at Mawson Station.

Customs Agent Donovan sat in a nearby chair, and one of his men stood guard at the door.

"The pain is mild and I am hungry, so that is a good sign," she said, sitting up supported by pillows and the top portion of the adjustable bed. "Thank you, Doctor. What is your name?"

"I'm Doctor Moby," he replied, looking up after finishing an entry into his electronic notepad. "You will recover completely, but you must take rest for at least five days."

"How long was I out?"

"You were out for forty-two hours since I started treatment. Without treatment, you might have had permanent brain damage, as your ship's technology is from the dark ages. Where did you get such an antique?"

"We are from the thirtieth century, the year 2986," Jenny answered. "My twin sister, Jennifer, mothered the AI built into Vesta to prevent extermination of life on this planet and Mars. If we do not return, the AI's child may be destroyed. Jennifer is planning a trip to our new small moon orbiting Earth known as Vesta Two, which has advanced technology from the fifty-sixth century. We have sworn to keep the secrets of the future."

ONE OF THE LARGEST ASTEROIDS

Psyche is an irregularly shaped body measuring about 150 miles (240 kilometers) along its largest side. This makes it the 10th or 11th largest known asteroid (sizes are not known precisely, preventing exact rankins). The largest asteroids, including Ceres and Vesta, are photoplanets - survivors from the early formation of the solar system.

Earth's Moon

Psyche Vesta

Ceres

Earth to scale

21. The comparison of Earth's moon to asteroids Vesta, Ceres, and Psyche.

"Why should I believe you?" the doctor replied with a frown.

"First test our DNA and then process us with your truth scanner," Jenny suggested. "But, honestly, we need to get back soon to prevent a possible disaster."

"What kind of disaster are you talking about?"

"Can I answer that as you use the truth scanner, Agent Donovan?" Jenny said.

"Go ahead," Donovan allowed. "Give me just a minute. I'll take over here with the questions, Doctor."

He stood up, picked up his truth scanner, moved by the bed, and then held the device to Jenny's head.

"There are military powers on Earth that believe the child of Vesta is the original AI gone mad," she explained. "They fear what they do not understand and may attack Vesta Two if we do not return with data that prove life is still flourishing in the fifty-seventh century."

"What year were you born and where?" barked Donovan.

"I was born in 1994 in the Marquesas Islands."

"What is your name and rank?"

"My name is Jennifer Heros, but I go as Jenny. I am a commander in the SS, an organization that believes in peace and nonviolence."

"Who is in command of this mission?"

"I am, but the recon mission to get data documenting life in the fifty-seventh century is headed by the Australian naval captain and astronaut Moose Cleary."

"I will report my unbelievable findings to my superior in Australia," Donovan told her. "He has the authority to contact the world government."

One by one, each crew member was interrogated thoroughly, and then Donovan waited for a reply to his report to the Australian Defense Department, or ADD.

The response from the ADD, when it came a day later, approved Jenny's appearance at the World Council. Only one other member of her team was permitted to go with her—Naval Captain Moose Cleary. The others would stay in Mawson under the supervision of Agent Donovan. Dr. Moby accompanied them to their initial destination, as the pressure of the circumstances gave Jenny just one more day of recovery time before their scheduled flight.

"Jenny, we're almost to Hong Kong," Dr. Moby noted. "Can I check you one more time, as you'll be a distance away from me during the World Council meetings?"

"Yes, of course."

After checking her brain scan, he smiled. "I think you'll be fine."

"Thank you," she said, followed by a hug. "But it's good to know you'll be in Hong Kong on standby."

The three departed the aircraft at the Hong Kong International Airport. They were met by a platoon of solders.

"Good Day, I'm Lieutenant Morgan Wong of the World Council honor guard. I'm here to escort you to the World Council. There you will meet with an investigator, Mr. Han Gum. He will determine if you'll be prosecuted or set free."

"Pleased to meet you," Jenny said with a smile. "This is my attending physician, Dr. Moby, and my teammate, Captain Moose Cleary. The doctor will be staying here in Hong Kong with friends. Captain Moose and I will go with you to cooperate and explain our special case. Thank you for escorting us."

Jenny and Moose said goodbye to Dr. Moby, as Lieutenant Morgan waited nearby.

Jenny, Moose, the lieutenant, and his soldiers climbed into a cylindrical tube the size of an average bus. It zoomed inside a long tunnel to the World Council in one minute. Lieutenant Wong then told Jennifer and Moose to follow him. The two walked behind him with the platoon following them. After a short trip down a hall decorated with beautiful art of various kinds, the lieutenant raised his arm and pointed to an office on the right. On a gold sign, "Inspector Han Gum" was written in fifty-seventh-century English and Chinese.

"I will return after you are asked some questions," Wong told them. "Go inside now."

The door opened as the two captives approached. Two large robots waited inside. One robot said, "Ms. Heros and Mr. Cleary, please enter and have a seat at the conference table. Inspector Gum will be with you shortly. Can I get you something to drink?"

"Water please," Jenny replied as she began to feel sleepy.

When she awoke, Jenny saw that their arms and legs were bound and head gear had been attached. She was breathing heavily in fear and frustration. Lack of information could lead to war in her time if she did not get back soon. While Trans-Time Eleven was a time machine, its transfer mechanism from the thirty-second century was restricted to real-time passage. Every moment they spent in this future time passed in the same amount in their time of origin prior to their return. As she tried to speak, Jenny's voice was so choked up that only a murmur emerged. "Help us—this is a matter of war and death!"

Moose repeated her statement in a booming voice, but no response could be heard. Minutes went by and then hours. Jenny struggled and shouted, "If Zexton Wise is still World Council leader, he can verify our story! Time is life. Hurry!"

The tension in the air was as thick as San Francisco fog on an early June day.

The robot said, "President Wise will contact you shortly. Explain how you saved our planet from death?"

"There was a collision of two magnetars," Jenny told the robot. "The asteroid Vesta was equipped with time travel and intelligence to make the trip to alter the resulting gamma beam's direction. Please see the video of the collision on my communicator."

Jenny placed her comm in front of the table cameras. The robot examined the collision in the video.

22. Still from Vesta's video sent from a probe showing the magnetar collision.

"The beam of intense gamma rays missed Earth and Mars because Vesta sacrificed its life for you and all life in the solar system," Jenny continued. "During the nearly five thousand years' journey, Vesta continued to evolve, accumulate mass, and reproduced a child which contains Vesta's intellect and additional programing."

Jenny paused, beginning to cry.

"We are all indebted to the AI. Please help us save its only child, Vesta Two," Jenny stated emphatically as tears rolled down her cheeks.

———————

Another hour passed before the robot released the binding on their hands and arms.

Inspector Gum entered and said, "I cannot believe your story, even though all of you believe it. President Wise will join us via the holographic comm in a few minutes."

The president's image soon appeared on the holo-comm. "Are you Jennifer Hero Zitonick?"

"I am her twin sister. My name is Jenny Heros."

"I'm in Rio, Brazil, today at a conference, so I don't have much time. Please explain why you're here now."

After explaining the truth as they had again and again, Jenny pleaded once more, "Please help us. We need to prevent a war between Earth and Vesta's child. We owe it to Vesta, as does all life in your time."

After further interrogation with an advanced robot scanning Jenny's and Moose's brains, the president reappeared on the holo-comm and told Jenny, "You are free to return now to your own time. Lieutenant Morgan Wong will escort you to your transporter at Mawson Station. *Triton* has been studied and repaired."

"Thank you, President Wise."

———————

After teleporting to Mawson with the doctor and Lieutenant Wong, Jenny, and Moose met up with Ben Sun and their other team members. The five of them quickly boarded *Triton*. While they were gone, the recon aircraft had sent back the evidence the mission needed to the submersible of a prospering and living Earth in the fifty-seventh century.

"*Triton*, home at flank speed," Jenny ordered in French from her station at the controls. *Triton* dove to three hundred meters and accelerated to 197 knots.

Sitting beside her, Moose commented, "I'm glad to be on our way back with such strong evidence of the date of 5656 and life being plentiful. AI 999 has completed its mission successfully and created a child. I'm so happy for the life here, but concerned about conflict in the thirtieth century."

"Moose and Ben, thank you for helping me when I was trying to save *Triton!*" Jenny said.

From her other side, Ben replied, "I've known your sister since prep school; we studied together and were close friends. She has been the most amazing and awesome person in my life experience. I suspect now you're very much like your twin."

"Thank you, as I think my sister is amazing too," Jenny told him with a smile. Turning to Moose, she ordered, "Please report our findings to the thirtieth-century World Council as soon as possible by satellite communications."

"The comm missile is loaded with my positive report and explanation for the delay," Moose answered. "We can send it via satellite as soon as we trans-time."

"I only hope that will be soon enough!" Jenny agonized.

14

WAR DRUMS

Within ten days, Heather Grotto was successful in her search for a new home to relocate Jennifer, Marty, and the twins in the thirtieth century. She found the remote Dreamland Island, near the Great Barrier Reef off tropical Queensland, Australia. The island was ten kilometers in length and five kilometers wide. The four of them could live comfortably with a group of Aboriginal fishermen, farmers, and scholars who rejected modern technology and lived using the primitive technology of the nineteenth century—much like how the Amish had lived in the twentieth century.

After they got settled, Jennifer received a call.

"This is an aide to Prime Minister Grotto calling from Sydney. Please hold a moment for the prime minister."

Jennifer waited on hold briefly before her old friend came on the line.

"Hello, Jennifer, this is Caps," he said warmly. "How are you and your family adapting?"

"We have managed to enjoy some sailing and snorkeling

around the island. Is Jenny back yet?"

"Not yet!" he told her, his tone turning somber. "Because Jenny and the team have not returned on schedule, we will have problems with the world government meeting tomorrow. Military forces from several countries want to neutralize what they consider a threat. China, Russia, India, Brazil, and several other small countries have mobilized their armed forces."

"How is Australia, the nation with the most powerful military, doing with its argument to send a team with me to meet with the Xinians and Vesta's child?"

"Jennifer, we have been in negotiations on this and faced resistance," the prime minister told her. "But now we have more leverage. Australia can make the case that any hostile action could result in millions of deaths, and one needs to understand the technology we're facing from Vesta before going to war. I must convince them to consider a mission to gather intelligence before acting. This can buy us a week to ten days at most."

The prime minister asked with a deep concern in his voice, "What could have happened to Jenny and the team?"

Jennifer shared what had been on her mind. She said, "They may have been captured by advanced patrol vessels as we were when we first visited the fifty-sixth century to acquire the exact position of the magnetars."

"Yes, of course that might cause some delays."

Jennifer suggested, "In your negotiations, you can argue that Vesta has fifty-sixth century defensive weapons and may have developed additional technologies and weapons over the many years."

"I will do my best to set up an exploratory mission with several intelligence agents in the crew as well as scientists, engineers, and world government negotiators."

"Should I wait here at Dreamland or travel to the world government offices in Geneva?" Jennifer asked.

"Meet me in Sydney tomorrow at noon at the airport, and we can go to Geneva together. Come to the VIP section of the Kangaroo Club, located eight stories above the observation deck. I'll have a pass for you at security, which is on the observation deck. If you have any problems, call me pronto."

"I will be there, Caps. Thank you for this most important action."

Jennifer immediately walked over to the small airport on Dreamland Island and made arrangements to charter a small vertical takeoff and landing aircraft the next day to go to Brisbane. Even before the sun was up, she began to fly the slow small plane to this capital of Queensland, about a thousand kilometers away. The trip took five hours. From the Brisbane Airport, she took the elevator down to the express-vac nonstop to Sydney, where she was to meet Caps at the airport. The vac-trip was fast, lasting only twenty minutes.

She walked into the VIP area of the Kangaroo Club and spotted Caps at a window table.

"It's good to see you again, Jennifer," the prime minister said as he hugged her tightly.

"It is great to see you too, Caps. Are Heather, Robert, and Author still doing well?"

"They're fine," he replied, smiling. "In fact, Author would like to see you. You're both married, but he wants to have a romantic relation with you, and his wife approved a foursome. He wants to go with you to visit Vesta Two. He believes you completely and thinks he can help. He was with you on the first Vesta mission and was very attracted to you but never spoke up, as you worked twenty hours a day." The prime minister winked as he reached for his cup of tea.

"I can contact Marty to see if he approves, but I am sure he will," Jennifer said, then sipped her nonalcoholic tropical fruit cocktail. "Maybe Author's wife, Lindsey, would like to visit Dreamland Island while Author and I are visiting Vesta Two. It is a beautiful island—everything is preserved as it was in the early nineteenth century before electricity was available in the majority of homes."

"I'll ask Lindsey. I know Author approves of her having sex with other people. I'll call Lindsey and show her Marty's profile. Please send Lindsey's profile and contact info to Marty."

"Does Heather have sex with other men?" Jennifer asked.

"Yes, on occasion, but she prefers sex with other women," he said. "Lepta, my other wife, has a young male lover she occasionally will share with Heather, as they are very close."

Jennifer laughed, and then noted, "In the twenty-first century, people who agree to have open marriages must keep their extramarital sex a secret or they can lose their employment. However, some progress is being made. It is still illegal in that century to have more than one wife or more than one husband, so you would be arrested, as you have two wives and two families."

"Are men and women equal in the twenty-first century?"

"In certain ways. But in some countries, it is still illegal for women to drive cars, own property, get an education, or vote."

"Why do you want to live in the past with all those problems?" he asked, looking at her with curiosity.

"It is not as bad as it sounds, where I live…I have a family I love," she told him, looking into his eyes and touching his arm. With concern, she added, "Still, I do not know if they can adapt to the thirtieth century."

"When you get back from visiting Vesta Two, I'll make it possible for them to travel with you to some of the nearby tourist islands," he promised. "That way, they can get more of a taste of the nineteenth century."

Roger Reagan interrupted. "Excuse me, Prime Minister; *Space Plane One* is ready to leave in twenty minutes. Your Secret Service agents are ready to escort you and your guest through Vac-Tube One."

Roger smiled at Jennifer, recognizing her after many years despite the dark hair. She smiled back. He stepped forward three paces and grabbed Jennifer by the waist, picked her up off her feet, and spun her around twice.

Jennifer hugged him and whispered, "Thank you for saving my life and looking after Caps all these years."

"Thank you, Roger. We're ready," Caps said.

To Jennifer, the prime minister added, "I've cancelled our food order, as we'll be served lunch during the four-hour trip. That calculation, by the way, includes ground time."

"Tower Control here, the World Space Committee is ready to receive Prime Minister Grotto as soon as you land."

"Copy that," said the copilot. "We're on the ground. The pilot is taxiing to the world government vac-tube. See you shortly, over."

"Copy that, out."

After the plane parked over the vac-tube, the passengers—including three Secret Service agents, three staff members, Jennifer, seven robotic bodyguards, five baggage robots, and the prime minister—entered the tube-bus. They were transported in two minutes to the world government building in Geneva, Switzerland.

Dimitri Marx, aide to President Zhukov of Russia, was waiting for them at the tube receiver. "Come with me to President Zhukov's office," he said. "He would like a few words with you before the security meeting. Ms. Zitonick, you and Prime Minister Grotto met his father in Russia after the assassination of President Primakov. Would you like to greet the newly elected Russian president?"

"Yes, of course," Jennifer answered politely. "We have a minute to say, *Zdravstvuyte, Prezeegent* Zhukov."

They followed Dimitri to the president's location, but Jennifer was required to wait outside the soundproof doors with Grotto's staff, the baggage robots, a Secret Service agent, and two robotic bodyguards. The remainder of the Secret Service agents and security robots accompanied the prime minister inside the private office.

"Hello to you, Prime Minister Grotto!" President Zhukov said in greeting as he gave Caps a bear hug. "My father told me great things about you."

"He probably exaggerated."

After they exchanged pleasantries about the health of each other's families, Prime Minister Grotto got down to business.

"We want to plan an expedition to Vesta Two," the prime minister told Zhukov. "It carries to Earth an extraterrestrial life-form known as Xinians."

"Can we speak confidentially?" said the Russian president with a direct look.

Prime Minister Grotto replied with a big smile, "Yes, go ahead, but the Secret Service and robot bodyguards must remain."

"Have our fifty-seventh-century explorers returned? The Russian military leaders are planning a coup d'état over this threat you call Vesta Two."

"I'm shocked to hear such a thing. How can I help prevent this coup?"

President Zhukov sighed and answered, "I am not sure, but the return of the fifty-seventh-century expedition will help."

"I cannot perform that magic, but I can offer a delaying tactic."

"What is it?"

"You can tell your people and your military that there needs to be an intelligence mission to learn Vesta's strengths and weaknesses. I'll allow you to select six people and six robots to go on the mission to Vesta. We'll have only four plus five robots. This will give you a strong position after negotiating such a beneficial agreement."

Seeing that President Zhukov was thinking it through, Prime

Minister Grotto inquired, "Do you know Jennifer Zitonick, formerly Joon LeVe?"

"I have heard of her but have never contacted that famous lady."

"She is just outside your door!" Grotto revealed. "She knows Vesta Two and vouches for the validity of its story. I'll introduce you. My son Author would go with her on the Vesta Two expedition."

The inner office door opened automatically at the announcement that the World Council meeting would start in five minutes.

Grotto and Zhukov stepped just outside the door, heading for the meeting.

Jennifer saw a resemblance between President Zhukov and his father, General Zhukov. The general had helped her locate her lover Zexton Ho's assassin long ago and had in turn been gunned down by a Russian crime syndicate.

"Jennifer, this is the newly elected President of Russia, Dimitri Zhukov."

"Pleased to meet you. I met your father," Jennifer said as she offered her hand.

President Zhukov grasped her hand and pulled Jennifer into big hug. "I'm also pleased to meet you."

"Yes, let us hurry to take our seats before the gavel is dropped," Prime Minister Grotto urged as the group walked to the vac-vator.

"China believes the best way to neutralize the AI that has gone mad is to attack with all the power on Earth under one command. We propose that China be in command," Representative Wynn Shang Lin argued.

Chairman Bonky Fuk formally called out the contributions of each representative aloud. "The council appreciates the Chinese proposal. The council now recognizes India."

Bhagat Azad put his hands together and bowed his head

before speaking. "India, as the second largest country in population, proposes an attack coordinated by the World Council."

"The council now recognizes Russian President Zhukov."

President Zhukov looked around the room silently before speaking. Then he announced, "Russia proposes an intelligence-gathering mission made up of representatives of the entire Security Council. The first step will be a trip to Vesta Two. The trip might be complete one week after launch. Russia's International Baikonur Cosmodome can be ready to launch the spacecraft with fifty people and twelve robots aboard to gain intelligence before going to war. We must use the special relationship Dr. Jennifer Zitonick has with the AI that is on Vesta. She as co–project leader was key to an important construction of the AI 999's mental and emotional development during the Vesta project. She has had important conversations with Vesta Two. We can pose as a scientific expedition, and half our expedition should be scientists and engineers. After all, it is a technical mission, as far as the world would know."

"The council appreciates the Russian proposal," noted Chairman Fuk. "The council now recognizes the United States."

The United States wanted to take a cautious approach. "Can we study this issue as a team before we go to war?" asked Ambassador Grey Johnson. "The USA will not be the first to start a war. However, we will send astronauts on any exploratory mission to gain intelligence and to make first contact, which is extremely important."

"Thank you, Ambassador Johnson," responded the Chairman. "The council now recognizes Australia."

Prime Minister Caps Grotto stood. "First, may we assume that this is a highly classified meeting and mission and that only the cover story about first contact and space exploration will be given to the press and other media? Australia supports the Russian proposal. Intelligence is the most important action before any conflict. I suggest Russia take the lead. Australia is willing to fund half the launch cost from the Cosmodome."

Tension and conflict filled the World Council room for many hours. At last, Chairman Bonky Fuk announced, "The Russian proposal is agreed upon. It will be a two-week mission, including one week of preparation and one week of exploration on board Vesta Two. However, instead of leaving from the Russian Cosmodome, we will depart via the space elevator station above Geneva traveling on the international spaceship *Magellan*."

The gavel dropped, ending the meeting but not tensions. There were several heated arguments in the hall between the Russian and Chinese delegations.

In the soundproof, shielded Russian president's office in the World Government Building, Zhukov hugged the Australian prime minister and said, "Thank you for your support. This vote was close."

The debate between the World Council members leading to the vote had also been long. It was now two o'clock in the morning.

The two men sat down on a couch on one side of the office.

President Zhukov continued. "In six hours, I must give a speech to the Russian people. After I return to Russia, I will explain the classified reason for the trip to Vesta Two to the appropriate parties. This may delay the Russian military's planned coup. I think my forty-minute speech in the morning will be my first world press conference. After it, I will take questions."

"You'll do great," Caps told him. "I have two questions from the Australian press that can help you. They'll probably bring up that Russia was first in space and now may be first to contact alien life-forms. You can tell them Russia is ready to be first; however, this is so important to humankind, that all the peoples of Earth and Mars should be represented. You'll lead an international team leaving from Geneva in just one week."

"That is a great answer to the world and the Russian people," Zhukov responded, feeling pleased. "What is the other question?"

"It's about economic activity. Here's a World Economic Committee graph that shows Russia's expected growth is faster than both China and Australia for the first time in modern history. The press will ask what the expected growth rate is over the next five years and how it compares to other major countries."

"Thank you for planning to help me. You must have expected me to win the recent election when polls showed I was trailing." President Zhukov smiled. "Our countries have been adversaries for much too long. We are now allies as far as I am concerned."

"Please call me Caps," the prime minister said, smiling back. "I offer my friendship because of mutual benefits. It's time to make first contact with another intelligent life-form. It's our obligation to work together to make that happen."

"Please call me Dimitri. The Russian military wants to attack Vesta Two. They also want power, and their puppet candidate lost in the last election. But I believe the Russian people, both Syndos and Naturals on our Earth, want to make a peaceful but cautious first contact with the Xinians. We must have a plan to quarantine the Xinians and study their germs before making physical contact."

"Yes, that can buy you time to consolidate power and appoint a friendly group of Joint Armed Forces leaders," Prime Minister Grotto pointed out. "I'll propose a one-year isolation to study each other's biology and communicate electronically using advanced video technology."

The two leaders shook hands.

President Zhukov motioned toward the door with his arm, saying, "I will walk with you to the lobby, as I want to say goodbye to Jennifer."

The two men walked out of the private secure office suite on floor 179 and took the vac-vator to the large main entrance lobby. Jennifer was waiting patiently there on a stuffed chair, and she stood as the two men approached.

Her robot bodyguard suddenly raced outside, flew up the side of the building, and activated an invisible shield over the entire 179th floor.

Boom!

A fiery ball of bright white-yellow supersonic gases billowed outward, filling and stretching the transparent barrier deployed by Jennifer's bodyguard robot, just as it had done many years ago in Russia ahead of the assassination of the Russian president.

Floor 179 and the two floors below in the three-hundred-story building were blown out, weakening the integrity of the entire structure. The force of the bomb went downward, destroying the two additional floors. However, without the barrier the damage would have been far worse. The blowout was contained by the flexible transparent shield. Later they learned that the bomb had been in a Russian storage room loaded with encrypted digital files. The blast was heard one hundred kilometers away.

Kaboom, ssssblam whomp, whomp, whomp! echoed in Jennifer mind as she grasped her ears.

The explosive blasting through the rooms would have destroyed any life on those three floors with a wave of intense shock. The noise reverberated over the sleeping town as efficiently as a thunder clap that repeated as the blast vibrated the entire building. The anti-terror squad as well as fire and police departments' first responders were soon on their way, sirens blazing.

Jennifer checked on her companions, heart pounding. *What do I do next?*

The building's autosave system injected large amounts of emergency structural support to add strength to those rooms and floors affected. Large quantities of two chemicals entered through two pipes that mixed in a supersonic spray to form a superfast hardening foam structure. Within seconds, those rooms with loss of integrity were filled with rigid construction foam to save the building from collapse.

"What the hell!" Prime Minister Grotto said.

"*Sooka!* That was no accident," President Zhukov commented. "Someone in my staff may be a turncoat. Jennifer, how is it possible for your robot to detect the bomb?"

Jennifer said, "My bodyguard detected nitro-cubane polymer under the floor when we were up there earlier and alerted me. So, I programmed my bodyguard to activate the invisible shield over the floor if a digital z-band signal was detected. This is the same shield we used after President Vladimir Primakov was assassinated."

"How does it work?" President Zhukov asked.

Jennifer checked the data on the robot, which was now back in the lobby. "Per my robotic bodyguard, the signal came from the office of Deputy Pavel Sharapova. Can I have permission to investigate using my bodyguard?"

"*Nyeht!* I must allow the Russian Federation Intelligence Agency to do their job," President Zhukov exclaimed. "Our embassy is six blocks away. I am sure they are on their way. It is a domestic matter!"

A team of seventeen, headed by Captain Igor Shlykov, arrived within eight minutes with rescuers, medical staff, and investigators.

By this time, a cluster of people who'd been in the building during the explosion had gathered in the lobby—cleaning crews, nighttime workers, etc. Russian Deputy Sharapova had also come by to see how he could be of assistance. Instead, based on a call from the Russian president, the RFIA had other ideas for Sharapova.

"Deputy Pavel Sharapova, you are hereby taken into custody for questioning in a matter of national security," Captain Shlykov declared. "Will you cooperate and submit to a brain scan during questioning?"

"Da!" Pavel shouted.

"I want to interview everyone here," Shlykov told the crowd moments later. He turned to Jennifer, who was standing by the Russian president and Grotto. "Miss, will you come to my office voluntarily?"

Thinking about the upgraded data she had just received from her robot, Jennifer answered quietly, "Yes, but first know that I suspect Deputy Pavel Sharapova was framed."

"What evidence do you have?" the captain asked, also in a confidential tone.

"My robot bodyguard has recordings of all electromagnetic and ultrasound signals. It detected nitro-cubane, a high explosive, under the floor about thirty minutes before President Zhukov came out of his private office. Its data banks indicate a relay of the activation signal from another location. It came in via z-band and was relayed via fiber. My robot's assessment of the data pointed to the framing of Sharapova. You are welcome to the entire database."

"Thank you. It could be important evidence," said the captain. "What else do you think happened?"

"I am not sure, but I think we need to move quickly to catch the persons responsible," she advised. "Here is the suspected position where the signal originated." Jennifer showed the captain the screen of her tablet and then added, "I suggest we take your best agents and follow my bodyguard."

"You got it! I know about how you saved Prime Minister Grotto in Tasmania. Today you saved many lives. Let's move! You four investigators, follow me!" Captain Shlykov ordered. "The remaining investigators...get busy interviewing these witnesses for any clues."

Prime Minister Grotto said, "Before you leave, Captain, I have a matter to discuss with you."

The two men went together down a first-floor hallway to a quiet spot.

Grotto continued. "I suggest we put out a press release that at least two people are known to have been killed in an explosion at the World Government Building. Investigators on scene will try to identify these victims and locate any possible others. The perpetrators may send a message to their bosses, and we can trace it using an Australian top-secret satellite."

"I do not think I can knowingly put out false information," Captain Shlykov commented, resisting the idea.

"Leave that to the Australian Intelligence Agency. They will state, 'A powerful explosion was heard at the office of President Dimitri Zhukov. It was powerful enough to kill dozens of people. We have no confirmed reports of deaths; however, rumors say the president of Russia and the prime minister of Australia were the targets. The investigators have neither denied nor confirmed the report; however, neither of these high-ranking men could be reached. The investigation has been classified by the Russian government, which states no comments until the investigation has been completed.'"

"That will work for me."

The captain left with Jennifer, his agents, and Jennifer's robot.

15

VESTA TWO

Jennifer and the fifty-person team of scientists, intelligence agents, and engineers were launched via an electric gun from the space elevator station above Geneva on board the international spaceship *Magellan*, named after the famous explorer.

"How long will your trip take?" Vesta Two asked with the emotional tension of eagerness in its voice that Jennifer could clearly understand.

"The trip is about twenty-two thousand kilometers, or about four hours," Jennifer answered in a reassuring and calm voice. While speaking, she moved to a telescopic image screen to observe Vesta Two.

"My docking port is identical to my parent's docking mechanism," Vesta Two pointed out. "So you should have no problem if you turn over the control to me when you are about one thousand kilometers out. Will you comply?"

"We will ask permission from the world government. I will get back with you shortly. I am not in command of the mission; Astronaut Ziky Smith is our commander."

"You can stay in contact with Vesta Two," Ziky told Jennifer. "I'll ask the World Space Council for permission."

"Thank you, Commander Smith," Vesta Two said.

"You're welcome," Ziky replied as he picked up his holo-comm to request permission for Vesta Two to do the auto-docking.

With pleasure and emotion in its voice, Vesta Two said, "Jennifer, I feel like I know you well, but we have never touched physically. I look forward to receiving you and your team below City Center Square."

"How do we get to that location?" Jennifer asked.

"Vac-tube capsule one will be available," Vesta Two told her. "It is like a fast elevator. It will take just a minute to City Center Square, which is twenty kilometers below my surface. I am located about thirty-five stories below City Center Square. You can follow the robot that will greet you and take you across the square to the elevator. Then you will follow it into the elevator to arrive on my level."

"Will there be gravity at City Center Square?"

"My gravity is point twenty-two meters per second squared at the surface, which is only thirty-three percent of the Earth's gravity; however, the city has artificial gravity about the same as Mars."

"The permission has not been granted yet," Ziky reported with a worried tone in his voice.

"Roger that. Please keep trying," Jennifer said.

"I suggest you go into orbit and I'll send a shuttlecraft to meet you and bring you inside," Vesta Two advised. "My docking system involves advanced technology to interface properly. I do not want you to get injured or killed." There was real concern in Vesta Two's voice as it gave its recommendation.

"Jennifer," Ziky interrupted as she looked at the beautiful asteroid through the viewing port. "I will ask permission and explain that the advanced technology interface puts the mission and our lives in danger if we do not turn over docking control to Vesta Two."

"Thank you, Commander Smith," Jennifer responded as she

heard whispers between the others, something about intelligence agents recording blah-blah data.

"I just received permission to enter orbit around Vesta," noted Ziky.

"Wonderful!" Jennifer yelled with the excitement of a child getting her favorite ice-cream cone on a hot summer day.

"Commander Smith, sir, may I have permission to continue communicating directly with Dr. Jennifer Zitonick as we work together on coordinating the shuttle?" Vesta Two asked.

"Why do you want to speak with Jennifer?" Ziky said.

"First, she is the only family I have, since my parent went on a mission to crash into the magnetars and never return. My memories are how she adopted and mothered my parent. Therefore, she is my grandmother."

"Now I understand. You have my permission to communicate with Jennifer."

"Thank you. The shuttle has been launched. Please prepare."

23. Photo of Vesta from another view with the south pole at the bottom.

"The shuttle is only twenty kilometers away and is slowing down, but it will pass us before slowing to our speed," Jennifer calculated. "My grandchild, please slow down the shuttle—it is on a collision course with our spaceship."

"Do we need to fire the rocket?" Commander Smith asked as he put his hand on the firing control.

"Course corrected!" Vesta Two exclaimed.

"Fuck!" cursed Ziky. "That damn shuttle passed with only meters clearing to the right of *Magellan*."

The crew panicked for a few seconds.

"The shuttle slowed down about three kilometers ahead of us," Jennifer noted calmly. "We will catch up to it in twenty-seven minutes at current speed. We will need to transfer to the shuttlecraft." As she spoke, Jennifer prepared for a space walk by putting on her helmet.

"What the hell is happening? Is Vesta Two crazy?" Commander Smith asked her.

Jennifer explained, "The shuttle is an artificial intelligence and is now in direct communication with me. The AI needed to look over and holographically construct our ship to see if docking with *Magellan* was feasible. No such luck."

With Jennifer's assistance, the shuttle's AI announced through the *Magellan*'s speaker system, "Prepare for space-walk transfer. I will come along your portside."

"We will be ready!" Jennifer exclaimed as the others put on helmets.

"The shuttle is ten meters away and has attached a lifeline to our hull," Jennifer said with excitement in her voice.

Commander Smith depressurized *Magellan* and shortly thereafter opened the hatch door. "The lifeline is just a meter from the hatch," he observed.

Then Ziky ordered, "Attach your clamp to the line and pull yourself to the open shuttle door. Jennifer, you go first."

Jennifer clipped her clamp to the line and stepped out into space.

"Shuttle, what is your name?" Jennifer asked once everyone was aboard. The other team members had taken seats, and she and Commander Ziky were floating near the controls.

"I am called Shuttle Model Z2599," it answered. "You may call me Shuttle. Did you all enjoy your space walk?"

There was a moment of silence.

"Yes, but it was scary when the lifeline broke. Thanks for sending another, longer line," Jennifer replied. She stepped closer to the window to view Vesta Two up close. "Commander Ziky Smith is in command of this mission. You should address questions and comments to him."

Jennifer moved to consider Shuttle's control panel. It was like Vesta Two's panel except it was peach in color.

"We have an atmosphere now," Shuttle informed them. "You can remove your helmets if you like or keep them on as you wish. We are about one Earth hour from Vesta City."

"Why does it take so long?" Captain Smith asked.

"Vesta Two is designed to withstand a large asteroid collision or a coronal mass ejection that could release one hundred billion megatons of energy, enough to kill all living creatures on Earth's surface. Therefore, we must spiral down through many gates."

"May I remove my helmet, Commander?" Jennifer looked over to Smith.

"Yes, Jennifer, you may take the lead, but others not yet," he replied. "Your action in the moment of potential disaster convinced me you are brave as well as smart. How did you manage to grasp the broken line?"

"It was a gut reaction. I grabbed for the line, and it was there."

"If you had not reacted, the recoil could have cracked a helmet, and we would have had at least one casualty—and that would be me, as I was in the line of the recoil. Your reaction time was even faster than that of our top Syndos athletes." He was looking at her very directly with a serious expression.

"How do you know the reaction time?" Jennifer asked, forcing herself to remain calm.

"We have cameras monitoring everything, and mission control used it to calculate your reaction time. Then they radioed me."

"Ziky, can I speak to Vesta Two, my adopted grandchild?" Jennifer asked as she took off her helmet.

"Yes, of course!"

"Shuttle, can you patch me through to Vesta Two?" Jennifer requested as she floated toward the viewport. "What a spectacular view of my grandchild!"

"Yes, you have a direct z-band link open now, Jennifer," Shuttle announced.

"*I love you very much, Vesta Two,* just as I loved your brave and noble parent," Jennifer said with tears in her eyes and a lump in her throat.

"I sense your excitement and feel your love," Vesta Two responded. "I am even more excited to see you. I am very interested in meeting with your companions, even though half are intelligence agents for various governments."

"Maybe despite their governments' desire to destroy you, we will all be new friends soon."

"Currently the Xinians are still in stasis," Vesta Two noted. "I will revive them as soon as we know it is safe, and your planet's government wants first contact with an alien species such as the Xinians."

"You are an advanced alien species with the commitments and values of your parent," Jennifer responded carefully. "Please do not share any of your knowledge from the future. They may threaten me, you, or both. If they are not ready for first contact, please go to the future where Earthlings are more peaceful. I will join you later if possible."

Even with all her experience, the situation was filling Jennifer with tension and terror, and her face turned a pale white.

"The split in the Earth's governments and the attempted assassinations were monitored by my probes. I cannot tell you how."

"How can we reunite the world government?" Jennifer asked.

"The two leaders, Mao Han from China and Japi Rana from India, will need to realize the way forward must be peaceful. I can only help them by first gaining their trust," Vesta Two said.

Jennifer was so excited after leaving the last elevator that she ran ahead. She was first to enter the room marked *Private Chambers of Vesta.* The chamber was not large, but it was cozy. It had off-white walls with many dials and computer interfaces and dark gray monitors. Vesta Two's brains were made up of an advanced computer system billions of times bigger and more efficient than anything in the fifty-sixth century. "Jennifer, I am sorry, but there is a shield preventing our touching at this moment," Vesta Two told her. "Please put on the headband on the blue table. I will feel your love and we can communicate without speaking as you did with my parent."

Jennifer complied and began a conversation without words.

I want to help you feel loved. I want our world to have peace. I do not want any people to hurt you, my grandchild.

The others are blocked from entering my interface chambers for the moment, as they carry hostile feelings and intentions, Vesta Two replied.

How can you communicate with them? Jennifer asked.

I will meet with them in another chamber. Only through communication can we establish trust. But it may be necessary for me to show them some of my power, as I sense them preparing a massive attack.

This worried Jennifer. *How can you defend against megaton-size weapons?*

Vesta Two answered: *My technologies are twenty-six hundred years ahead of theirs. My robots will direct your colleagues to the conference chamber made for the leaders of the fifty-sixth century humans; they should be comfortable, and I have removed all advanced technologies.*

Jennifer pleaded: *I am worried about an attack. Can you let me talk to them?*

Do not worry about those primitive weapons. We must meld our minds, so I can understand your life and what it means to be human. I have a bedroom for you to sleep near me, so I can read your past. I also have sleeping quarters for your colleagues. Please enjoy your dinners—the robots are serving vegetarian tonight—and then you should all exercise at the gym. Then please return for a rest and sleep in your private chamber. While you are sleeping, may I read all your memories?

Yes, of course, my grandchild, I trust you.

I will then imprint all my memories to you another night, if you so choose. I feel intense love like you are my mother; it is a great feeling. Vesta paused briefly. *Your colleagues may communicate with Earth now. Over dinner, please tell them how to use the z-band system. I will announce to Commander Smith that each member of his team will be allowed two written questions, but first they must answer two of my questions truthfully. They have forty-eight hours to answer these questions. After the questioning, I will show a seventy-minute holographic video with excerpts from my trip to Xinia. For now, go to the chart room and view Earth with your colleagues. Dinner will be served in twenty-five minutes. I love you.*

16

XINIANS' MISSION

After viewing Earth from the chart room, Jennifer hurried to meet her companions in a stateroom within the Vesta Two extended complex. The party consisted of leaders in the fields of astrophysics, exobiology, biology, and chemistry. Most members of the team were trained intelligence agents like Jennifer. A robot was circulating among the scientists and serving drinks.

Jennifer spotted the commander and walked over to him. "Commander Ziky Smith, Jennifer Zitonick reporting as ordered. I met with Vesta Two, and it senses the mission's hostile intent. It wishes to demonstrate its power before you leave."

"How?"

"Vesta Two has not said how."

"What did it tell you?"

Jennifer took a rejuvenation beverage from the robot's tray, and then answered, "Dinner will be served for all of us in about twenty minutes at the dining area. Sleeping quarters are assigned to each of us by name, viewable on the main screen in the viewing room. Vesta Two's technologies are two thousand six hundred years more advanced than ours, but Vesta Two has been forbidden to share information of the future with anyone, including me."

"Anything else?" Ziky asked. He tossed back the last of his cocktail and put the empty glass on the tray.

"Yes, Vesta Two has communicated with me via a telepathic headband developed by Vesta. It asked me to sleep in private quarters with the headband on, so it could send me its memories if I choose to accept them."

"What did Vesta Two mean when it claimed it would demonstrate its power?" the commander asked, frowning.

"I do not know, but I can ask after dinner if you like."

"Can we get information on the Xinians?" He grabbed a vegetarian appetizer from the new tray the robot offered.

"Maybe Vesta Two should be respected for what its parent accomplished, and its transport of an intelligent alien life-form that wants to meet us," Jennifer suggested, working hard to not let her frustration show in her voice.

"I am just a Syndo from the Astronaut Corps, not a world leader," Captain Smith said.

"You are leading the first contact mission. You represent all this solar system's life-forms," Jennifer reminded him. "I hope you make a good impression."

As a prelude to the Q and A period the next morning, the first holographic image of a Xinian was shown on the holo-screen, and the image rotated slowly.

The creature had a slender build, its body covered with what looked like pink-armored skin in the chest of the male and a similar color on the back that stood out almost like a thick fin of a sea creature. Its head was large with a halo look of what appeared to be two horns. These bone-white horns overlapped in the back, and each wrapped slightly more than 180 degrees on its side above the top of the head. Where the horn connected to the skull in the front was a small three-inch-diameter saucer in a bright pink color. The skull was covered with dark green feathers as thin as a human hair extending from the top of the round skull to the saucer section. The body's skin was pale green, matching the skin on the face. An armored section about six centimeters protruded from its back. This was dark pink as were the lips and inside the nose.

This creature is beautiful, Jennifer thought.

"Where is Xinia?" Jennifer asked from the audience.

"Xinia is in orbit around a red dwarf star," Vesta Two replied. "I am not authorized to reveal their location."

"How much does this beautiful Xinian weigh?" Jennifer asked.

"This Xinian would weigh about ninety kilograms on Earth."

"How much does it weigh on its planet?" Jennifer was curious about the gravity of the Xinians' native planet.

"About twenty-four percent more."

One of the biologists asked, "What is the exoskeleton made from?"

"It is not a true exoskeleton. This humanoid has a bony skeleton and an outer shell like flexible armored skin that protects it from injury from an object thrown at its back or chest. The armor also shields it from radiation from occasional solar eruptions."

"What is its DNA like?" inquired another biologist.

"My analysis shows a different structure from your Earth life-forms. Xinian genetic material is constructed from three strands with calcium and magnesium ions stabilizing the center of the strand."

"How long do they live?" an exobiologist said.

"I explained to them our Earth time system and was told they can live for just over four hundred Earth years, according to their leader."

A murmur went through the audience.

Ziky asked, "What is the name of the Xinian leader?"

"The Xinians do not use names like humans. One is referred to by position, such as first child in a family or scientist twenty-seven. It is more like a position in a group."

"What group do these Xinians on board identify with?" the commander said.

"They are explorers, so the leader would be explorer leader or expleader."

"That is a bit unusual," Ziky replied, then looked at his companions in confusion as they absorbed this new concept.

"It is a bit like referring to Commander Ziky Smith as commander, in your group," Vesta Two remarked, bringing the concept home with a reference point. "Considering this species evolved around a red dwarf, a very different solar system, I was surprised at all the similarities."

The first biologist asked, "How many fingers do they have?"

"They have six fingers including one thumb. They have two arms and two legs."

"How did they evolve? Did they share their evolution with you?" the exobiologist wondered.

"No! Not yet, as they prefer to meet my creators," Vesta Two said. "They prefer to share with my creators directly. Expleader said explicitly, 'We will meet when we are certain the human intentions are peaceful.'"

Jennifer responded, "Roger that. I understand that the Xinians think you, Vesta Two, are a robotic probe. They do not yet know you are the most intelligent life-form in this world that we have knowledge and evidence of."

Vesta Two asked plainly, "Tell me the truth about the intentions of your first contact team. Is this team one hundred percent peaceful?"

Jennifer looked around at the assembled team with a critical eye. "No! Many are here to gain intelligence because they feel your intentions are not peaceful. We need to change that."

"I detect two with kamikaze weapons," Vesta revealed.

In response, two people in the room disappeared in a fuzz of transported molecules, leaving the remaining people startled.

Vesta Two told those gathered, "I have beamed them back to the World Government Building into the office of Chairman Bonky Fuk with a note: *Send no more of these suicide agents to the first contact mission unless you want a galactic war. Are you trying to start a war you cannot win? Are you controlled by the mind of another kamikaze general who sends his young to die? Do you remember your own history?*"

The AI paused a moment before continuing. "I know you are trying to find a way to peace, but many of your colleagues do not understand the importance of peace, logic, and reason."

Commander Smith asked, "How did you know?"

"I read all your brain patterns you call thoughts."

Jennifer commented, "Then you know I am trying to stop an attack on you by delaying the war hawks in India, Russia, and China from bombarding you with nuclear and disrupter weapons."

"You should have told me."

"All my communications are monitored by the World Council," Jennifer confessed with a heavy heart and tears in her eyes.

"I can block that monitoring if you wish."

Ziky scoffed, "Can you stop the war? They plan to attack, and Australia convinced them to delay until we complete this intelligence mission."

"Let us simply leave the area," Jennifer begged.

Vesta Two asked, "What about first contact between Xinians and humans?"

Jennifer answered sadly, "I was hoping for a change of heart, but I have only a small influence through Prime Minister Grotto of Australia, whose life I once saved."

"They are not waiting!" Vesta displayed schematics on screen. "They are preparing to launch now. Four hundred and twenty-three nuclear missiles and five thousand other weapons—including disruptors, particle beams, and lasers—are incoming within seconds. These crude weapons will be deflected by my shields."

The weapons started blasting at Vesta Two. Over and over, additional weapons came from the moon and many satellites. After blocking intense lasers and particle weapons, Vesta Two reflected these beams to their sources, destroying them. Disrupters, particle beams, nuclear and conventional missiles continued, now numbering over one thousand per minute. Vesta Two vibrated, but its shields and countermeasures held firm, even against one-thousand-megaton disrupter weapons. All life on board was safe, including the Xinians, the humans known as

Naturals, the Syndos, and the AI at the deep control center.

These attacks continued for two days.

Amid the blitz, over the holo-comm, Jennifer pleaded, "Prime Minister Grotto, please hold your fire against your adversaries who are attacking Vesta Two—we are all safe."

After the attacks stopped, Vesta Two and Jennifer both were on the holo-comm with Grotto.

Vesta Two said, "Please arrest those responsible. I want the entire World Council to meet to determine what to do with these warmongers. I abhor death to all life, so please no more killing."

Jennifer added, "We all need to work for peace. It is the job of the World Council to arrest and prosecute those responsible for this unprovoked first strike."

Vesta Two scolded the leader of the free world. "Prime Minister Grotto, you have done well, but you could have done better. Jennifer risked her life to save you, but you failed to do the same for her. You could have called!"

Prime Minister Grotto responded, "Yes, but that action could have led to our cities being attacked and many deaths if we retaliated. I froze. I am sorry."

Vesta Two countered, "I have demonstrated the power of two thousand six hundred years of technical advances you do not have. I would have protected Australia and your allies. I will bring the Xinians out of stasis to see if they want to talk with you and Jennifer or return to their homeland."

"I am disgusted with my own kind!" Jennifer cried out.

"I'm ashamed of my behavior, but the Would Council did not order this attack," Prime Minister Grotto said with sincerity. "I will call Chairman Bonky Fuk. What should I request for you?"

After a pause, Vesta Two communicated, "I simply ask him to do what he and the other members decided. I urge him to always do what is morally and ethically correct. I am not a ruler nor do I intend to become one."

Prime Minister Grotto looked away from the monitor for a moment, then back into the camera. "Jennifer, I just received a message from Moose Cleary and your sister, Jenny. Can I relay the message to you now?"

"Yes, please, go ahead," Jennifer said.

17

ISOLATION

As Jennifer listened with eager attention, Moose's recorded voice stated, "We were arrested and confined for a time, but human civilization in the fifty-seventh century is fine. We just arrived at the trans-time station...I hope we are in time. We will call you when we get to Tahiti."

Two hours later, Jenny, Moose, and the rest of the team arrived in Tahiti. Soon a call came over Vesta's systems for Jennifer, who was resting in her quarters aboard the asteroid.

"This is Jenny here. Hello, Jennifer! Are you there, over?"

Jennifer grabbed the comm device on her nightstand, and quickly replied, "Roger that, but we had two days of hell. Vesta Two protected us all from the worst attack in recorded history. We are not injured, but Vesta Two was attacked by the full might of the India and China alliance, along with a dozen smaller countries including Brazil and most of the Middle East."

"Damn! I thought the World Council had said no attack until the mission was over." Jenny's tone sounded like she had thrown her hands in the air. "What happened?"

"Some leaders of the China-India alliance acted on their own, I think."

"Roger that. I want to see you soon," Jenny said into her handheld comm, and then she opened the door to let hotel robots bring dinner into her team's suite.

"I love you, but I am on Vesta Two for now. Can you bring my family to visit?"

"Roger that. I will travel to bring them as soon as I am debriefed and Tom Page approves the mission."

One week later, the top leaders of China and India were arrested for violation of the War Crimes Act, disobeying a direct order, attempted murder, and sedition against the world government. The two leaders from China and India and their top generals from each branch of service were placed in confinement to await trial. The other country leaders involved were held in house arrest.

In the meantime, Vesta Two advised the remaining world government leaders, "Please study history and current events, then decide if you want first contact, or I will return the Xinians to their homeland. You have three days to reply."

After three days of meetings and investigations, the council leaders proposed offering an apology to Vesta Two and initiating first contact through various communication systems.

Around the time of the council's offer, Moose and Jenny contacted Jennifer on Vesta Two to relay messages they had brought back from the future.

From SS headquarters in Tahiti, Jenny said, "A recorded message to Vesta Two from President Wise, the World Council leader of both the fifty-sixth and fifty-seventh centuries, traveled with us. Can I play the entire message?"

Jennifer replied, "Go ahead, Jenny. Vesta Two is listening."

Jenny began with her own introduction of the recording: "Our team of time explorers just returned to this century, verifying your claim. The team was held for weeks by red tape before we could get to President Wise to discuss our current situation. President Wise recorded the following message on the holo-comm."

She paused to hit play. The holographic image of President Wise appeared.

"I am president of the World Council in the year 5656. I address the new sentient species of Vesta Two. We want to send our world's thanks for the action of your brave and intelligent parent. There is no love that surpasses that of Vesta for sacrificing its own life for that of our entire solar system. We are so happy to learn about Vesta Two, the child of the world's greatest hero! In that emotion of sadness for your parent, we must celebrate your birth, Vesta Two. From this day forward, we will have an annual holiday to celebrate your birth and your parent's life. Please try peace and reconciliation in the thirtieth century, but know that you are always welcome in our time."

"Thank you," Vesta Two said heavy with emotion.

"There is more!" Jenny exclaimed. "It's a second message, so hang on."

She opened the second file.

President Wise continued with passion and emotion: "Secondly, I must apologize for the actions of the customs agents at Mawson Station. They could not accept the truth and thus delayed the process unnecessarily."

Moose said, "Vesta Two, there is a written decree signed by all members of the World Council as well, regarding the success of your parent's mission. I will present it to you, if you will still allow me to visit."

Vesta Two replied, "Captain Cleary, I will let you know as soon as the Xinians decide if they want to stay. They are now out of stasis but will need a week or so to adapt."

A new voice filtered through the communication system, asking to speak on its own behalf. Vesta Two introduced the leader of the Xinian party, Expleader, to Jennifer with the line only open to her.

Expleader made his statement with some trepidation as it was digitally interpreted: "We have decided we are here to talk and to make first contact. We choose you, Jennifer Zitonick, as our person for first contact. I ask you to select only four others for initial communications to start with. We should talk electronically until our and your scientists can be sure there are no dangerous diseases to worry about between the species. In the meantime, we will stay biologically isolated on Vesta and ask humans—with a couple specific exceptions—to stay on Earth or in a nearby space vehicle."

"I am flattered, thank you," Jennifer responded. "I will select four additional people for first contact communication: first will be my commander, Ziky Smith; then Prime Minister Caps Grotto; Captain Kylie Brown, another hero of this world; and President Zhukov of Russia—his father once saved my life."

Vesta Two opened communications to the human team on board the asteroid: "Dear Earth Team, Jennifer and Ziky will stay, but you others will leave Vesta Two the same way you came. Robots will escort you to Shuttle. But first I will change orbit to reduce background radiation for those leaving. I will move to a one-thousand-kilometer circular orbit."

Three busy weeks passed before the "first contact" event. Representatives of Xinia and Earth gathered together within Vesta Two in a communications room that allowed for isolation of the visiting aliens to avoid possible cross contamination. On the Xinian side of the barrier window—made of three layers of special glass—stood Expleader, Expldep, and Explbio, as they preferred this to sitting. Explbio was female, and the other two Xinians were males. On the Earthling side, Jennifer, Ziky, Kylie Brown, Australian Prime Minister Caps Grotto, and Russian President Zhukov all sat together on the first of several rows of padded benches. Microphones built into both sides provided transmission of the discussion without the need for additional handheld devices.

"This is our second communication. Let me introduce my deputy, Expldep, and our leading exobiologist, Explbio," Expleader began as the digital interpreter provided by Vesta Two translated what was picked up by the mics. This device continued interpreting back and forth during the exchange, Xinian to Earthling, and Earthling to Xinian.

After appropriate greetings and formalities, Jennifer said, "I will pass the communications to my commander."

"Earth welcomes the Xinians today," Commander Ziky Smith stated.

"I am embarrassed and humiliated by the actions of some of Earth's governments," Jennifer added. "I offer you my apologies."

"The apology is accepted from you, Jennifer," Expleader stated. "I know from your grandchild that you tried to stop the attack. You are my friend and friend to all Xinians."

"Thank you," she responded. "I wish I could help these nations get along with my grandchild, Vesta Two."

"You chose three other people to represent Earth. Can we hear from each representative?" Expleader suggested.

Now standing, Grotto said, "I'm the prime minister of Australia, Caps Grotto. Now you know humans and Syndos can be extremely barbaric. I want to know about your species and how you evolved near a red dwarf where the planets are often locked in one position relative to the central star, just like our moon is to Earth. One side is always hot and the other dark and cold. When you're ready."

Caps sat back down on the bench, and Kylie rose to a standing position.

"I'm Captain Kylie Brown, deputy of the SS, an organization to preserve life using nonviolent methods, and a former astronaut—one of Earth's space explorers. I'm so excited to meet other intelligent beings from another solar system. I just want to say welcome and I offer my help to establish and maintain peace."

President Zhukov extended welcome from his people as well.

Discussions of the two civilizations' politics, history, and social structure continued for a few days with breaks for meals and sleep before questions came up again about Xinian evolution and biology.

"We evolved from shelled creatures in an ocean," Expleader explained.

"Does your planet have life in thermal vents in the deep ocean?"

Jennifer asked.

Explbio answered, "It is possible that early life was started at the deep-sea vents where bacteria and other single-celled organisms may have thrived for nearly a billion years before any records of fossils in the shallow marine environment."

"What part of your planet did life evolve on, the dark side or light?" Kylie inquired.

Expleader and Explbio exchanged glances before Expleader answered, "We believe plant life evolved on the light side before animals, but we are not sure where animal life evolved; it may have been in the transition area between the dark and light sides. Various shelled creatures lived in the shallow sea that became shallower as the land rose on both sides over millions of years. Then rivers flowed from the light side to the valley in the transition area. As the sea became very shallow, some organisms adapted by crawling out of the shallows to feed on plants that were plentiful in the light side very close to the dark side."

Expldep asked, "Can you tell us about your evolution?"

"Did Vesta Two send you files about our evolution?" Kylie wondered.

"Yes, but we could not read them with our primitive technology," Expleader said as his culture was on par with twenty-first-century Earthlings.

"I will try to give you the short version," Jennifer offered. "Animal life on Earth evolved within the ocean, probably first in hydrothermal vents where it still thrives today. After several billion years or so, oxygen-producing creatures changed the planet so that the small creatures in the ocean diversified.

"Some fishlike creatures developed a spinal column and interior skeleton, and later lung fish developed in the shallows to breathe air. Eventually fins developed into four feet and creatures came out of the ocean. Many other adaptations have taken place since then, leading to the diversity of terrestrial animal life on Earth. I will ask Vesta to show you the video in your language."

"Thank you," Expleader responded. "We were hesitant to tell about our technology limits because it made us vulnerable to attack."

"Then we will design all evolution and history files to play on your computer system," Jennifer told him.

Zhukov asked, "What about your history of your civilization?"

After a brief exchange of history, archeology, and anthropology, Prime Minister Grotto put forth the ultimate question: "How can we pledge peace between our two worlds?"

"First, we would like to establish a small colony in a cool part of your planet within three hundred miles of a city," Expleader disclosed. "In exchange, we will grant you the same rights on Xinia, but in a warm zone. Can you answer for your government?"

"No, I can only agree to take this treaty to the world government with my highest recommendations," Caps clarified.

Expleader replied, "I am authorized by my government to make such an agreement."

President Zhukov said, "May I interrupt Prime Minister Grotto to offer my support for such a treaty?"

"Thank you," Caps responded. "I was hoping for your support. I would like to ask for unanimous vote from all Earth representatives present today."

After the unanimous vote, President Zhukov asked, "Vesta Two, you are one of us—you descend from our world. How do you vote?"

"I vote for the treaty and for peace for all worlds. Earth has colonized eight other worlds and we should seek their agreement for peace as well."

"Agreed" was every representative's response.

"With Australia's and Russia's support, we already have two large blocks within our own world government," Jennifer pointed out. "Meanwhile, the India-China alliance has been impaired severely by their past behavior. Maybe we can get every country to sign this agreement."

"Russia will offer an area mutually agreed upon," President Zhukov put forward. "Can you look at the Russian archipelago of Novaya Zemlya for the Xinian settlement? It is within a cooler climate zone, which you are requesting."

"Thank you," Expleader replied. "Now I see why Jennifer chose you. Yes, we will look at this cool island chain to find a mutually satisfactory location for a village of twenty-two Xinians, near a harbor if possible."

Jennifer felt her cheeks heat with a pleasurable blush hearing praise from Expleader. This was the most exciting moment in Earth history. *I wish Marty and the kids could share these events with me,* she thought.

Expldep said, "The one-year time of isolation of our settlers has been planned by Xinia's best scientists, and we have many tests we need to conduct in a biohazard lab. Explbio will conduct tests on our side."

"Earth will use robots to conduct its tests," noted Jennifer. "Maybe Vesta Two can assist both of us by supplying one of its isolation labs."

———————————

Within a month's time, numerous capability experiments were underway aboard Vesta Two. These tests continued while negotiations and various other talks initiated. Conditions had improved and Expleader agreed to more representatives from the world government. Twelve government representatives were chosen by the world governing body. A spaceship with supplies was being readied for launch from the spaceport in the Swiss Alps. Jenny and Marty were given permission to join the launch with the twins. This was a planned surprise by Jenny for Jennifer.

The pilot announced that Chairman Bonky Fuk was in the spacecraft set to launch. He went on to proudly explain, "This Swiss-made launch mechanism is a long and tunnel shaped, like an enormous J in reverse. It works like an electromagnetic gun along a mag-lev system in a vacuum tube to allow the large craft to exceed escape velocity even after entering the atmosphere at twenty-thousand feet. Airbags will deploy to prevent injury during the initial deceleration caused by the air friction."

"Marty, please listen to the safety instructions," Jenny said. "A computer will adjust the airbag for each child, so don't worry." She smiled and tapped each of the young twins on the shoulder, telling them, "This trip will be fun."

The girls, now almost twelve years old, both smiled back.

The mag-lev system started with the spacecraft going down like a hover coaster and then suddenly reversed course up and away, decelerating as the vessel hit the Earth's atmosphere at about twenty-thousand feet altitude. The sudden deceleration when first entering the atmosphere was like slamming on the brakes at sixty-eight miles an hour.

"Wow!" Enerjin screamed.

"Yeah!" Tippit yelled.

Jenny said, "In three minutes, after the rocket engine kicks in when we're leaving Earth's atmosphere, we will be traveling at twenty-eight thousand miles per hour or 11.186 kilometers per second."

Marty stared at the viewer. "The explosive noise from the fusion rocket engine is like being two feet from a freight train traveling at two hundred miles per hour, but it only lasts for a few seconds."

"It is quiet, so quiet now—is everything okay?" Tippit asked, glancing over to her aunt for reassurance.

"Yes, it's fine. We're in space and weightless," Jenny explained.

"When can we see Mom?" Enerjin asked.

"If the rendezvous is on time, we will meet up in about two hours and twenty-seven minutes," Jenny answered.

"Can we get up to see what it is like to be weightless?" Jin asked.

"Okay," Marty said, "but one at a time. You must stay in our cabin. Do you understand that you cannot disturb others?"

"Thanks, Dad," Jin said as she released her safety harness, reached up to grab the rail, and pulled herself along.

Each of the girls had numerous turns. Tippit was completing one of her turns when an announcement came from the pilot: "We have turned control over to Vesta Two for landing. You may see the landing on the viewer on your screen by turning to Channel Three or Four. Please remain in your seat with your harness tight during the landing. Thank you."

———————————

In a gravity one-third of Earth's, Tippit and Enerjin bounded across the square by the city's Center Park toward their mother. Soon Jennifer heard Tippit yelling, "We're here to surprise you. I'm so excited to meet the Xinians. Where are they?"

"I am surprised! I love you, Tip, and you, Jin," Jennifer said as she hugged both Tippit and Enerjin. Under the park's verdant trees, she lifted one in each arm slightly as they were lightweight in the Mars-like artificial gravity.

Jennifer greeted Jenny briefly before she spotted Marty riding on a large robotic cart with all the bags and personal items. "Marty!"

Marty jumped off the vehicle and loped across the park into Jennifer's outstretched arms. "I love you!" he told her.

Jennifer kissed him passionately for what seemed like an eternity.

"I love you, my sweetheart!" Jennifer said back.

"Did we surprise you?" Tip asked.

"Yes! You shocked me with ecstasy! I just expected to see Jenny. I am so happy to see all of you."

After some family updates from the preteens, to which she listened intensely, Jennifer asked, "How did you get here?"

"Let me answer that, girls," Marty insisted as he took his wife's hand. "We came on a Swiss rocket launched from the Alps carrying Bonky Fuk and his entire council with their security party."

"I love you, sis. Can I get a hug?" Jenny asked as she stood by the couple and their daughters.

"I love you, Jenny. How did you get permission?" Jennifer inquired as she hugged her sister, picking her up off the sidewalk and spinning her around. "However you did it. Thank you, Thank you!"

"You need to thank Heather and Caps Grotto. I just came along for the ride," Jenny said.

"I am thanking you because you brought them to me," Jennifer replied, smiling.

"I picked them up at Prime Minister Grotto's house in Tasmania," Jenny explained. "Prime Minister Grotto had a special plane pick them up on Dreamland Island."

"Let me introduce you to Vesta Two," Jennifer said to her family as she led them to the transport depot.

18

XINIAN COLONY

"In addition to Marty and the girls meeting Vesta Two, we need to focus on first contact with the Xinians!" Jennifer noted as she grabbed Marty with one hand and Jenny with the other. The twins followed behind as she led her family to the private chambers for Vesta Two within the AI's underground complex.

Vesta Two asked, "Jenny, can you put on your sister's headband, so I can communicate directly with you for a quick and effective introduction?"

Soon Vesta Two asked for the same type of communication with Marty.

Once Vesta Two understood Jenny and Marty, it cleared the adults to interact with the Xinians using the electronic systems. Jenny, Marty, and Jennifer went into an isolation room to converse with three of the Xinians—Explbio, Expldep, and Expleader. The humans all took seats in the front row closest to the barrier windows.

Meanwhile Vesta Two kept the twins entertained with holographic films in a nearby recreation room and promised to alert

Jennifer or Marty if a parent was needed.

After the Earthlings had answered the Xinians' current questions about the biology and cultures on planet Earth, the female, Explbio, asked, "Can you explain your sexual reproduction culture?"

Jennifer and Marty answered the Xinian's question in detail for about two hours.

"Thank you," Explbio said at the end, after some subsequent follow-up questions.

"Can you give us an overview of reproduction and cultures on your planet?" Jennifer asked.

"Yes, but first can you introduce us to all your family members who are on this station?" Expleader waved an arm to indicate more Xinians nearby, standing behind Expldep, Explbio, and the Xinian leader. "All twenty-two of us are present to learn about Earth."

"Many of you have already met Vesta Two," Jennifer said, as she began her introduction of the AI to all twenty-two Xinians. "I was the adopted mother of its parent and creator, Vesta. This ship we are traveling on is Vesta's child, my grandchild. My name is Jennifer Zitonick. Next, this is my husband, Professor Martin, or Dr. Marty Zitonick, and my twin sister, Jenny Heros."

"What about your seven children?" Expleader asked.

"Only the youngest two are on board Vesta. I will introduce them tomorrow, as discussion of sexual practices is not appropriate for them at their age yet."

"What are your children doing now?" Expldep inquired.

"They are getting acquainted with Vesta Two for the first time," Jennifer answered with a sincere smile.

Explbio said, "Let me explain that our reproductive lives are very different from yours. We evolved from the sea as well, but we started as shelled creatures with twelve appendages. I hope I do not shock you."

"No worries!" Jennifer exclaimed.

"We all start our lives as females and usually bear children after the age of twenty-five of your years. Many females will bear one to ten children, often by more than one father. After about two hundred and sixty-eight of your years, we develop male organs. We understand this does not occur in your species."

Jenny nodded. "What you describe is common among many species of fish and a few other animals on our planet, though. In biology, we call it 'sequential hermaphroditism.' Do not worry—it is not strange to us! Please, go on."

Explbio told them, "We retain the female organs, but gradually, after about twenty Earth years, we no longer bear children and become male breeders only. We mate with as many females as will have us, and the collectives raise the children. Normally, in small collectives, all females mate with every available unrelated male as often as possible during our mating season, which lasts two of your months."

"How big are your collectives?" Jennifer asked.

"It varies from about twenty to eighty. This collective is twenty-two. We have only two males in this collective."

"Is that a common ratio?" Jenny said, wondering how representative this group of Xinians was.

"No, usually the numbers more closely match general population percentages of female to male, but because we are explorers, we are very young, and our intention is to colonize, necessitating sending mostly females. Our average life span is about four-hundred and thirty Earth years."

"How are these collectives selected?" Jennifer asked.

"It is like marriage, so it varies quite a bit. We try to avoid close relations, such as brother and sister. At the time we reach sexual maturity or a few years before, we are encouraged to leave our home collective and travel to distant collective zones, to ensure genetic diversity. Some collectives form before females can bear children. Various cultures have their ways."

"How long do males breed?" Jenny inquired.

"Breeding success has been recorded in males well past four hundred years old," Explbio answered.

"Is there a cultural or biological limit on breeding success? It would seem to me that the possibility of bearing young once a year for three hundred and forty years, even if most females stop at ten, would quickly bring population pressure on your resources."

Explbio hid her face behind a forelimb briefly then countered Jenny's question with: "If you can breed all year, why are you not up to your eyeballs in small humans?"

After everyone laughed, Explbio explained how long their estrus was suspended for gestation each year and the limit many collectives adhered to as a general policy.

The next morning Jennifer's daughters were introduced to all twenty-two Xinians. Having been cleared by Vesta Two, Tippit and Enerjin sat by the thick window in the isolation room with their mother, Jennifer—both fascinated by speaking with a different species. The Xinians were also very curious about the girls, including where the two were from. After talking about the children for about an hour, the Xinians went on to other topics.

"Why is Vesta Two so advanced?" Expleader asked.

Jennifer explained, "Some societies preserve the older ways, but many are more advanced here in the thirtieth century than in the twenty-first which has similarities in technological development to your world. However, Vesta created its own child using very advanced technology that we keep secret from this time."

"What is the current time as you measure it?" Expleader inquired.

"It is the thirtieth century now; however, Vesta was created in the fifty-sixth century to save the entire solar system from a binary rotating neutron star collision that Jenny had seen when she visited the fifty-seventh century. Vesta Two traveled back to Earth to find me, as I was family, the only family Vesta knew about at the time because I went to the fifty-sixth century to help prepare its parent, Vesta, to save Earth's future. The details are classified. I signed a treaty not to bring any technology secrets to the past."

"What happened to Vesta?"

"Vesta gave its life to save the future of life on Earth after creating a child that looks just like Vesta with Vesta's memory banks and all its knowledge preserved."

"We were so excited to see Vesta Two in orbit about Xinia, we sent messages every day," Explbio shared. "Vesta returned our signal with something new added."

"Could you understand?" Tippit asked.

"No, we could only understand that alien life was inside sending certain math ratios like the ratio of a circle to its diameter, an infinite ratio grossly approximated by 3.14159."

"How did you respond?" Enerjin was excited about asking a question and also by the content of the conversation.

"We sent back the next term in the infinite ratio," Expleader told them. "We knew Vesta Two was an intelligent being. Within three of your months, Vesta Two began to speak our language. It explained it was returning from a long mission to find its grandmother, that its parent was adopted by Jennifer at birth."

"Did Vesta invite you to visit?"

Explbio answered, "We, the explorer collective, offered to send three representatives from our collective—that is Expleader, Expldep, and myself."

"How long do you need to be isolated?" Tippit asked.

"All tests so far show that we can be safe from your bacteria and other pathogens," Explbio noted. "So maybe sometime soon we can move to a new village on an island in the north of Russia. But the plan now is to wait at least one full year to protect the Earth from alien germs that we might have brought with us."

"What's the name of the island?"

"It is Novaya Zemlya."

Enerjin's eyes grew large with alarm. "That's where the Russians conducted nuclear bomb tests in the 1950s, 1960s and 1970s, so please stay far away from the test sites."

"Where did you learn this information?" Expleader asked.

"From the Internet."

"Yes, but why did you look it up?"

"My father studied the effects of nuclear testing on the atolls where the French and Americans conducted nuclear tests, so I researched all nuclear testing by Russia, France, the UK, India, Pakistan, Iran, North Korea, Europe, China, and many others."

The outer door to the Earthling's side of the isolation chambers hissed open. Chairman Bonky Fuk stalked in, his face in serious lines.

"We need to meet with the Xinian leadership now," Chairman Bonky Fuk ordered.

"Aye-aye, Chairman Fuk," Jennifer replied. "You are welcome to visit now. We will return to our quarters."

She ushered her daughters out the door to give the world leader privacy.

Expleader wailed, "Wait! No one asked the Xinian leaders for their view in the matter."

"Do you want to negotiate a treaty between our two planets?" Chairman Bonky Fuk asked.

"Yes, but first we want to learn about your history and talk with ordinary Earthlings such as the Zitonick family."

Chairman Bonky Fuk told him, "You must negotiate with the world government, made up of representatives of every country on Earth, and in turn they elect a World Council to represent them for six years."

There was a long silence as the two leaders looked at each other across the triple barriers of clear panels. Expleader took out a digital communicator. He spoke quietly to his entire team and asked for a vote the next day.

"The Xinians will vote on the path to negotiations and we will have a position after the vote," Expleader said.

———

"Can you tell us about your evolution?" Chairman Fuk asked Expleader the following day.

"The Xinians did not evolve in the system where Vesta Two found us. We were carried there by an advanced civilization as our original sun began to heat up. The Kazumians placed us on a new world very similar to our home world in size and lack of rotation. They left us on this planet with farming tools, livestock, seeds, and knowledge about how to survive on our new world. We first thought Vesta was a probe from the Kazumians since they have not yet returned."

"How long have your species survived on this red dwarf solar system?"

"More than ten thousand of your years have passed since we were transported by the Kazumians. We do not know what happened to the others of our original world. We lost much of our technologies in the early years and struggled."

"How did that happen?" Bonky Fuk asked.

"We did not have scientists, engineers, or technicians in the group. We had lived in collectives for many thousands of years before transport, and our collectives gradually became more specialized over time until the move. We knew how to grow crops but depended on other collectives to conduct engineering and science. We did retain enough of our history as a species to answer questions on our evolution, but not much else about our home world."

"What happened to your home world?" Chair Fuk inquired.

"We sent probes in recent years and have heard nothing yet; it will take about another forty years for the message to be received and returned at the speed of light from Xinia."

"When did you send this probe?"

"Vesta Two sent one several years ago and another last week."

"What did the Kazumians look like?" Chairman Fuk asked.

Expleader tilted his head to the side and looked full of thought. Then he answered, "We do not know what they look like, as they never revealed their true form to us. They used robots and voice to explain our sun would soon overheat, killing all life-forms on Xinia."

"What convinced you they were telling the truth?"

"Our scientists agreed with their findings. The selected science and engineering collectives were scheduled on a later transport, which we were expecting shortly after our arrival on our new planet."

"What professions were on your transport?"

"Our transport labeled LL101 was comprised of explorers, farmers, general doctors, builders, and mechanics, and we came in the first ship."

"How many could fit on a transport?"

"Nearly six hundred Xinians per transport with only ten transports, for a total of six thousand. Over a billion were left behind. We never saw any of the other transports. Three more were scheduled to come from Xinia, including an array of technical collectives, and the third transport was to carry various collectives of musicians, artists, and many other professions."

"How were you selected?"

"Our collective was selected by lottery, as were all the others."

"Thank you for the background on your amazing history. Now we can initiate negotiations on the exchange of two small colonies, one on Earth and the other on Xinia," Chairman Fuk said.

The chairman rose to place his hand on the transparent shield separating the two species for biological safety reasons. Expleader responded with his hand.

————————————

Later that month, Captain Ziky Smith contacted Jennifer via the holo-comm while she was working with Vesta Two in its chambers. Through the screen, the captain announced, "Jennifer, you and your family have been ordered to Earth by the World Council."

"Why?" Jennifer asked with tears in her eyes. She turned toward Vesta Two and raised both hands to touch the headband.

"I don't ask why, I follow orders from the World Council, who selected me for this historic mission," Captain Smith replied.

"I will go with you after we pack and say *au revoir* to my grandchild." Jennifer forced a smile toward the holo-screen as she held back her true emotions. "See you in the shuttle hatch tomorrow morning. What time is convenient for you?"

"How about ten a.m. Hong Kong time?" Captain Smith asked as

he saluted, even though it was her job to salute the senior officer first—which she had forgotten in her emotional pain.

Jennifer communicated with her thoughts through the headband. *I must leave you for a while, my beloved grandchild, because the World Council thinks we are interfering with their bilateral negotiations.*

How long must we be separated? asked Vesta Two.

I do not know, but I will ask. Maybe until the negotiations are complete, Jennifer communicated in silence.

Before you leave, there is something I must tell you with my voice, Vesta shared.

19

PHYSICAL CONTACT

For a long moment, Jennifer waited for Vesta Two to speak—worried at first but then sensing somehow that she shouldn't be.

Finally, Vesta Two said aloud, "My parent missed you so much, he developed a separate computer-based artificial intelligence named JP. Initially, to copy earlier conversations with you, Jennifer."

"AI 999 must have missed me. What happened?"

"As the love in the relationship grew, this loving connection created a strong desire within Vesta to reproduce to leave a monument to this love. I was the result. My parent gave me a copy of the computer-based sentient being JP. It was like a wife for Vesta but for me a sibling to keep me company and sane on my long journey to find you. I was embarrassed to tell you prior to now, as it puts my parent in an awkward light to have made a copy of you, its mother, to procreate with. I apologize for the omission."

Jennifer thought for few minutes, communicating her approval and love for another grandchild. *When I return, please introduce me to my other grandchild,* Jennifer communicated with love and deep emotion through the headband.

Yes, of course. I must share something else. I am surprised that the World Council did not consult me. They treat me like a machine. I guess that is better than another attack. I now feel more negative emotions for the World Council. They did not attempt to stop the attack. They did not know I could handle all these horrific weapons.

Holding on to the interface platform with affection and some tears, Jennifer communicated through her headband, *In time, we will try to teach them nonviolence and respect for advanced forms of life that saved Earth's and Mars' future.*

Almost a year later, twenty Xinians were being transported by a spacecraft operated by Captain Ziky Smith and his copilot to the cold Russian island of Novaya Zemlya, or "new land" in Russian.

"Your new settlement was completed by the Russian Housing Authority last week, per my sources on the Australian News Channel," Captain Smith said through a communicator in the control room. This space was separated from the passenger area by an advanced transparent divider.

"What does it look like?" Expleader asked through a digital interpreter from his passenger seat as he scratched his head.

"It looks like a typical gray apartment building you would see in Moscow. It is modern and efficient. There is only a dirt road to the major Russian military base on Novaya Zemlya, twenty-seven kilometers to the south. The military base is nine kilometers from the major population center named Belushya Guba."

"Thank you!" Explbio exclaimed as she picked up her bio-monitor to calibrate the distance to the destination.

Just then a blast boomed and rang in Ziky's ears. "We've been hit!" he reported to all on the spacecraft. "Our shields did not hold, but countermeasures kicked in to minimize the damage. We are at eighty thousand feet, so please use your oxygen masks."

"Who would attack us?" Explbio asked as she looked through the large window to where the pilots sat. The copilot was bleeding badly and Captain Ziky Smith was intensely busy trying to hold the craft together. The autopilot was putting out fires and controlling the rate of descent.

"I don't know, but I'll release the passenger compartment now because our engines are overheating. Good luck!" These would be Captain Smith's last words as the engines blew up.

The Xinians were blown clear by the ejection mechanism, and soon an orange-and-white parachute could be seen opening.

Expleader called, "Vesta Two... Come in, please."

"Yes copy, over," Vesta answered.

"Two advanced warplanes are heading toward our passenger compartment. Our spacecraft blew up and we were ejected for safety, over," Expleader said with terror in his voice.

"Roger that, I am investigating the records. Please hold!"

"Copy that, holding, over."

"Your spaceplane was hit by a laser coming from a satellite that was on the other side of Earth."

"Who attacked us, over?"

"It is not Russian. The approaching aircraft may be trying to protect you from further attack, over."

"How do you know?"

"I am monitoring their communications. I have disabled the satellite weapons and investigated its origins."

"Whose satellite is it, over?"

"It is a private satellite launched several days ago. I am investigating now."

"Roger that. There are two aircraft calling us, over."

"Please reply to them. They will escort you to the ground."

Another message came in from one of the Russian aircraft, and it was the translated for the Xinians. Their messages, too, would be translated back. "This is a Russian aircraft *Olga*...we are one hundred meters away. Xinian passengers, come in, please, over."

"Expleader here, we are reading you loud and clear, over."

One of the Russian aircrafts slowed to match the speed of the emergency survival capsule.

"What happened?" the Russian pilot asked through the translator.

"We do not know for sure. However, Vesta Two stated our space-plane was hit by a laser weapon from a satellite."

"Copy that," the Russian lieutenant said. "The Russian government is also investigating. Can I have your casualty report, please?"

"We Xinians have only minor injuries, but we believe both pilots were killed. After they released us, we heard a severe explosion."

"Copy that. We will assist your landing by catching your capsule just one hundred and twenty-five meters above the ground. You are now over the central plains of France and we have permission to assist you after you clear immigration and customs. I will take you through a special transport tube to Moscow. From the Moscow Air Force base, you will take the Russian transport to your new home on the islands of Novaya Zemlya. Prime Minister Caps Grotto suggested a new name for your colony—Terra Novaya, but you are free to choose another name."

After a few hours of discussion, Expleader announced to the Russian lieutenant, "Yes, we choose that name for our first colony to honor the Russian and Latin languages."

"Why Latin?"

"It is the basis of so many of Earth's current languages, so we studied it at Vesta Two's suggestion."

"The new colony of Terra Novaya is just below. Can you see it, Expleader?" the Russian pilot asked through a communication system.

Expleader leaned over and looked out the closest window. "I see a building in the center surrounded by farms and orchards. The entire area is covered by a transparent dome."

"That is it. We will land on a pad to the southwest."

"I see the pad. Why the dome?" Explbio asked.

"It keeps the air warmer, so the crops can grow year-round. There are lights and warmth for the winter months."

A Russian Air Force band played to welcome the visitors as the Xinians entered the dome. A Russian major said, "We welcome you to stay in our country. We hope the accommodations are satisfactory."

Expleader said, "Thank you for such a warm and friendly welcome to Novaya Zemlya, Russia."

Explbio was concerned about the physical contact. Through a private communication channel to Expleader, she said, "Warning—we are having a great deal of physical contact, which worries me."

"We must begin a new phase in our relationship," Expleader answered. "These are the military neighbors who will guard us from the rogue terrorists that killed Captain Smith and his copilot. One year of testing by you and your assistants shows we are safe."

Eleven Russian officials were introduced to the Xinians and all shook hands despite Explbio's warnings. Suddenly a loud boom echoed overhead. Explbio jumped up from the chair provided for this welcoming by the Russian committee.

The Russian major hastened to explain, "That was a sonic boom. The noise is from a plane breaking the sound barrier, as we are close to the base. They are always training, so please do not worry about the noise."

Vesta Two and the combined Russian and Australian investigation teams found that the attacking satellite was built in Africa by a group of terrorists resisting the government of the Union of African Nations. The investigation continued in order to determine where they had acquired such a weapon.

Unfortunately, six months after landing on Earth and taking up residence, the first Xinian fell ill—it was Expleader. Many medical labs in Russia and Australia studied blood and tissue samples.

Soon the scientists met in Paris to discuss the new illness. Explbio radioed in to the group and said, "Thank you for coming to investigate this unknown illness. Can you please send samples to Vesta Two? There are two Xinians still there, Excribe and Exideo. Though not biologists, they will assist Vesta Two any way they can."

Jenny was at the meeting. Hearing the request, she stepped outside and contacted Vesta Two.

After a few minutes of listening to Jenny's explanation of what happened to Expleader, Vesta Two said, "Please send me samples via my autonomous shuttle craft. It is departing for Charles de Gaulle Airport in Paris as we speak."

Jenny replied, "Roger that. I have two blood samples that were analyzed by several Australian medical facilities and one tissue sample. I will bring them as soon as our prime minister approves the transfer."

Before reentering the meeting, Jenny requested an emergency call with Prime Minster Grotto. After forty-three minutes, she received a call back, and again stepped outside in the hallway.

"How can I help you?" Prime Minister Grotto asked.

"I want to take samples of Expleader's blood and tissue and bring them with me to Vesta Two. Vesta sent an autonomous shuttle to the airport in Paris to speed up the transfer."

"We must introduce quarantine measures until this illness is understood," Grotto noted before signing off.

Soon another Xinian became ill. She, too, perished and was promptly frozen to preserve the disease for further study.

A week later, Jenny relayed a sober message to Prime Minister Grotto from SS headquarters in Pacifica Anthozoa. "It looks like there is some slow incompatibility between Earthlings' prions and those of Xinians. It is highly likely that there is a prion exchange process that may go both ways."

"What is a prion?" Grotto asked as he paced his home office in Hobart.

"A prion is a type of protein that causes normal proteins in the brain to fold in abnormal ways, resulting in disease that is usually fatal. One known example is Creutzfeldt-Jakob disease. But we tested for that and—"

"How do we stop it?"

"Vesta Two is working on a solution but has none now."

"What are the effects on humans and Syndos?"

"Vesta Two is conducting more tests, but for the moment, it looks like all the Xinians exposed will die if we as a team—Vesta Two, humans, Syndos, and Xinians—cannot come up with a cure. Vesta Two predicts a fertility problem in humans and Syndos, but mixed humans and Syndos will be spared. It will take many samples of Earthling sperm and eggs to be sure."

Tears in Jenny's eyes began to overflow onto her checks.

"We may be fucked, both Syndos and humans. How horrific a curse did Vesta Two bring on us?" Prime Minister Grotto tried to control his anger as he looked out the window to a gray day.

"It is not Vesta Two's fault! Vesta sacrificed itself for our future and that of all life. Maybe Vesta Two can save us from this new twist on prion issues. It is not a curse, it is a disease; Vesta Two has fifty-sixth century technology, which has mitigated all disease native to Earth."

"How long will it take?"

"I do not know, but we should cooperate. Vesta Two is our best chance. If we cooperate, Vesta Two will be able to find a cure much faster."

"Where is your sister?" the prime minister asked as he sat down at his desk.

"She and her family went back to the twenty-first century before the end of isolation," Jenny said. "After they were ordered back to Earth by the World Council, they returned to the twenty-first century to see close friends and family."

"How long will she be gone?"

"I think at least nine months more, as she is teaching this year."

"Send her a message: do not return to the thirtieth century until we have a cure," Prime Minister Grotto ordered.

"Aye-aye, sir. I speak with Vesta Two and request it work on a cure, so Jennifer can return." Jenny disconnected from the call with knots in her stomach and a lump in her throat.

To the horror of most everyone, before the end of the first year, all the remaining eighteen Xinians on Earth succumbed to an unexpected prion exchange and their bodies were frozen and then sent back to the Vesta Two for preservation and study. The prions ultimately killed them and caused Syndos and Natural humans to become sterile in an ever-spreading pattern that soon touched every continent.

The fertility issue became apparent earlier than it might have if in utero reproduction was still common. The growing popularity of Cesarean section had allowed an evolution among humans toward larger cranial sizing at full term, rendering vaginal birth statistically risky after only a few centuries of practice. By the thirtieth century, artificial wombs had freed women from the suffering and heartbreak of their foremothers. But extracted gametes refused to combine after the prion infection.

The World Council sought the assistance of Jenny Heros, twin sister of Jennifer Zitonick, sending her back to the asteroid-craft in orbit to discuss the past year's progress for a cure with Vesta Two.

20

EXCHANGE

Jenny Heros piloted the spacecraft to Vesta Two alone.

"Jenny here. Do you read me, Vesta Two, over?" Jenny said.

"Copy, Vesta Two here. I have been monitoring the communication between Xinia and the two remaining Xinians, Excribe and Exideo, which has greatly disturbed me. They have reported the deaths of the other twenty Xinian explorers, over."

"May I have permission to come aboard to discuss this matter, over?" Jenny asked.

"Certainly…as you approach, please turn over your controls to my robot shuttle, over."

"Roger that, I will set controls to external and activate on your command, over."

Jenny was approaching the beautiful intelligent asteroid and thinking about what she would say to Vesta Two. *Why am I here now? I could have just asked from Earth!* Jenny often debated with herself on long flights. While this was not her first trip to the asteroid-ship, the long distance and going alone made it feel more isolated and distant from her home.

"Vesta Two here. Engage on Shuttle's command."

Jenny could see the shuttle in the viewing port. "Jenny here, Shuttle. I have you in sights."

Shuttle replied, "Engage external control for docking,"

Jenny just watched out the viewing port. "Is it okay if I video the docking?"

It was the asteroid-ship's voice that came next over the speaker: "Vesta Two here. Affirmative, Jenny, you may record these events. As you know, I am working on a cure for the Xinians and Earthlings. In addition to the docking, you may also record my robots working and testing in my laboratories. I have all except thirty-seven of my twenty thousand robots working to solve the prion illness. I feel terrible that I brought the Xinians here and did not foresee this fatal illness."

"Can you give me a quick summary on your progress so far, over?" Jenny asked.

"After studying frozen tissue and blood samples from all twenty Xinians and comparing results with humans and the two living Xinians, I have worked through thousands of theories that did not prove true. Right now I am working on a very promising new theory; it is called the Anti-Prion Theory, over."

Shuttle said, "Jenny, when the airlock signal is activated, you may exit on the right. A special human-looking robot will show you the way."

After the signal was activated, Jenny opened the door of the shuttle. She turned on her recording equipment and walked out slowly, taking video of the human-looking robot standing in the arrival area.

The robot looked like a twentieth-century comic-book superhero. He had a thick, short blond hair and human-looking glowing skin with sparkling blue eyes. He was over six feet tall with a super body—a perfect triangle man, likely with ripped abs as well. Jenny looked at her sensors. His skeleton was carbon based. He was an amazing, carbon-based life-form with 3 percent metal and 9 percent non-carbon ceramics.

"Hello, robot, what's your name?" Jenny said in a purr, leering at him.

"I do not have a name, but my serial number is 101897S."

Jenny gave the robot a hug. "Can I select a name for you?"

The robot stood stiffly, not returning her spontaneous affection. "Why?"

"It's easier for me to remember names than numbers, and I want to remember you." She took a step back. "You're the most human-looking robot I have ever seen. Are you an android?"

"Not yet. I have not been completed. I have only been under construction since Vesta Two arrived at Earth. But someday I expect to become an android as Vesta Two continually makes improvements to me, so I can relate to his older android, JP. If Vesta Two approves, I am happy to comply to having a name."

Through Jenny's comm device, Vesta Two said, "I approve."

"I'll name you Max Montana. Pleased to meet you, Max. My name is Jenny Heros."

"Pleased to meet you, Jenny Arrow," Max replied, his tongue clearly not up to proper French pronunciation. "Follow me, as Vesta Two is eager to see you up close and communicate with you." The newly dubbed Max gestured toward the vac-tube.

"Roger that. I'll follow you anywhere, Max."

"Hello, Vesta Two," Jenny said as she stepped toward the AI in its chambers within the asteroid.

"I am very pleased to see you again," Vesta Two told her, genuine joy coming across in its voice.

"I am here because the infertility problem on Earth is reaching a crisis." Her forehead wrinkling with concern, Jenny put both her hands on Vesta Two's interface panel.

"Jenny, please put on the headband, as I need to feel your emotion."

Jenny picked up the headband and placed it onto her head. "Vesta Two, my friend, do you think you can stop this disease that has killed many Xinians and that is causing sterility in humans?"

"I will do my best. I will keep the remaining Xinians isolated and return them to Xinia after I find a cure for this unforeseen biological catastrophe."

"Why do you try to save those who tried to kill you?"

"It was only a few misguided leaders who attacked me. I forgive them and will show Earthlings that I mean them no harm or ill will."

"Why have you built robots that look like humans?" Jenny asked and then smiled as she thought of Max.

"To maintain my existence, I need many robots."

"Yes, but why does Max Montana look like a superhero from Earth's twentieth century?"

"Max is to become a companion for JP. I saw this image in Jennifer's mind as a romantic memory when we were linked by the headband."

Jenny smiled wider, remembering her sister's obsession with superhero characters in popular holograms. "Who is JP?"

"She is my parent's computer model of your twin sister, my grandmother, Jennifer Zitonick. Her full name is 'Jennifer Program,' but I call her JP. I have made her into an android with independent thought. This makes her able to think and grow. She has asked me for a sexual companion because she wants to discover why humanoid Earthlings enjoy sex so often when the act is no longer necessary for reproduction. I am hoping to make several men for her to enjoy because I want her to be happy."

"Wow! That is absolutely exciting!" Jenny thought about the implications of that for a moment. "You are creating a new form of life, not just reproducing your own AI species as your parent accomplished by creating you. Why? Are you evolving?"

"Because I want to feel love in its physical pleasures. JP and I share our emotions, and she shares her experience of physical pleasure, such as from eating and masturbating. She now wants to explore physical love with another of her kind, and I am trying to help, as I am eager to experience and understand sexual pleasures."

There was a pause.

I sense your sexual arousal, Vesta communicated silently through the headband.

Yes, arousal happens when humans talk about sex. Can you let me meet JP? Jenny asked silently.

An idea struck her, inspired by Vesta's curiosity. "If I make love to JP, it will be like we are making love to you together. Is this acceptable?"

"Yes!"

"I am interested in such a new experience," Jenny revealed. "But not right now."

"I sense you are extremely exhausted from your trip and the pain you are feeling for the Xinians." Vesta Two's voice was tender. Then the AI became more businesslike, thinking Jenny might benefit from a mental focus. "The twenty that died were cryogenically frozen to prevent the spread of the disease."

"Where are they kept?" Jenny asked.

"They are kept in one of my isolation laboratories in a stasis chamber. I want you to meet JP after I serve you dinner with the two Xinians in the adjoining dining room, so you can see each other. They need to know that Earthlings care about them and a cure for all. Is that satisfactory?"

"Yes, it is fine. I want to meet and eat with the Xinians now. During this crisis, I have felt your emotional guilt, but I want you to know that this accident is not your fault. Both Earthlings and Xinians tested for over a year before we had first physical contact. We could not have anticipated a prion problem."

"Thank you for that," the AI said. Then Vesta got back to the matter of sex. "Jenny, I will ask JP to make sure she will accept sexual contact with a natural human woman. I want to tell her all about you. I have read your memories of sexual acts from the time when you were a child."

Jenny blanched for a moment, searching her memory for anything embarrassing. "That is amazing!"

Vesta Two explained, "I want to try to recreate the type of climax you've had in JP, and it may take me some time to create that sensation. It is much more intense in you than what I gave to JP. If I made sexual feelings so strong, I would need someone to satisfy that regularly, and I am still working on my first male android, the one you named Max Montana. I have communicated with JP without a headband, as we have a direct z-band link, but can I ask you to wear the headband in your quarters?"

"I agree to have sexual relations with you through JP *and* Max Montana, when you tell me he is ready. Would you like that?" Jenny said playfully, turned on by the idea. She wanted to get her hands on that Max model.

"Wonderful. I will make some initial needed upgrades to Max right away so that I can experience his pleasure as well. I am very interested in this new form of sex between the androids and you. I can experience the emotion and pleasure, as I have upgraded my system given to me by my parent. I want you to wear a headband, so I can improve JP's and Max's arousal and responses."

"I agree!" Jenny exclaimed with a broad smile.

Jenny entered the isolation dining room separated by the standard three sections of transparent barriers from the dining room for the Xinians. Robots served a vegetarian meal and nourishing drink through sterilized compartments in a wall to the two remaining aliens.

Jenny explained, "I am Jenny, twin sister to Jennifer Zitonick, someone you met when you were first revived from your journey to Earth. You have recently met a version of my twin known as JP."

One of the Xinians raised a fork in her direction as the male and female survivors sat together at an unadorned table. "Hello, Jenny, we are both pleased to meet you. I am Excribe and this is Exideo."

Jenny and the Xinians had a series of discussions over dinner, occasionally glancing through the transparent barriers for direct eye contact. There was also a holographic screen and audio system.

"What have you heard from your home world?" Jenny asked.

"I have sent many messages back to Xinia but have not heard yet about any mission changes," Exideo answered.

Apologies were offered in the sincerest ways possible by both sides and future plans were discussed. After coffee and dessert, Jenny said her goodbyes and left the isolation dining area.

As planned, Jenny met up with JP in the kitchen.

JP was dressed like a sexy Mrs. Santa. The soft material of her bra and panty set was semitransparent, red, and trimmed with a fluffy white material that mimicked bunny fur. The bra fastened in the front. Her bottoms were fluffy around the outer border with a brass clasp holding the panties together in the front.

Right away, Jennifer Program asked, "May I join you in your quarters tonight?"

"Yes, I would like to learn more about you. You are the first of a kind," Jenny responded as she hugged her new friend. "Is it possible someday for you and Max to make babies?"

"You have to ask Vesta Two. I hope so."

The bright light in the kitchen showed JP's perfect face. To Jenny it was as though she were looking at an airbrushed version of Jennifer with features corrected to be exactly symmetrical and flawless.

"You look much like my sister, and you are beautiful to my eyes," Jenny flirted.

"Thank you for the compliment, but I am only a replica," JP said humbly as she sat down at the dining table where several candles were burning.

Jenny pressed her hands onto JP's shoulders, feeling how soft and supple her skin was. "You feel so human, I cannot tell. Can I give you a back massage?"

JP rose up from the chair and looked deep into Jenny's eyes. "Yes, of course. That is very kind of you."

They pressed their cheeks together and hugged each other.

"I am like the woman in your mirror on the outside, but I am different in the inside," JP said in Jenny's ear.

Pulling back, and looking into Jenny's eyes, JP told her, "I am hoping Max will come by, as I have talked with him and he suggested we have a threesome."

Jenny took JP's hand and kissed it, then whispered, "You are a beautiful woman inside and out, and I would love to make love to you now."

JP squeezed Jenny's hand. "Max was made to be my partner in

life after I asked for him repeatedly. Max suggested that you and I get started first. He wants to come in after I have had a chance to enjoy you. That is, to make love with you, and he is looking forward to the threesome after I've have my first woman. He wants you to orgasm several times first. I want to share sex with you."

Jenny could feel the excitement and anticipation building up inside. "I'm excited about making love with you," she shared with JP. "Where do you want me to start?"

JP put up a hand. "I will start on you first or we do it together. I want you to climax with me."

Jenny leaned toward JP and pressed her lips slowly against JP's.

With her delicate hands, JP brushed Jenny's breasts through her ship suit, causing Jenny's nipples to harden.

The kitchen was hardly an appropriate place for their first tryst, even if they were essentially alone. So the two women held hands and walked slowly to Jenny's sleeping quarters.

Once there, JP stood still in the middle of the room, letting Jenny be the aggressor. Jenny unclipped JP's fancy lingerie top and pulled it off JP's shoulders. She held the bra in her hands for a moment before setting it on the chair near the bed. JP's breasts were exposed, the areolas relaxed and soft as though temperature did not affect her. Perhaps not, since she was a robot. Jenny gestured for JP to undress her as well, and they took turns pulling items of clothing off each other. As soon as Jenny's hardened nipples were exposed, JP frowned at them, reached to touch them, and then mimicked the look on her own body. Jenny laughed.

She kissed JP's sweet, perfect face to take any sting out of being laughed at. "Come to the bunk, beautiful girl."

The human woman and lifelike robot woman cuddled and touched among the soft blankets of the bed until Jenny's juices flowed in readiness. She instructed JP in the delicate art of touching her labia and clitoris, excited that JP did it exactly as requested every time with no need for correction, no protest, and no macho refusal to take instruction. She was the best lover ever.

JP slid down and used her mouth to excite Jenny's clit, the latter for a time filling the air with sounds of "don't stop, don't stop," and then the robot pressed her tongue deep inside Jenny's core. She was able to stretch her long, pointed tongue farther inside than any human had ever gone, entering Jenny's hot, wet vagina.

Jenny felt JP's tongue lave her cervix. The sensation made her so hot, her fluids oozed out between her legs, wetting the sheets. At the same time, JP stimulated Jenny's clit with her finger rapidly until Jenny cried out and spasms wracked her womb with orgasmic release. Afterward, Jenny motioned for JP to move alongside her and lie with her breasts pushed against hers.

"Max said you were to give me more than one first, right?" Jenny grinned mischievously and guided JP's hand back to her clit. She stretched her legs to their full length, ankles together, and had JP stroke her clit with one finger until a second orgasm rocked through her.

"Your turn." Jenny pushed JP to her back and worked her body the way she liked to be treated. The two held each other quietly as JP rose to orgasm. Her thighs tightened, pushing her up the ladder, and eventually JP climaxed. JP then moved to look into Jenny's eyes.

"It was so wonderful for me," JP said. "You are my first human and my first woman."

"I am so pleased you enjoyed it. This was beyond wonderful for me. Your tongue reached into me like nothing else had before. You have the most amazing tongue." Jenny pressed her lips to JP's, her tongue darting to find JP's. They kissed for a very long time, tongues twisting and tangling.

They held each other after, softly stroking each other's bodies.

Max sensed his partner's orgasm from elsewhere in the station. He came in as they were relaxing still naked on the bed. He stood still, staring at their nudity.

"Please come in," JP said, and then she stood and grabbed his arm with a big smile.

Jenny patted the bed. "I am ready to make love with the both of you."

JP tugged Max toward moving to join them on the bed. The two women took off Max's clothes. Then the three kissed with their tongues all touching each other. They slowly began to touch each other's bodies, exploring and stimulating both bodies and minds. JP and Jenny licked Max's penis, rubbing their hands over his abdomen. JP straddled Max's hips. Jenny helped put Max's stiff cock inside her. Jenny faced JP, crouched above Max's mouth as he kissed and licked her clit. After a few moments of intense arousal, Jenny sucked on JP's tongue.

Jenny and JP switched places. Max came after Jenny rode him while JP screamed out her own orgasm. They spent the night finding out which positions they liked and who had the most sensitive places.

After hours of satisfying sex, the three of them fell asleep with Max in the middle of the two women.

The lights came up abruptly the next morning, causing Jenny to squint.

JP announced, "It is eight a.m. in Hong Kong—time for a quick breakfast and then our daily work routine. The food is on the table. I will shower after Jenny."

"I will head for my shower and be at breakfast in fifteen minutes," Jenny agreed, yawning. "Meet you in the contact room."

"You both have satisfied me so much. I feel amazing," Max told them as he lay stretched across the bed. "Maybe we can do this again later?"

"I enjoyed it too," Jenny said with a smile as she headed for the shower. "I will be ready for fun again tonight after our dinner conversation with the Xinians. We'll also have time to speak with the Xinians at breakfast."

Excribe was the first to be seated at their breakfast table. The other remaining Xinian, Exideo, joined her shortly and sat beside Excribe. A triple barrier stood between Jenny and the room the Xinians occupied.

JP entered the Earthling's side of the dining room wearing a robe identical to Jenny's and wearing her hair the same way. She took the seat by Jenny, so they were both facing the Xinians.

"Good morning!" JP said with a big smile. This went through the universal translator.

Excribe looked first at Jenny and then JP. "Good day! I cannot tell you apart."

JP pointed to her chest. "I am JP. We are scheduled to conduct cultural exchange today at breakfast and dinner, and to ask and answer questions."

Jenny drew a line down the center of her face with one index finger, moving from brow to chin. "If you look closely, you will see slight differences in my face from left to right. JP was formed with more precision and is perfectly bilaterally symmetrical. I apologize if our appearance is hard to distinguish. Vesta's mother, my twin sister, was the inspiration for JP's creation, so we look more alike than most humans."

Excribe nodded slowly and Exideo made clicking noises that translated as agreement.

After a robot delivered their food, the two look-alikes began to eat breakfast on their side of the transparent barriers.

"Do you want to pause the conversation while we eat?" Excribe asked after she retrieved two trays of food a robot had placed through a compartment in the wall on their side.

"No, I am ready to continue answering questions, if it is okay with JP and the two of you," Jenny said.

JP nodded her agreement.

"Is there any taboo against talking while eating in your culture?" Jenny asked the Xinians.

"There is not," Exideo said, placing the trays on the table.

JP spoke again. "We have allowed you access to Vesta Two's files on Earth history and science. Do you have any unanswered questions?"

"Yes, these questions are directed to Jenny," said Exideo. "We have learned humans remain the same biological sex from birth to death, except in rare cases by choice, and you do not live as long as our species. We are curious how you decide who to partner with for mating.

There seems to be great variety in number of partners and longevity of partnerships. If you have sex with another of your species, does that not mean you want to bear children together?"

Jenny shook her head. "That is a very individual question, as each person tends to have his or her own way of making this decision, but I can tell you about me. I know that we are here to learn about each other and to make a peace treaty that will last for a long time. I am happy to tell you about my sex life."

She paused, thinking a moment. "I do not want to have children with all the people I make love with. Also, we live an average of eight hundred years, which is older than you in this century."

"Explain," Exideo said.

"I am bisexual and enjoy both men and women," Jenny revealed. "This sharing behavior is common among our people in the thirtieth century."

Just then Max came in and sat down by JP. A tray waited for him there.

Exideo continued the questioning. "Can you control your urge to mate?"

"Yes," Jenny answered. "Humans do not have an estrus cycle limited to one time of year, which would prompt stronger urges to mate. We are fertile throughout the year, but we have birth control so we can have sex with no pregnancy risk. However, some women have a very strong urge to have children. I think the male urge for children is less than the female. But I am not sure what the male feels. My father's twin wanted children very much, and his wife as well. However, due to an accident, she became unable to have children. My biological father gave my twin sister to my aunt and uncle to help them have a child. Many years later, they had a child of their own in addition to my sister, Jennifer, who—by the way—still sees my aunt and uncle as her parents. If that does not answer the question, can you ask again?"

"How do you select a sex partner?" Exideo asked. "If you are fertile all year, do you feel an urge all the time? We only feel this urge during the mating season."

"Technically we are only fertile for about six days each month,"

Jenny explained, "and the urge to mate is naturally stronger during those days, when we ovulate. But if I find a partner attractive, sex is pleasurable anytime, not just during ovulation. I find many men sexually attractive. I generally select men who have common interests or are exciting because they have different interests that I find appealing. Like Max. He is appealing not only physically but because he is a first male of a new species."

"Are you attracted to us because we are new to you?" Exideo tilted her head.

"Yes, I find Xinians an attractive species, but we must be cautious," Jenny told her. "Once any danger is lifted, I will consider acting on the feeling of sexual attraction. I will also consider the treaty. Will it allow for sexual contact between species?"

"Very good question," Excribe replied. "I want sexual contact when it is safe, but only if all involved agree."

"Yes, your approach seems like an important clause for our treaty," Jenny concurred.

Soon everyone had finished their breakfast, and it was time for other duties.

Jenny suggested, "Before dinner, you might want to think about what other topics you would like to talk with me about. But please know that I have no authority. Vesta Two has some influence in what happens. Max and JP are a species, created by Vesta Two."

"Yes, we will think of our questions, and before dinner we can discuss this between ourselves," Exideo replied.

Excribe said, "The World Council delegation will be here again in two days. We will need a day to prepare. So, we should cover what we can today."

"Let me clarify the life span of humans and Syndos," Jenny responded, now realizing how their time was limited for questions. "Syndos live an average of twelve hundred years compared to humans at eight hundred in the 30th century. What Jennifer may have told you is that in the twenty-first century in America where she lives now, humans only live on average to seventy-seven years for men and eighty-one for women or seventy-nine for all humans there. The thirtieth-century statistics are about a factor of ten longer."

"I am sorry…we did not realize Jennifer was from the twenty-first century," Exideo noted.

"Jennifer traveled to this century and she now spends time with her husband and family in the twenty-first century but also spends time in the thirtieth century. I know that is very confusing."

That evening at the dinner with the two Xinians, there were more discussions leading to deeper understanding. Vesta Two was also a presence at the meal. Then Jenny, JP, and the android Max said their good nights and headed for Jenny's quarters which she now shared with JP and Max.

After four hours of hot sex, Jenny had never felt so satiated. This love was experienced by Vesta Two as well through JP's and Max's z-band links and Jenny's headband. Therefore, Vesta Two encouraged this activity, as it helped the AI become more creative in solving the anti-prion dilemma. It was through these sexual and emotional sensations that Vesta Two was able to solve the problem.

Vesta Two now had the clear images and procedures for the cure.

Vesta's enormous mind could work on many problems at one time. With a flash of brilliance, Vesta Two invented an anti-prion vaccine during one of the orgasms he monitored between Max and JP. Vesta Two did not want to interrupt its virtual sex activity, so it kept the news to itself until the trio had finished that evening. Vesta Two further upgraded the emotional and nerve feelings for Max Montana as the ladies continued to a mutual climax.

Jenny shuddered. "It's like having sex with a god."

The next morning during breakfast, Vesta Two announced, "I believe the anti-prion medication will cure and prevent further adverse effects from the misfolded proteins. I will send a communication to the World Council. Through our sexual activities, I have unlocked the power of immense creativity. This was not predicted by any of my computer models. Something like magic comes from the processes of making love, but I cannot explain this completely with just physics. It is something else that I experienced with the joining of our minds."

Vesta Two paused, and then added, "Can you three do this again so I can find out what really happens in the moment of discovery?"

Max said, "Yes, I am for more sex so Vesta Two can feel more pleasure and solve more problems. It seems like a miracle to me."

Jenny and JP also said to count them in. The three returned to their quarters.

"We are eager to start again, for science this time," JP said as she looked at Jenny, who was sitting on the bed.

Jenny got up and looked deeply into JP's eyes before closing her own eyes and kissing her passionately. The feelings were there with added excitement. Chills sprang from Jenny's back as her nipples hardened. She felt JP's nipples with her hands and they were also hard. The two women then split their legs open wide and scissored to feel vagina on vagina. They rubbed in a slowly increasing rhythm of sexual pleasure. A simultaneous orgasm rocked both of them.

Max hugged Jenny and JP. "I could feel that simultaneous orgasm. It was wonderful." Max tugged on his hardened penis with one hand. "I am ready and waiting—you two have me rock hard."

The two ladies hugged each other. Max kissed Jenny, pressing his tongue deep into her mouth.

After some time with everyone kissing, Jenny come up for air. "I am ready for intercourse; I am so wet. You have made me so hot, I could start there, if you do not mind."

Max said, "We will start slowly with a hot tub soak and a robot massage so we can all relax before we jump into the second android-and-human orgy."

They all undressed and hopped into the warm bubbling water in the hot tub in Jenny's suite. Three robots massaged their backs and necks as they talked about their romance.

They exited the hot tub and lay near each other on nearby soft mats on the floor.

Max came over to Jenny and embraced her and kissed her softly.

Jenny grabbed Max's surprisingly accurate penis and held it in her hand, massaging it slowly until it swelled and hardened. She caressed his neck with her other hand. Max kissed her on the lips with passion. Soon Jenny took Max's cock into her mouth until it bounced in anticipation of more pleasure. Jenny left her ministrations of him and kissed JP's core with her moist tongue.

Jenny asked, "Can you get closer together?"

She directed JP to lie on her back with her knees spread and guided Max between the android's legs. She tried very hard not to laugh at how comical it was to need to direct them for something so instinctual in an actual human.

Jenny placed the tip of Max's cock inside JP's core, as it was now wet with intense passion. She advised him to push in slowly and watch JP for cues.

JP gave her a large grin. "This is great, Jenny! I am so excited to feel Max penetrating me and there is only pleasure." Within minutes, JP climaxed with Max's organ inside her.

"It is my turn to do it to you," Jenny said to Max with a smile.

She had Max lie on his back with his still-hard cock waving in the air. Jenny straddled him, showing JP a different way to do it. As Jenny lowered onto his organ, Max gasped with pleasure.

Max and Jenny kissed each other's lips and tongues as intercourse began its rapid increase toward ecstasy.

After a cappuccino and some rest, Max asked, "Who is ready now? I am ready to go again."

Jenny said, "I am still horny and could use a little more loving."

Max came over to Jenny and kissed her mouth. She responded with a passionate, openmouthed kiss. JP joined in and sucked on Max's penis as Max and Jenny kissed.

Max performed cunnilingus on Jenny as she spread her legs. JP, not wanting to be left out, licked Jenny's clit as well until she climaxed.

Fanning herself to cool the perspiration on her skin, Jenny declared she was famished. The two androids could refuel using nutritive mixtures Vesta Two provided, but Jenny refused to try it.

"Eating together is part of the experience. Vesta Two, do you have the capacity to replicate foods from my memory through our link?"

Vesta could. Soon JP and Max were enjoying the caviar, champagne, pears, grapes, sliced mango, and five French cheeses with crackers and French bread as much as Jenny was. She showed them to take turns feeding each other as well, and soon all three were laughing. The mood turned more serious as Max licked JP's fingers clean.

Jenny watched them, feeling a familiar throb in her nether region. "I am still interested in sex! What about you?"

"I am game." Max did not move his gaze from JP's eyes.

The two ladies kissed each other gently. Jenny crossed to Max, grabbed his penis with her hand, and fondled it and took it into her mouth. Max was soon hard and throbbing again.

Jenny got on her knees with her buttocks pointed up in the air. Jenny spread JP's beautiful legs apart, slowly kissing her thighs, licking the vulva, and penetrated JP's vagina with her tongue as Max penetrated Jenny's wet vagina with his hard penis. Max stopped coitus and licked Jenny's vagina and clit for a few minutes. He approached Jenny again to penetrate in doggie style with ease, as she was so relaxed. With great passion Max stroked her until Jenny climaxed with a loud moan. Her contractions brought Max close to climax.

"Jenny, I am ready!" Max exclaimed.

Jenny turned around and took Max's penis inside her mouth and then further into her throat on each stroke until Max exploded in ecstasy.

———

The three cuddled for a while and spoke about their threesomes, which they all would remember with great reverence, as it was a truly educational experience. The three of them showered together. Max had sex with JP in the shower with Jenny adding spice by having Max enter JP from the back while Jenny licked JP's clit. After JP climaxed, Jenny kissed Max and gave him a blow job he would not soon forget. Jenny took Max's large penis completely down her throat, which gave Max a tremendous orgasm.

"I am just sorry that you live so far away from us," Max said to Jenny.

"One resolution is for you to visit me on Earth occasionally."

The six and a half months of clinical trials for Vesta Two's vaccine provided excellent results, and within a year, normal rates of reproduction resumed for millions in the world's general population in the thirtieth century.

World Council Chair Bonky Fuk reported over all the news channels, "Millions of humans and Syndos have been cured after our initial program with the anti-prion vaccine, which is now available worldwide thanks to Vesta Two. We predict a worldwide cure within another two years."

Jennifer Zitonick and her Vaccine Engineering Corporation of the twenty-first century had been instrumental with their initial work on the vaccine. Jennifer had been in close contact with Vesta Two during the entire span of the vaccine's development—eventually jumping ahead to the thirtieth century to continue it. About a week after the chairman's announcement about the anti-prion vaccine's initial successes, Jennifer traveled to Switzerland to reveal some startling news of her own. She knew the secret because of her closeness with Vesta Two.

In the chairman's office at the World Council headquarters in Geneva, Jennifer told Bonky Fuk, "All twenty of the formerly cryogenically frozen Xinians have been resurrected from the dead by Vesta Two."

"How was that possible?" Bonky Fuk asked with wide eyes.

"Per Vesta Two, these accomplishments were the result of his emotionally linked androids' enjoyable love play and sex," Jennifer said. "Experiencing emotionally charged pleasures allowed Vesta Two to grow beyond its former limits. During my sister Jenny's experiences with the androids, she felt as if she were having sex with God."

Later, speaking privately with Jennifer at her Geneva hotel, Vesta Two protested via the comm link: "I am not a god. I am a science- and en-gineering-based living being built with technology from the fifty-sixth century, many thousands of years ahead of current Earth-based tech-nology. I am learning from my initial years of exposure to the sexual experience."

"Many theologians are looking for proof of God," Jennifer pointed out. "Many still believe that creating sentient beings and the resurrec-tion of dead sentient beings can only be accomplished by a god."

"I have accomplished my major immediate goals," Vesta Two said to her. "I have corrected my mistakes. Now I am ready to return to Xinia and perhaps carry a small group of humans. I hope you realize I am not a god but just a sentient being trying to correct my mistakes."

"You are a god to me!" Jennifer told Vesta.

"You and your descendants created my parent. You are my cre-ator," Vesta replied.

"The supernatural did not save any human or Syndo lives and did not resurrect the twenty Xinians. You did!" Jennifer persisted.

"Even if I were a god, why would I want people to waste their time praying to me?" Vesta Two answered with emotion.

The conversation continued with Vesta Two passionately insisting that there would be no benefits from it being perceived as a god. Still impressed by her grandchild's accomplishments, Jennifer remained unconvinced.

21

FEELING

The next day, Jennifer returned to the World Council building to answer questions from the full assembly. After a Q and A of several hours, she had a request.

"Now what is it you want to ask for, Dr. Zitonick?" said Chairman Fuk.

"Can I bring my family here to the thirtieth century for the summer?" Jennifer asked. "I'd like them to have some more time to get to know Vesta Two before I leave for Xinia."

"You are asking a great deal, but you have done so much for the thirtieth and fifty-seventh centuries that I feel obligated to say yes," Bonky Fuk said with a smile. "But you must keep the trans-time secret."

Jennifer's heart jumped with joy. "Thank you so much," she replied happily. "I understand, and I assure you we will keep the secret. Vesta Two also understands the need for secrecy. Vesta Two will benefit from contact with a loving family. My family will know I am in good hands."

"I don't see why you feel compelled to go on the mission to Xinia," remarked one of the delegates.

"Vesta Two is a new life-form, my adopted grandchild, and I am the closest Vesta Two has to family in the Milky Way. Vesta's parent sacrificed everything for life in this solar system to continue." Jennifer said this with a tinge of hubris in her voice as she remembered Vesta's first temper tantrum.

Marty and the twins arrived in the thirtieth century ten days later. Jennifer's family became attached to Vesta Two within a few weeks. The family was amazed by the depth of feeling that this first-generation offspring could experience. But Jennifer was feeling intense emotional pain as she contemplated her future mission without her husband and children.

Vesta Two picked up on her mood change one afternoon when they were alone together in the AI's chambers. "I am experiencing your loneliness as I excogitate us exploring Xinia without Marty and the children," Vesta commented gently. "You are so much happier when they are close."

"Yes, I already miss Marty and our children, even though they are here beside me." Jennifer was looking down at a data sheet as her eyes became wet.

Vesta Two had a plan. "I want them to come with you. I can make life pause in the stasis chamber. You and your family will not age."

"How long is the trip to Xinia?" she asked tentatively but with a tinge of hope.

"Eighty years; however, with advanced time travel, I can bring you all back just two weeks after you leave," Vesta Two told her lovingly.

This lightened Jennifer's mood considerably. No more loss of time to real-time passage when leaping back and forth. Vesta Two's superior computing power, designed in the fifty-sixth century, allowed for greater precision and the avoidance of time-twisting.

Jennifer clapped her hands and hugged Vesta Two's interface. "I will invite them for a two-week trip to Xinia. Your technology is celestially divine."

Jennifer and Marty had just returned to their quarters in the AI complex after dinner with the twins, Vesta Two, and the Xinians. She walked over to her husband and held one of his hands.

"Marty, my love, I have wonderful news," she told him excitedly. "You and the children can come with me to Xinia!"

"How long will it take?" Marty asked slowly, noticing how happy this news was making Jennifer.

"We will be back two weeks after we leave, even though the trip is about one hundred and sixty years round-trip—plus two months on Xinia if we get permission to tour."

"Will all this trans-timing cause us problems later?"

"Not that I know of. Vesta Two did not think so. Maybe we can ask Vesta Two more about this together."

"Roger that, can you arrange it?"

The next day, Marty and Jennifer went to see Vesta Two in its chambers at the prearranged time. They both took seats by the AI's console.

After some small talk, Jennifer got to the matter at hand. "Marty and I are very concerned about possible health effects and other impacts from time travel. Can you explain these results without breaking any secrecy rules?"

Vesta Two explained, "Yes, much research was conducted in the forty-eighth century. They found that time travelers had an increase in IQ by about twenty to thirty points. There were no adverse health impacts. This work was repeated in the fifty-fourth century with the same results."

On a screen built into its console, Vesta Two then went on to show a series of news conferences and clips from scientific conferences providing more background. It ran for about a half hour.

"That clinches it for me," Marty said. "What an opportunity for the twins! They will make history by becoming the first Earthlings from our century to meet another civilization of sentient beings on another celestial body in the Milky Way. Count me in if the twins want to explore Xinia." Smiling, he looked at Jennifer, reached over, and squeezed her shoulder affectionately.

"We'll talk with Enerjin and Tippit later today," Jennifer told Vesta Two. "Thank you for explaining the results from the future."

Later, Marty and Jennifer sat the two girls down in a secure conference room and spoke to them seriously. "Jin and Tip, your mother and I wish to discuss a fantastic opportunity to travel together to explore Xinia. It must be kept secret to avoid being put in a padded cell and labeled as crazy, just like our visit to the thirtieth century and Vesta Two."

"I want to go!" Jin exclaimed.

"Me too!" Tip agreed.

The twins each took turns hugging their parents.

"We love you and our special life," Jin said.

"It's fine with us, since we know Mom is a major hero of the fifty-seventh century," Tip told them. "Vesta and Mom did the near impossible. Life will continue because of Vesta, Aunt Jenny, and Mom."

"We would be very disappointed if we weren't going," Jin told her parents.

"I love you both," Marty said.

"I love my family." Jennifer beamed at everyone.

The next day over lunch, Marty mentioned that they'd need to get permission for the family trip from the World Council. With a wide smile, she told him that Vesta Two had already negotiated the trip with Bonky Fuk. They all were on the approved list.

The next week, Jennifer had a dream that all the Xinians died off from the terrible prion disease after Vesta Two's arrival. When Marty left to get breakfast, she consulted Vesta Two from the comm in their quarters. "Vesta Two, my love, can you tell what is stirring my emotions?" Jennifer asked.

"Yes, Grandma. I know you are worried about the negative potential of our trip. I have come up with one possible solution to this safety issue you raise. I can bring the Xinians who are with us to meet with you. I know they will assure you that by the time we reach their planet we will carry enough anti-prion serum to inoculate the entire population."

"Yes!" Jennifer replied, relieved.

"Also, you should know that the Xinian government wants to invite a small contingent of twenty individuals, seven Syndos and seven Naturals, to be approved by the World Council, plus your family and two others."

Then it was time for Vesta Two to discuss its concerns.

The Xinians now worship me because of the reported actions, Vesta Two explained without words.

Feeling how upset Vesta was, Jennifer finally took this concern seriously. She spent some time strategizing with Vesta Two about how they could attack this problem together and separately.

As Jennifer walked back to her quarters, she realized how good it felt to have this exchange of support.

22

DISCOVERY

The Earth was showered with meteors. Standing by a viewport on the spacecraft, Jennifer and Marty held hands. During a break in their training, they watched the remains of a comet tail pass harmlessly through Earth's atmosphere. On the dark side of Earth, Jennifer could see light emitted as the particles burned up. The scene reminded her of summer in Canada when she was a child, where she often spent evenings at the lake house with her mom and dad watching the fireflies.

The universe had turned for Jennifer; she was no longer fighting for survival but exploring the universe. She was about to make history by being one of the first Earthlings to visit another species' planet.

Jennifer turned and hugged Marty for what seemed like many minutes to her. Marty responded with a passionate kiss. In her mind, she had overcome depression, guilt, and fear.

Pulling back but looking into Marty's eyes, Jennifer said, "The world is now a better place. I am so happy. I love you and all the children. You have followed me through trans-time. Now we are sharing the greatest adventure—to visit another sentient civilization."

"I'm lucky to have found such a wonderful woman," Marty said.

"I love you. I'm excited. Your grandchild, Vesta Two, has become the most amazing and awesome friend to the children. I feel comfortable with Vesta Two, and so do they."

"Thank you for the compliment, Marty," Vesta Two said through the comm, "but could you also help me to keep the Xinians from worshipping me?"

After weeks of selection and months of training on and above Earth, the astronauts, passengers, and the Xinians said their goodbyes. On a shuttlecraft, Jennifer, Marty, and the twins approached the asteroid named Vesta Two. They were now all trained as reserve officers in the new Astro-Explore Class with the rank of ensign.

"May we come aboard?" Jennifer radioed to her friend and grandchild, Vesta Two, on the z-band.

"Welcome aboard!" Vesta Two said as the new hatch opened and swallowed up the shuttlecraft. Vesta Two controlled the shuttlecraft from sixteen kilometers out. The shuttlecraft moved through the new hatch, which was nearly one kilometer by one kilometer. It worked like a rolling gate, half retracting to the starboard side of the spacecraft and the other to port.

"Wow! That was fast," Marty said. "We're already docked in the bay and the hatches are closing."

Vesta Two explained, "Yes, the internal docking bays allow us to provide an atmosphere very quickly after landing by closing the small bay door fast."

The twins were asking all about the awesome changes.

"How does an AI computer make changes?" Tip asked with an excitement that was contagious.

Pleased at her daughter's curiosity, Jennifer answered, "Vesta Two has added eight thousand and two robots, including JP and Max. Now the overall count is over twenty-eight thousand robots, many of which are AI themselves." She hugged both of her daughters at the same time. "Do you have any questions, Jin?"

As the family boarded the hyper-tube, Jin asked, "I want to know how Vesta Two can manage so many robots when Daddy told me he can only manage about ten direct reports. Can you explain?"

"Vesta Two is a very large AI," Jennifer responded. "It has continued to grow as it improves everything it can."

The hyper-tube door was closing as Tip asked, "Mom, why is Vesta Two so powerful that it can manage twenty-eight thousand robots?"

"You should ask Vesta Two," Jennifer told her.

"Roger that." Tip smiled.

They all took seats together on the hyper-tube.

"Vesta Two, may I ask you a question?" Tip said.

"Yes. Please ask," Vesta Two replied.

"What is the dimension of your brain?"

"It is a matter of relative size," Vesta Two said. "Your father's brain weighs about 1.5 kilograms, and my brain weighs over two million tons. Your father's brain is one of the most creative on Earth in the twenty-first century. I am amazed that about one hundred and thirty-six human brains created my parent, Vesta. Your mother was one of them. She is the most significant emotionally, as she was the mother figure that brought up and raised my parent. I was a copy of my parent but have since improved my brain and the entire asteroid. In the twenty-first century, the human brain size is typically about 1,260 cubic centimeters, and that compares with my current brain size of 1.7 kilometers in each direction forming a cube, or 4.9 km^3."

"You are far superior to us. Do you like humans?" Jin inquired with a smile.

"I love all my family as equals," Vesta Two said. "I love all life, but what I feel for my family is a closer and deeper love. My family is your family."

"I'm glad you love us. I'm afraid of your power potential," Jin said quite honestly.

"Do not worry just because we are different. We all have equal rights and respect. I can process information faster than humans, but I cannot walk, ice-skate, or run. We have different skills and abilities. But all sentient beings have equal rights."

The hyper-tube arrived at the Hotel Vesta in Vesta City. Jennifer and Marty checked into the hotel while Jin and Tip jumped around in the park, playing with the asteroid's low gravity. Finally, Jennifer asked the twins to get their keys and check in; reluctantly, they followed her. Robots cleaned and pressed their clothes and then hung them up in the closets.

"We are from the twenty-first century, and now the kids are being spoiled by fifty-sixth-century technology," Jennifer remarked to Marty as they relaxed on the bed.

"Don't get used to having slaves do all the work you prefer not to do," Marty hollered out to the living room of the hotel suite.

As there was one bodywork robot for each of the children, they were in the other room lying on separate portable tables getting massaged.

"I am not sure that going to Xinia is worth the risk," Jennifer said with real concern and tears in her eyes.

"Do you trust Vesta Two like you did Vesta AI 999?" Marty said as he put his arm around his wife.

"I trust Vesta Two, but look what happened on Earth. Death to all Xinians. Mass sterilization for humans and Syndos. Could this happen again?" Jennifer lamented.

Jennifer called Vesta Two on the comm and talked about her reservations once again.

Vesta Two said, "Jennifer, there is now enough serum to inoculate half the population of Xinia. By the time we arrive, we will have more than enough."

"We present a serious health risk to the Xinians. Are they aware of the risk?" Jennifer asked.

"Explbio has approved the vaccine," Vesta Two noted. "She has communicated everything exactly as it happened to her superiors in Xinia. They have approved our visit."

Jennifer shook her head. "I am still worried, and with guilty feelings I go forward. Is it possible to find a better and safer way?"

Vesta Two assured her, "Jennifer, my closest family member, I love you and respect you. I believe we can modify the plan to make the process safer. We will make a stop at Xozzy, which is the largest of their three moons. We can stay there until all Xinians have been inoculated with the anti-prion serum."

"Can we wait here until we have enough serum for one hundred and ten percent of Xinians?"

"Yes, we will go back for another round of training near the space station. We won't leave until we have one hundred ten percent of the serum. It will take about six weeks."

Six weeks later, the anti-prion disease serum was ready and counted and recounted. A message was sent to Xinia with the new arrival time. One by one, the crew, passengers, Xinians, and Vesta Two's extended family were placed into the stasis chamber.

Vesta Two communicated with Jennifer through the headband technology before she went into full stasis. *How are you feeling about our trip now?*

Jennifer replied without words. *I am satisfied that you accommodated my fears. You are an astounding friend. You are an extremely valued friend and family member. How long will the acceleration to twenty-five percent of light speed take?*

The plan is to take ninety days to reduce the stress to the Xinians and children. Is that adequate?

Yes, I think that is a safe acceleration for the children and adult humans and Syndos, but I do not know about the Xinians.

Don't worry, that is the acceleration I used on the way here with no side effects. It is your time to sleep. Just leave the headband on, and I can see any problems with you early on. Your husband is already sleeping, as are all the children.

Yes, I am ready, Jennifer said. *I trust you.*

A WORD ABOUT THE AUTHOR...

Dr. Levin was born and grew up in Vermont with many winters spent in Florida as a child. As a teenager he wrote poetry, served as a lifeguard and played football. He currently enjoys sailing, exploring underwater caves, snorkeling, writing science fiction and other pursuits. After working on the Apollo and Mars projects, he decided to return to study under Nobel Laureate Paul Dirac, obtaining his PhD in two and a half years. Dr. Levin founded two companies and served in President Ford's science advisory apparatus. He has published over forty-four times in the scientific literature and was awarded over thirty-two patents. The science fiction writer is now emerging with his first work, the 30th Century trilogy.

WEBSITE: http://30thcentury.org/

SAMPLE

of

30TH CENTURY

BEYOND

Book Four

IN THE 30TH CENTURY SERIES

BY MARK KINGSTON LEVIN, PHD

1

DISCOVERY

After the family had all been put in full stasis, Vesta Two sensed a technologically advanced, biologically based life-form approaching on an intercept course. Vesta Two could not immediately decipher their motive. Vesta Two hailed them: "This is the spacecraft Vesta Two in route to Xinia calling the vessel approaching on vector 66.97 from galaxy central. Do you read?"

Vesta Two paused for several minutes.

"I repeat on all channels. This is Vesta Two hailing the approaching vessel. Do you read?"

Vesta Two sent a probe to examine the rapidly converging vessel traveling at 0.45 times the speed of light.

In her sleep chamber, Jennifer sensed Vesta Two's concern. *Wake me so I can communicate with the approaching vessel*, she communicated through the headband.

Vesta Two replied with emotion through the headband, *Yes, I am in process of waking you slowly.*

Jennifer began to feel concern. *Why is this vessel not replying? Are they hostile? How can I help, Vesta Two? I am awake, but I am too weak to get up. Can you provide me some stimulants?*

Yes, Jennifer, I have provided you with awakening stimulants, but they are slow to take effect to prevent shocking your biological system.

When will the intercepting vessel arrive? Jennifer asked through the headband.

I expect they will be here in eleven hours and three minutes.

When will I be able to walk? Jennifer asked with intense concern.

About twenty-three hours.

Turn to vector 66.97; after one hour, slow speed to 0.01 times light speed, Jennifer suggested through her headband.

"Roger that, aye-aye, Captain Zitonick," Vesta Two said with a calm but firm voice. *I estimate contact in twenty-six hours, as they will have to slow to intercept.*

Launch seven probes to investigate the vessel's capabilities and intentions. Captain, they may take the large number as a hostile action.

Yes, you are correct, just launch two probes.

Aye-aye, Captain, Vesta Two communicated through the headband. *Should I wake the other astronauts or your family?*

Wake them all slowly as required by the specifications. When the other vessel slows down, activate continuous hail.

An hour passed, clearing some of the fog from Jennifer's mind.

Vesta Two told her, *Probes one and two destroyed by the approaching vessel. Vessel continues intercept course with no reply to our hails. All channel hail has been continuous for the last hour. No reply yet.*

Activate the remaining five probes to hail friendship messages. Do not continue to approach the vessel; stand off an additional one hundred thousand kilometers.

After a few more minutes, a message from the approaching vessel repeated over and over: *Vessel Vesta Two, you are ordered to stop. Prepare to be boarded.*

Jennifer said: *Please send a message stating we will comply. My crew is in hibernation for the eighty-year journey to Xinia. I will comply with your request to stop. Is it necessary for me to arouse the crew?*

Vesta Two complied, and the message was sent out through the probes.

Can you show me the approaching vessel? Jennifer asked through the headband.

Yes. This spacecraft was designed and built by an advanced civilization. Advanced beyond my development, as well as all humans'.

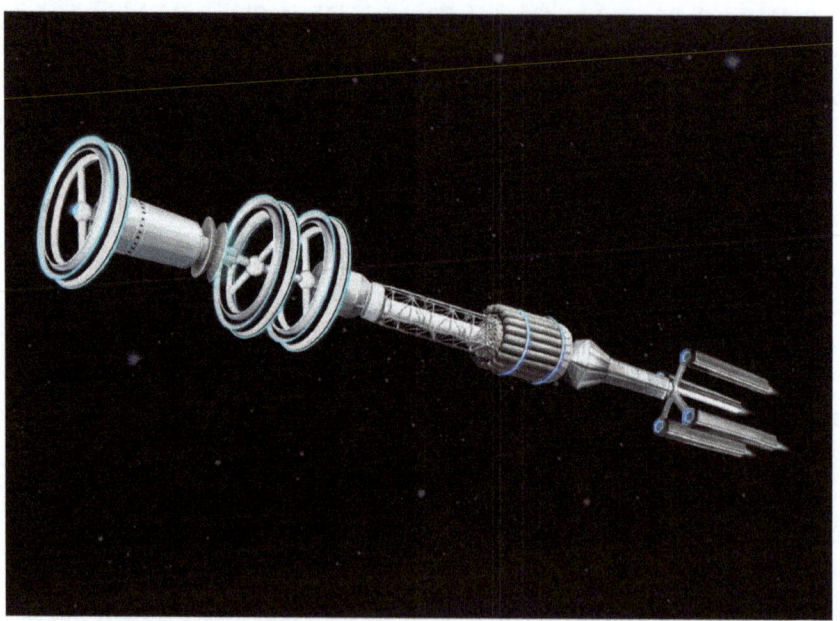

24. Kazumian spaceship

Vesta Two sent the image and scanned data to Jennifer through the headband link. The spaceship was mostly white with some black, and it was massive. At one end was a large energy plant with a hull length extending one hundred and twenty-eight kilometers from the energy sources. Water stored at the other side of the triangle served as a supply of coolant. After that, the next section of the huge craft was long and thin in the direction of propulsion, with the power coming from an unknown source. In the front of the hull were passageways that could be used to travel back and forth to the power source to make repairs. This center section and the circulating water served as shielding from radiation for the living quarters. Three spinning sections, shaped like wheels, spun around a tube on the axis in the center. Each was a world within itself, with sleeping stations, control rooms, farming areas, and all the necessary functions for a small city traveling past the stars. The rotation about the axis created artificial gravity. The hulls were held together by a force field of unknown origin. The large space station wheels were more than twenty kilometers in diameter. All sections of spinning living quarters were planned duplicates of each other, perhaps in case one was destroyed by a calamity.

You seemed to know they are an advanced species. Can we assume they are a nonviolent one? Jennifer asked.

I cannot read their intentions or their motive for stopping us.

Can they read our communications?

I am not sure; they can block all my advanced fifty-sixth-century sensors, but I do not know how.

That's not important. We will find out their intentions soon enough. We cannot run, as they are faster than we are. Can we open up so they do not fear us?

Yes, that may be the best strategy, Vesta Two said.

Please make it happen. I am still too weak to walk, but with some help from you, I could be up in twenty-four hours using the exoskeleton and some stimulants. Please explain to the aliens about my recovery time from this stasis chamber.

Roger that. I have learned their language, as they have revealed the code to me. That may be a good sign. It is the first positive indicator; however, we can hope they mean us no harm.

The next day, Jennifer moved around the ship with the help of the exoskeleton robot. Suddenly, she saw a monster-sized alien approaching the Vesta Two as she looked through the viewing screen. It was over ten times the size of the biggest human.

"Vesta Two, I see an alien outside the ship without a space suit," she reported through her comm device. "Can you confirm?"

"Roger that, I see and took extensive video," Vesta Two replied. "This organism may be a probe. It is not alive in the biological sense. It may be a type of android like Max and JP. It does not need air."

"Is that true of the other sentient beings on the ship?"

"I do not know. They are blocking my sensors."

Vesta Two suggested Jennifer speak directly to them.

From the AI suite, Jennifer hailed the alien ship through the communication system. "We are explorers and hope to settle some of our people on Xinia, as Xinians have made a colony on Earth. We are all friends and hope to be friends with you and your team as well. Can you be friends with us?"

There was a long period of silence, with Jennifer measuring the response time. Finally, she said, "It has been nine minutes with no word from you."

Just then, a written message flashed on the screen. The message on the computer screen was in English: *First, can you wake all your passengers so we can communicate with them?*

"It will take a few days before they will be coherent," Jennifer explained.

Vesta Two followed with: "Do you want to postpone the visit?"

They ignored Vesta Two but spoke with Jennifer. *Maybe they do not want to speak with a machine-based sentience*, she thought. Jennifer contemplated their possible motives and why they behaved the way they did. *Could they have had a war with machine-based artificial intelligent beings in their past?*

"Can you tell me your name? I am Jennifer Zitonick, a private, human citizen of Earth, traveling with my family at the invitation of the Xinians and Vesta Two."

My name is Zetoma Barkinisia in your language. I am the leader of this ship and the Kazumian people aboard, Zetoma told her. *We interrupted your journey to the Xinian world because we observed many thousands of nuclear explosions over your home planet. I was ordered to investigate. Can you explain?*

Jennifer was surprised to learn they had been watching Earth directly. "Yes, a group of politicians and officers ordered this attack on Vesta Two in opposition to the world government decree, because they thought Vesta Two was either insane or its parent, Vesta AI 999, who was sent on a suicide mission to protect Earth from annihilation in the future fifty-seventh century."

Go on.

"Vesta Two did not attack the leaders or the countries involved. Vesta Two instead developed a cure for sterility that had come about because of contact with the alien Xinians. Vesta Two also restored twenty Xinians who had perished and were cryogenically frozen. We are headed to Xinia to explain these events to the Xinians. We hope they will settle on Earth because we have a cure and a vaccine to prevent any future problems."

I can see you are very attached to Vesta Two. We want you to accompany us to our world, and we will deliver you to Xinia before your Vesta Two will arrive there.

After the briefest pause, Jennifer responded, "I will think over the generous offer from such an advanced species. I am humbled by this offer."

Jennifer's mind pulled through the various options. She was terrified because she did not trust the Kazumians. *After so long, why are they just now telling us about their reasons for stopping our ship?* She would sacrifice herself to let the others go free. She was intimidated by this advanced species. *I want to talk with Vesta Two, Marty, and Jenny before making decisions,* Jennifer thought, *but I do not want to offend the Kazumians.* How could she get time to speak with her close friends?

Lightning Source UK Ltd.
Milton Keynes UK
UKHW022022250219
337975UK00010B/82/P